George de Horne Vaizey

About Peggy Saville

Outlook

George de Horne Vaizey

About Peggy Saville

1. Auflage | ISBN: 978-3-73262-160-6

Erscheinungsort: Frankfurt am Main, Deutschland

Erscheinungsjahr: 2018

Outlook Verlag GmbH, Frankfurt.

George de Horne Vaizey

About Peggy Saville

Outlook

Mrs. G. de Horne Vaizey

"About Peggy Saville"

Chapter One.

A New Inmate.

The afternoon post had come in, and the Vicar of Renton stood in the bay window of his library reading his budget of letters. He was a tall, thin man, with a close-shaven face, which had no beauty of feature, but which was wonderfully attractive all the same. It was not an old face, but it was deeply lined, and those who knew and loved him best could tell the meaning of each of those eloquent tracings. The deep vertical mark running up the forehead meant sorrow. It had been stamped there for ever on the night when Hubert, his first-born, had been brought back, cold and lifeless, from the river to which he had hurried forth but an hour before, a picture of happy boyhood. The vicar's brow had been smooth enough before that day. The furrow was graven to the memory of Teddy, the golden-haired lad who had first taught him the joys of fatherhood. The network of lines about the eyes were caused by the hundred and one little worries of everyday life, and the strain of working a delicate body to its fullest pitch; and the two long, deep streaks down the cheeks bore testimony to that happy sense of humour which showed the bright side of a question, and helped him out of many a slough of despair. This afternoon, as he stood reading his letters one by one, the different lines deepened, or smoothed out, according to the nature of the missive. Now he smiled, now he sighed, anon he crumpled up his face in puzzled thought, until the last letter of all was reached, when he did all three in succession, ending up with a low whistle of surprise—

"Edith! This is from Mrs Saville. Just look at this!"

Instantly there came a sound of hurried rising from the other end of the room; a work-basket swayed to and fro on a rickety gipsy-table, and the vicar's wife walked towards him, rolling half a dozen reels of thread in her wake with an air of fine indifference.

"Mrs Saville!" she exclaimed eagerly. "How is my boy?" and without waiting for an answer she seized the letter, and began to devour its contents, while her husband went stooping about over the floor picking up the contents of the scattered basket and putting them carefully back in their places. He smiled to himself as he did so, and kept turning amused, tender glances at his wife as she stood in the uncarpeted space in the window, with the sunshine pouring in on her eager face. Mrs Asplin had been married for twenty years, and was the mother of three big children; but such was the buoyancy of her Irish nature and the irrepressible cheeriness of her heart, that she was in good truth the youngest person in the house, so that her own daughters were sometimes quite shocked at her levity of behaviour, and treated her with gentle, motherly restraint. She was tall and thin, like her husband, and he, at least, considered her every whit as beautiful as she had been a score of years before. Her hair was dark and curly; she had deep-set grey eyes, and a pretty fresh complexion. When she was well, and rushing about in her usual breathless fashion, she looked like the sister of her own tall girls; and when she was ill, and the dark lines showed under her eyes, she looked like a tired, wearied girl, but never for a moment as if she deserved such a title as an old, or elderly, woman. Now, as she read, her eyes glowed, and she uttered ecstatic little exclamations of triumph from time to time; for Arthur Saville, the son of the lady who was the writer of the letter, had been the first pupil whom her husband had taken into his house to coach, and as such had a special claim on her affection. For the first dozen years of their marriage all had gone smoothly with Mr and Mrs Asplin, and the vicar had had more work than he could manage in his busy city parish; then, alas, lung trouble had threatened; he had been obliged to take a year's rest, and to exchange his living for a sleepy little parish, where he could breathe fresh air, and take life at a slower pace. Illness, the doctor's bills, the year's holiday, ran away with a large sum of money; the stipend of the country church was by no means generous, and the vicar was lamenting the fact that he was shortest of money just when his children were growing up and he needed it most, when an old college friend requested, as a favour, that he would undertake the education of his only son, for a year at least, so that the boy might be well grounded in his studies before going on to the military tutor who was to prepare him for Sandhurst. Handsome terms were quoted, the vicar looked upon the offer as a leading of Providence, and Arthur Saville's stay at the vicarage proved a success in every sense of the word. He was a clever boy who was not afraid of work, and the vicar discovered in himself an unsuspected genius for teaching. Arthur's progress not only filled him with delight, but brought the offer of other pupils, so that he was but the forerunner of a succession of bright, handsome boys, who came from far and wide to be prepared for college, and to make their home at the vicarage. They were honest, healthy-minded lads, and Mrs Asplin loved them all, but no one had ever taken Arthur Saville's place. During the year which he had spent under her roof he had broken his collar-bone, sprained his ankle, nearly chopped off the top of one of his fingers, scalded his foot, and fallen crash through a plate-glass window. There had never been one moment's peace or quietness; she had gone about from morning to night in chronic fear of a disaster; and, as a matter of course, it followed that Arthur was her darling, ensconced in a little niche of his own, from which subsequent pupils tried in vain to oust him.

Mrs Saville dwelt upon the latest successes of her clever son with a mother's pride, and his second mother beamed, and smiled, and cried, "I told you so!"

"Dear boy!"

"Of course he did!" in delighted echo. But when she came to the second half of the letter her face changed, and she grew grave and anxious. "And now, dear Mr Asplin," Mrs Saville wrote, "I come to the real burden of my letter. I return to India in autumn, and am most anxious to see Peggy happily settled before I leave. She has been at this Brighton school for four years, and has done well with her lessons, but the poor child seems so unhappy at the thought of returning, that I am sorely troubled about her. Like most Indian children, she has had very little home life, and after being with me for the last six months she dreads the prospect of school, and I cannot bear the thought of sending her back against her will. I was puzzling over the question yesterday, when it suddenly occurred to me that perhaps you, dear Mr Asplin, could help me out of my difficulty. Could you—would you, take her in hand for the next three years, letting her share the lessons of your own two girls? I cannot tell you what a relief and joy it would be to feel that she was under your care. Arthur always looks back on the year spent with you as one of the brightest of his life; and I am sure Peggy would be equally happy. I write to you from force of habit, but really I think this letter should have been addressed to Mrs Asplin, for it is she who would be most concerned. I know her heart is large enough to mother my dear girl during my absence; and if strength and time will allow her to undertake this fresh charge, I think she will be glad to help another mother by doing so. Peggy is bright and clever, like her brother, and strong on the whole, though her throat needs care. She is nearly fifteen—the age, I think, of your youngest girl—and we should be pleased to pay the same terms as we did for Arthur. Now, please, dear Mr Asplin, talk the matter over with your wife, and let me know your decision as soon as possible."

Mrs Asplin dropped the letter on the floor, and turned to confront her husband.

"Well!"

"Well?"

"It is your affair, dear, not mine. You would have the trouble. Could you do with an extra child in the house?"

"Yes, yes, so far as that goes. The more the merrier. I should like to help Arthur's mother, but,"—Mrs Asplin leant her head on one side, and put on what her children described as her "Ways and Means" expression. She was saying to herself, —"Clear out the box-room over the study. Spare chest-of-drawers from dressing-room—cover a box with one of the old chintz curtains for an ottoman—enamel the old blue furniture —new carpet and bedstead, say five or six pounds outlay—yes! I think I could make it pretty for five pounds!..." The calculations lasted for about two minutes, at the end of which time her brow cleared, she nodded brightly, and said in a crisp, decisive tone, "Yes, we will take her! Arthur's throat was delicate too. She must use my gargle."

The vicar laughed softly.

"Ah! I thought that would decide it. I knew your soft heart would not be able to resist the thought of the delicate throat! Well, dear, if you are willing, so am I. I am glad to make hay while the sun shines, and lay by a little provision for the children. How will they take it, do you think? They are accustomed to strange boys, but a girl will be a new experience. She will come at once, I suppose, and settle down to work for the autumn. Dear me! dear me! It is the unexpected that happens. I hope she is a nice child."

"Of course she is. She is Arthur's sister. Come! the young folks are in the study. Let us go and tell them the news. I have always said it was my ambition to have half a dozen children, and now, at last, it is going to be gratified."

Mrs Asplin thrust her hand through her husband's arm, and led him down the wide, flagged hall, towards the room whence the sound of merry young voices fell pleasantly upon the ear.

Chapter Two.

Mellicent's Prophecy.

The schoolroom was a long, bare apartment running along one side of the house, and boasting three tall windows, through which the sun poured in on a shabby carpet and ink- stained tables. Everything looked well worn and, to a certain extent, dilapidated, yet there was an air of cheerful comfort about the whole which is not often found in rooms of the kind. Mrs Asplin revelled in beautiful colours, and would tolerate no drab and saffron papers in her house; so the walls were covered with a rich soft blue; the cushions on the wicker chairs rang the changes from rose to yellow; a brilliant

Japanese screen stood in one corner, and a wire stand before the open grate held a number of flowering plants. A young fellow of seventeen or eighteen was seated at one end of the table employed in arranging a selection of foreign stamps. This was Maxwell, the vicar's eldest surviving son, who was to go up to Oxford at the beginning of the year, and was at present reading under his father's supervision. His sister Mellicent was perched on the table itself, watching his movements, and vouchsafing scraps of advice. Her suggestions were received with sniffs of scornful superiority, but Mellicent prattled on unperturbed, being a plump, placid person, with flaxen hair, blue eyes, and somewhat obtuse sensibilities. The elder girl was sitting reading by the window, leaning her head on her hand, and showing a long, thin face, comically like her father's, with the same deep lines running down her cheeks. She was neither so pretty nor so even- tempered as her sister, but she had twice the character, and was a young person who made her individuality felt in the house; while Maxwell was the beauty of the family, with his mother's crisp, dark locks, grey eyes, and brunette colouring.

These three young people were the vicar's only surviving children; but there were two more occupants of the room—the two lads who were being coached to enter the University at the same time as his own son. Number one was a fair, dandified-looking youth, who sat astride a deck-chair, with his trousers hitched up so as to display long, narrow feet, shod in scarlet silk socks and patent-leather slippers. He had fair hair, curling over his forehead; bold blue eyes, an aquiline nose, and an air of being very well satisfied with the world in general and himself in particular. This was Oswald Elliston, the son of a country squire, who had heard of the successes of Mr Asplin's pupils, and was storing up disappointment for himself in expecting similar exploits from his own handsome, but by no means over-brilliant, son. The second pupil had a small microscope in his hand, and was poring over a collection of "specimens," with his shoulders hitched up to his ears, in a position the reverse of elegant. Every now and then he would bend his head to write down a few notes on the paper beside him, showing a square-chinned face, with heavy eyebrows and strong roughly-marked features. His clothes were worn, his cuffs invisible, and his hair ruffled into wild confusion by the unconscious rubbings of his hands; and this was the Honourable Robert Darcy, third son of Lord Darcy, a member of the Cabinet, and a politician of world-wide reputation.

The servants at the vicarage were fond of remarking, apropos of the Honourable Robert, that he "didn't look it"; which remark would have been a subject of sincere gratification to the lad himself, had it been overheard; for there was no surer way of annoying him than by referring to his position, or giving him the prefix to which he was entitled.

The young folks looked up inquiringly as Mr and Mrs Asplin entered the room, for the hour after tea was set apart for recreation, and the elders were usually only too glad to remain in their own quiet little sanctum. Oswald, the gallant, sprang to his feet and brought forward a chair for Mrs Asplin, but she waved him aside, and broke impetuously into words.

"Children! we have news for you. You are going to have a new companion. Father has had a letter this afternoon about another pupil—"

Mellicent yawned, and Esther looked calmly uninterested, but the three lads were full of interest. Their faces turned towards the vicar with expressions of eager curiosity.

"A new fellow! This term! From what school, sir?"

"A ladies' boarding-school at Brighton!" Mrs Asplin spoke rapidly, so as to be beforehand with her husband, and her eyes danced with mischievous enjoyment, as she saw the dismay depicted on the three watching faces. A ladies' school! Maxwell, Oswald, and Robert, had a vision of a pampered pet in curls, and round jacket, and their backs stiffened in horrified indignation at the idea that grown men of seventeen and eighteen should be expected to associate with a "kid" from a ladies' school!

The vicar could not restrain a smile, but he hastened to correct the mistake. "It's not a 'fellow' at all, this time. It's a girl! We have had a letter from Arthur Saville's mother, asking us to look after her daughter while she is in India. She will come to us very soon, and stay, I suppose, for three or four years, sharing your lessons, my dears, and studying with you —"

"A girl! Good gracious! Where will she sleep?" cried Mellicent, with characteristic matter-of-fact curiosity, while Esther chimed in with further inquiries.

"What is her name? How old is she? What is she like? When will she come? Why is she leaving school?"

"Not very happy. Peggy. In the little box-room over the study. About fifteen, I believe. Haven't the least idea. In a few weeks from now," said Mrs Asplin, answering all thequestions at once in her impulsive fashion, the while she walked round the table, stroked Maxwell's curls, bent an interested glance at Robert's collection, and laid a hand on Esther's back, to straighten bowed shoulders. "She is Arthur's sister, so she is sure to be nice, and both her parents will be in India, so you must all be kind to the poor little soul, and give her a hearty welcome."

Silence! Nobody had a word to say in response to this remark; but the eyes of the young people met furtively across the table, and Mr Asplin felt that they were only waiting until their seniors should withdraw before bursting into eager conversation.

"Better leave them to have it out by themselves," he whispered significantly to his wife; then added aloud, "Well, we won't interrupt you any longer. Don't turn the play-hour into work, Rob! You will study all the better for a little relaxation. You have proved the truth of that axiom, Oswald— eh?" and he went laughing out of the room, while Oswald held the door open for his wife, smiling assent in lazy fashion.

"Another girl!" he exclaimed, as he reseated himself on his chair, and looked with satisfaction at his well-shod feet. "This is an unexpected blow! A sister of the redoubtable Saville! From all I have heard of him, I should imagine a female edition would be rather a terror in a quiet household. I never saw Saville,—what sort of a fellow was he to look at, don't you know?"

Mellicent reflected.

"He had a nose!" she said solemnly. Then, as the others burst into hilarious laughter, "Oh, it's no use shrieking at me; I mean what I say," she insisted. "A big nose—like Wellington's! When people are very clever, they always have big noses. I imagine Peggy small, with a little thin face, because she was born in India, and lived there until she was six years old, and a great big nose in the middle—"

"Sounds appetising," said Maxwell shortly. "I don't! I imagine Peggy like her mother, with blue eyes and brown hair. Mrs Saville is awfully pretty. I have seen her often, and if her daughter is like her—"

"I don't care in the least how she looks," said Esther severely. "It's her character that matters. Indian children are generally spoiled, and if she has been to a boarding-school she may give herself airs. Then we shall quarrel. I am not going to be patronised by a girl of fourteen. I expect she will be Mellicent's friend, not mine."

"I wonder what sums she is in!" said Mellicent dreamily. "Rob! what do you think about it? Are you glad or sorry? You haven't said anything yet."

Robert raised his eyes from his microscope, and looked her up and down, very much as a big Newfoundland dog looks at the terrier which disturbs its slumber.

"It's nothing to me," he said loftily. "She may come if she likes." Then, with sudden recollection, "Does she learn the violin? Because we have already *one* girl in this house who is learning the violin, and life won't be worth living if there is a second."

He tucked his big notebook under his chin as he spoke, and began sawing across it with a pencil, wagging his head and rolling his eyes, in imitation of Mellicent's own manner of practising, producing at the same time such long-drawn, catlike wails from between his closed lips as made the listeners shriek with laughter. Mellicent, however, felt bound to expostulate.

"It's not the tune at all," she cried loudly. "Not like any of my pieces; and if I *do* roll my eyes, I don't rumple up my hair and pull faces at the ceiling, as *some* people do, and I know who they are, but I am too polite to say so! I hope Peggy will be my friend, because then there will be two of us, and you won't dare to tease me any more. When Arthur was here, a boy pulled my hair, and he carried him upstairs and held his head underneath the shower-bath."

"I'll pull it again, and see if Peggy will do the same," said Rob pleasantly; and poor Mellicent stared from one smiling face to another, conscious that she was being laughed at, but unable to see the point of the joke.

"When Peggy comes," she said, in an injured tone, "I hope she will be sympathetic. I'm the youngest, and I think you ought all to do what I want; instead of which you make fun, and laugh among yourselves, and send me messages. For instance, when Max wanted his stamps brought down—"

Maxwell passed his big hand over her hair and face, then, reversing the direction, rubbed up the point of the little snub nose.

"Never mind, chubby, your day is over! We will make Peggy the message-boy now. Peggy will be a nice, meek little girl, who will like to run messages for her betters! She shall be my fag, and attend to me. I'll give her my stamps to sort."

"I rather thought of having her for fag myself; we can't admit a girl to our study unless she makes herself useful," said Oswald languidly; whereupon Rob banged the notebook on the table with clanging decision.

"Peggy belongs to me," he announced firmly. "It's no use you two fellows quarrelling. That matter is settled once for all. Peggy will be my fag; I've barleyed her for myself, and you have nothing to say in the matter."

But Esther tossed her head with an air of superior wisdom.

"Wait till she comes," she said sagely. "If Peggy is anything like her brother, you may spare yourself the trouble of planning as to what she must or must not do. It is waste of time. Peggy will be mistress over us all!"

Chapter Three.

Enter Miss Saville!

A fortnight later Peggy Saville arrived at the vicarage. Her mother brought her, stayed for a couple of hours, and then left for the time being; but as she was to pay some visits in the neighbourhood it was understood that this was not the final parting, and that she would spend several afternoons with her daughter before sailing for India. On this occasion, however, none of the young people saw her, for they were out during the afternoon, and were just settling down to tea in the schoolroom when the wheels of the departing carriage crunched down the drive.

"Now for it!" cried Maxwell, and they looked at one another in silence, knowing full well what would happen. Mrs Asplin would think an introduction to her young friends the best distraction for the strange girl after her mother's departure, and the next item in the programme would be the appearance of Miss Peggy herself. Esther rearranged the scattered tea-things; Oswald felt to see if his necktie was in position, and Robert hunched his shoulders and rolled his eyes at Mellicent in distracting fashion. Each one sat with head cocked on one side, in an attitude of eager attention. The front door banged, footsteps approached, and Mrs Asplin's high, cheerful tones were heard drawing nearer and nearer.

"This way, dear," she was saying. "They are longing to see you!"

The listeners gave a simultaneous gulp of excitement, the door opened, and—Peggy entered!

She was not in the least what they had expected! This was neither the blonde beauty of Maxwell's foretelling, nor the black-haired elf described by Mellicent. The first glance was unmitigated disappointment.

"She is not a bit pretty," was the mental comment of the two girls. "What a funny little soul!" that of the three big boys, who had risen on Mrs Asplin's entrance, and now stood staring at the new-comer with curious eyes.

Peggy was slight and pale, and at the first sight her face gave a comical impression of being made up of a succession of peaks. Her hair hung in a pigtail down her back, and grew in a deep point on her forehead; her finely-marked eyebrows were shaped like eaves, and her chin was for all the world like that of a playful kitten. Even the velvet trimming on her dress accentuated this peculiarity, as it zigzagged round the sleeves and neck. The hazel eyes were light and bright, and flitted from one figure to another with a suspicious twinkling; but nothing could have been more composed, more demure, or patronisingly grown-up than the manner in which this strange girl bore the scrutiny which was bent upon her.

"Here are your new friends, Peggy," cried Mrs Asplin cheerily. "They always have tea by themselves in the schoolroom, and do what they please from four to five o'clock. Now just sit down, dear, and take your place among them at once. Esther will make room for you by her side, and introduce you to the others. I will leave you to make friends. I know young people get on better when they are left alone."

She whisked out of the room in her impetuous fashion, and Peggy Saville seated herself in the midst of a ghastly silence. The young people had been prepared to cheer and encourage a bashful stranger, but the self-possession of this thin, pale-faced girl took them by surprise, so that they sat round the table playing uncomfortably with teaspoons and knives, and irritably conscious that they, and not the new-comer, were the ones to be overcome with confusion. The silence lasted for a good two minutes, and was broken at last by Miss Peggy herself.

"Cream *and* sugar!" she said, in a tone of sweet insinuation. "Two lumps, if you please. Not very strong, and as hot as possible. Thank you! So sorry to be a trouble."

Esther fairly jumped with surprise, and seizing the teapot, filled the empty cup in haste. Then she remembered the dreaded airs of the boarding-school miss, and her own vows of independence, and made a gallant effort to regain composure.

"No trouble at all. I hope that will be right. Please help yourself. Bread—and—butter—scones—cake! I must introduce you to the rest, and then you will feel more at home! I am Esther, the eldest, a year older than you, I think. This is Mellicent, my younger sister, fourteen last February. I think you are about the same age." She paused a moment, and Peggy looked across the table and said, "How do you do, dear?" in an affable, grandmotherly fashion, which left poor Mellicent speechless, and filled the others with delighted amusement. But their own turn was coming. Esther pulled herself together, and went on steadily with her introductions. "This is Maxwell, my brother, and these are father's two pupils—Oswald Elliston, and Robert—the Honourable Robert Darcy." She was not without hope that the imposing sound of the latter name would shake the self-possession of the stranger, but Peggy inclined her head with the air of a queen, drawled out a languid, "Pleased to see you!" and dropped her eyes with an air of indifference, which seemed to imply that an "Honourable" was an object of no interest whatever, and that she was really bored by the number of her titled acquaintances. The boys looked at each other with furtive glances of astonishment. Mellicent spread jam all over her plate, and Esther unconsciously turned on the handle of the urn and deluged the tray with water, but no one ventured a second remark, and once again it was Peggy's voice that opened the conversation.

"And is this the room in which you pursue your avocations? It has a warm and cheerful exposure."

"Er—yes! This is the schoolroom. Mellicent and I have lessons here in the morning from our German governess, while the boys are in the study with father. In the afternoon, from two to four, they use it for preparation, and we go out to classes. We have music lessons on Monday, painting on Tuesday, calisthenics and wood-carving on Thursday and Friday. Wednesday and Saturday are half-holidays. Then from four to six the room is common property, and we have tea together and amuse ourselves as we choose."

"A most desirable arrangement. Thank you! Yes,—I *will* take a scone, as you are so kind!" said Peggy blandly; a remark which covered the five young people with confusion, since none of them had noticed that her plate was empty. Each one made a grab in the direction of the plate of scones; the girls failed to reach it, while Oswald, twitching it from Robert's hands, jerked half the contents on the table, and had to pick them up, while Miss Saville looked on with a smile of indulgent superiority.

"Accidents will happen, will they not?" she said sweetly, as she lifted a scone from the plate, with her little finger cocked well in the air, and nibbled it daintily between her small white teeth. "A most delicious cake! Home-made, I presume? Perhaps of your own concoction?"

Esther muttered an inarticulate assent, and once more the conversation languished. She looked appealingly at Maxwell. As the son of the house, the eldest of the boys, it was his place to take the lead, but Maxwell looked the picture of embarrassment. He did not suffer from bashfulness as a rule, but since Peggy Saville had come into the room he had been seized with an appalling self-consciousness. His feet felt in the way, his arms seemed too long for practical purposes, his elbows had a way of invading other people's precincts, and his hands looked red and clammy. It occurred to him dimly that he was not a man after all, but only a big overgrown schoolboy, and that little Miss Saville knew as much, and was mildly pitiful of his shortcomings. He was not at all anxious to attract the attention of the sharp little tongue, so he passed on the signal to Mellicent, kicking her foot under the table, and frowning vigorously in the direction of the stranger.

"Er,"—began Mellicent, anxious to respond to the signal, but lamentably short of ideas,—"Er,—Peggy! Are you fond of sums? I'm in decimals. Do you like fractions? I think they are hateful. I could do vulgars pretty well, but decimals are fearful. They never come right. So awfully difficult."

"Patience and perseverance overcome difficulties. Keep up your courage. I'll help you with them, dear," said Peggy encouragingly, closing her eyes the while, and coughing in a faint and ladylike manner.

She could not really be only fourteen, Mellicent reflected. She talked as if she were quite grown-up,—older than Esther, seventeen or eighteen at the very least. What a little white face she had! what a great thick plait of hair! How erect she held herself! Fräulein would never have to rebuke her new pupil for stooping shoulders. It was kind of her to promise help with those troublesome decimals! Quite too good an offer to refuse.

"Thank you very much," she said heartily, "I'll show you some after tea. Perhaps you may be able to make me understand better than Fräulein. It's very good of you, P—" A quick change of expression warned her that something was wrong, and she checked herself to add hastily, "You want to be called 'Peggy,' don't you? No? Then what must we call you? What is your real name?"

"Mariquita!" sighed the damsel pensively, "after my grandmother—Spanish. A beautiful and unscrupulous woman at the court of Philip the Second." She said "unscrupulous" with an air of pride, as though it had been "virtuous," or some other word of a similar meaning, and pronounced the name of the king with a confidence that made Robert gasp.

"Philip the Second? Surely not? He was the husband of our Mary in 1572. That would make it just a trifle too far back for your grandmother, wouldn't it?" he inquired sceptically; but Mariquita remained absolutely unperturbed.

"It must have been someone else, then, I suppose. How clever of you to remember! I see you know something about history," she said suavely; a remark which caused an amused glance to pass between the young people, for Robert had a craze for history of all description, and had serious thought of becoming a second Carlyle so soon as his college course was over.

Maxwell put his handkerchief to his mouth to stifle a laugh, and kicked out vigorously beneath the table, with the intention of sharing his amusement with his friend Oswald. It seemed, however, that he had aimed amiss, for Mariquita fell back in her chair, and laid her hand on her heart.

"I think there must be some slight misunderstanding. That's my foot that you are kicking! I cut it very badly on the ice last winter, and the least touch causes acute suffering. Please don't apologise; it doesn't matter in the least," and she rolled her eyes to the ceiling, like one in mortal agony.

It was the last straw. Maxwell's embarrassment had reached such a pitch that he could bear no more. He murmured some unintelligible words, and bolted from the room, and the other two boys lost no time in following his example.

In subsequent conversations, Mellicent always referred to this occasion as "the night when Robert had *one cup*," it being, in truth, the only occasion since this young gentleman entered the vicarage when he had neglected to patronise the teapot three or four times in succession.

Chapter Four.

Good-Bye, Mariquita!

For four long days had Mariquita Saville dwelt beneath Mr Asplin's roof, and her companions still gazed upon her with fear and trembling, as a mysterious and extraordinary creature whom they altogether failed to understand. She talked like a book; she behaved like a well-conducted old lady of seventy, and she sat with folded hands gazing around, with a curious, dancing light in her hazel eyes, which seemed to imply that there was some tremendous joke on hand, the secret of which was known only to herself. Esther and Mellicent had confided their impressions to their mother; but in Mrs Asplin's presence Peggy was just a quiet, modest girl, a trifle shy, as was natural under the circumstances, but with no marked peculiarity of any kind. She answered to the name of "Peggy," to which address she was at other times persistently deaf, and sat with neat little feet crossed before her, the picture of a demure, well-behaved young schoolgirl. The sisters assured their mother that Mariquita was a very different person in the schoolroom, but when she inquired as to the nature of the difference, it was not easy to explain.

She talked so grandly, and used such great big words!—"A good thing, too," Mrs Asplin averred. She wished the rest would follow her example, and not use so much foolish, meaningless slang.—Her eyes looked so bright and mocking, as if she were laughing at something all the time.—Poor, dear child! could she not talk as she liked? It was a great blessing she *could* be bright, poor lamb, with such a parting before her!—She was so grown-up, and patronising, and superior!—Tut! tut! Nonsense! Peggy had come from a boarding-school, and her ways were different from theirs—that was all. They must not take stupid notions, but be kind and friendly, and make the poor girl feel at home.

Fräulein on her side reported that her new pupil was docile and obedient, and anxious to get on with her studies, though not so far advanced as might have been expected. Esther was far ahead of her in most subjects, and Mellicent learned with pained surprise that she knew nothing whatever about decimal fractions.

"Circumstances, dear," she explained, "circumstances over which I had no control prevented an acquaintance, but no doubt I shall soon know all about them, and then I shall be pleased to give you the promised help;" and Mellicent found herself saying, "Thank you," in a meek and submissive manner, instead of indulging in a well-merited rebuke.

No amount of ignorance seemed to daunt Mariquita, or to shake her belief in herself. When Maxwell came to grief in a Latin essay, she looked up and said, "Can I assist you?" and when Robert read aloud a passage from Carlyle, she laid her head on one side and said, "Now, do you know, I am not altogether sure that I am with him on that point!" with an assurance which paralysed the hearers.

Esther and Mellicent discussed seriously together as to whether they liked, or disliked, this extraordinary creature, and had great difficulty in coming to a conclusion. She teased, puzzled, aggravated, and provoked them; therefore, if they had any claim to be logical, they should dislike her cordially, yet somehow or other they could not bring themselves to say that they disliked Mariquita. There were moments when they came perilously near loving the aggravating creature. Already it gave them quite a shock to look back upon the time when there was no Peggy Saville to occupy their thoughts, and life without the interest of her presence would have seemed unspeakably flat and uninteresting. She was a bundle of mystery. Even her looks seemed to exercise an uncanny fascination. On the evening of her arrival the unanimous opinion had been that she was decidedly plain, but there was something about the pale little face which always seemed to invite a second glance, and the more closely you gazed, the more complete was the feeling of satisfaction.

"Her face is so *neat*," Mellicent said to herself; and the adjective was not inappropriate, for Peggy's small features looked as though they had been modelled by the hand of a fastidious artist, and the air of dainty finish extended to her hands and feet and slight, graceful figure.

The subject came up for discussion on the third evening after Peggy's arrival, when she had been called out of the room to speak to Mrs Asplin for a few minutes. Esther gazed after her as she walked across the floor with her dignified tread, and when the door was closed she said slowly—

"I don't think Mariquita is as plain now as I did at first; do you, Oswald?"

"N–no! I don't think I do. I should not call her exactly plain. She is a funny little thing, but there's something nice about her face."

"Very nice!"

"Last night in the pink dress she looked almost pretty."

"Y–es!"

"Quite pretty!"

"Y–es! really quite pretty."

"We shall think her lovely in another week," said Mellicent tragically. "Those awful Savilles! They are all alike—there is something Indian about them. Indian people have a lot of secrets that we know nothing about; they use spells, and poisons, and incantations that no English person can understand, and they can charm snakes. I've read about it in books. Arthur and Peggy were born in India, and it's my opinion that they are bewitched. Perhaps the ayahs did it when they were in their cradles. I don't say it is their own fault, but they are not like other people, and they use their charms on us, as there are no snakes in England. Look at Arthur! He was the naughtiest boy—always hurting himself, and spilling things, and getting into trouble, and yet everyone in the house bowed down before him, and did what he wanted.—Now mark my words, Peggy will be the same!"

Mellicent's companions were not in the habit of "marking her words," but on this occasion they looked thoughtful, for there was no denying that they were already more or less under the spell of the remorseless stranger.

On the afternoon of the fourth day Miss Peggy came down to tea with her pigtail smoother and more glossy than ever, and the light of war shining in her eyes. She drew her chair to the table, and looked blandly at each of her companions in turn.

"I have been thinking," she said sweetly, and the listeners quaked at the thought of what was coming. "The thought has been weighing on my mind that we neglect many valuable and precious opportunities. This hour, which is given to us for our own use, might be turned to profit and advantage, instead of being idly frittered away—

"'In work, in work, in work alway,
Let my young days be spent.'

"It was the estimable Dr Watts, I think, who wrote those immortal lines! I think it would be a desirable thing to carry on all conversation at this table in the French language for the future. *Passez-moi le beurre, s'il vous plait*, Mellicent, *ma très chère. J'aime beaucoup le beurre, quand il est frais. Est- ce que vous aimez le beurre plus de la*,—I forget at the moment how you translate *jam, il fait très beau, ce après- midi, n'est pas*?"

She was so absolutely, imperturbably grave that no one dared to laugh. Mellicent, who took everything in deadly earnest, summoned up courage to give a mild little squeak of a reply. "*Wee—mais hier soir, il pleut*;" and in the silence that followed Robert was visited with a mischievous inspiration. He had had French nursery governesses in his childhood, and had, moreover, spent two years abroad, so that French came as naturally to him as his own mother-tongue. The temptation to discompose Miss Peggy was too strong to be resisted. He raised his dark, square-chinned face, looked straight into her eyes, and rattled off a breathless sentence to the effect that there was nothing so necessary as conversation, if one wished to master a foreign language; that he had talked French in the nursery; and that the same Marie who had nursed him as a baby was still in his father's service, acting as maid to his sister. She was getting old now, but was a most faithful creature, devoted to the family, though she had never overcome her prejudices against England and English ways. He rattled on until he was fairly out of breath, and Peggy leant her little chin on her hand, and stared at him with an expression of absorbing attention. Esther felt convinced that she did not understand a word of what was being said, but the moment that Robert stopped, she threw back her head, clasped her hands together, and exclaimed—

"*Mais certainement, avec* pleasure!" with such vivacity and Frenchiness of manner that she was forced into unwilling admiration.

"Has no one else a remark to make?" continued this terrible girl, collapsing suddenly into English, and looking inquiringly round the table. "Perhaps there is some other language which you would prefer to French. It is all the same to me. We ought to strive to become proficient in foreign tongues. At the school where I was at Brighton there was a little girl in the fourth form who could write, and even speak, Greek with admirable fluency. It impressed me very much, for I myself knew so little of the language. And she was only six—"

"Six!" The boys straightened themselves at that, roused into eager protest. "Six years old! And spoke Greek! And wrote Greek! Impossible!"

"I have heard her talking for half an hour at a time. I have known the girls in the first form ask her to help them with their exercises. She knew more than anyone in the school."

"Then she is a human prodigy. She ought to be exhibited. Six years old! Oh, I say—that child ought to turn out something great when she grows up. What did you say her name was, by the bye?"

ROUND AND ROUND SHE WENT, FASTER AND FASTER, WHILE THE FIVE BEHOLDERS GASPED AND STARED.

[*See page* 29.

Peggy lowered her eyelids, and pursed up her lips. "Andromeda Michaelides," she said slowly. "She was six last Christmas. Her father is Greek Consul in Manchester."

There was a pause of stunned surprise; and then, suddenly, an extraordinary thing happened. Mariquita bounded from her seat, and began flying wildly round and round the table. Her pigtail flew out behind her; her arms waved like the sails of a windmill, and as she raced along she seized upon every loose article which she could reach, and tossed it upon the floor.

Cushions from chairs and sofa went flying into the window; books were knocked off the table with one rapid sweep of the hand; magazines went tossing up in the air, and were kicked about like so many footballs. Round and round she went, faster and faster, while the five beholders gasped and stared, with visions of madhouses, strait-jackets, and padded rooms, rushing through their bewildered brains. Her pale cheeks glowed with colour; her eyes shone; she gave a wild shriek of laughter, and threw herself, panting, into a chair by the fireside.

"Three cheers for Mariquita! Ho! ho! he! Didn't I do it well? If you could have *seen* your faces!"

"P–P–P–eggy! Do you mean to say you have been pretending all this time? What do you mean? Have you been putting on all those airs and graces for a joke?" asked Esther severely; and Peggy gave a feeble splutter of laughter.

"W–wanted to see what you were like! Oh, my heart! Ho! ho! ho! wasn't it lovely? Can't keep it up any longer! Good-bye, Mariquita! I'm Peggy now, my dears.—Give me some more tea!"

Chapter Five.

Explanations.

In the explanations that followed, no one showed a livelier interest than Peggy herself. She was in her element answering the questions which were showered upon her, and took an artistic pleasure in the success of her plot.

"You see," she explained, "I knew you would all be talking about me, and wondering what I was like, just as I was thinking about you. As I was Arthur's sister, I knew you would be sure to imagine me a mischievous tom-boy, so I came to the conclusion that the best way to shock you would be to be quite too awfully proper and well-behaved. I never enjoyed anything so much in my life as that first tea-time, when you all looked dumb with astonishment. I had made up my mind to go on for a week, but mother is coming to-morrow, and I couldn't keep it up before her, so I was obliged to explode to-night. Besides, I'm really quite fatigued with being good—"

"And are you—are you—really not proper, after all?" gasped Mellicent blankly; whereat Peggy clasped her hands in emphatic protest.

"Proper! Oh, my dear, I am the most awful person. I am always getting into trouble. You know what Arthur was? Well, I tell you truly, he is nothing to me. It's an extraordinary thing. I have excellent intentions, but I seem bound to get into scrapes. There was a teacher at Brighton, Miss Baker,—a dear old thing. I called her 'Buns.'—She vowed and declared that I shortened her life by bringing on palpitation of the heart. I set the dressing-table on fire by spilling matches and crunching them beneath my heels. It was not a proper dressing-table, you know—just a wooden thing frilled round with muslin. We had two blazes in the last term. And a dreadful thing occurred! Would you believe that I was actually careless enough to sit down on the top of her best Sunday hat, and squash it as flat as a pancake!"

Despite her protestations of remorse, Peggy's voice had an exultant ring as she detailed the history of her escapades, and Esther shrewdly suspected that she was by no means so penitent as she declared. She put on her most severe expression, and said sternly—

"You must be dreadfully careless. It is to be hoped you will be more careful here, for your room is far-away from ours, and you might be burned to death before anyone discovered you. Mother never allows anyone to read in bed in this house, and she is most particular about matches. You wouldn't like to be burned to a cinder all by yourself some fine night, I should say?"

"No, I shouldn't—or on a wet one either. It would be so lonely," said Peggy calmly. "No; I am a reformed character about matches. I support home industries, and go in for safeties, which 'strike only on the box.' But the boys would rescue me." She turned with a smile, and beamed upon the three tall lads. "Wouldn't you, boys? If you hear me squealing any night, don't stop to think. Just catch up your ewers of water, and rush to my bedroom. We might get up an amateur fire-brigade, to be in readiness. You three would be the brigade, and I would be the captain and train you. It would be capital fun. At any moment I could give the signal, and then, whatever you were doing—playing,—working,—eating, —or on cold frosty nights, just when you were going to bed, off you would have to rush, and get out your fire-buckets. Sometimes you might have to break the ice, but there's nothing like being prepared. We might have the first rehearsal to-night—"

"It's rather funny to hear you talking of being captain over the boys, because the day we heard that you were coming, they all said that if they were to be bothered with a third girl in the house, you would have to make yourself useful, and that you should be their fag. Max said so, and so did Oswald, and then Robert said they shouldn't have you. He had lots of little odd things he wanted done, and he could make you very useful. He said the other boys shouldn't have you; you were his property."

"Tut, tut!" said Peggy pleasantly. She looked at the three scowling, embarrassed faces, and the mocking light danced back into her eyes. "So they were all anxious to have me, were they? How nice! I'm gratified to hear it. Is there any little thing I can do for your honourable self now, Mr Darcy, before I dress for dinner?"

Robert looked across the room at Mellicent with an expression which made that young person tremble in her shoes.

"All right, young lady, I'll remember you!" he said quietly. "I've warned you before about repeating conversations. Now you'll see what happens. I'll cure you of that little habit, my dear, as sure as my name is Robert Darcy—"

"The Honourable Robert Darcy!" murmured a silvery voice from the other side of the fireplace. Robert turned his head sharply, but Peggy was gazing into the coals with an air of lamb-like innocence, and he subsided into himself with a grunt of displeasure.

The next day Mrs Saville came to lunch, and spent the afternoon at the vicarage. As Maxwell had said, she was a beautiful woman; tall, fair, and elegant, and looking a very fashionable lady when contrasted with Mrs Asplin in her well-worn serge, but her face was sad and anxious in expression. Esther noticed that her eyes filled with tears more than once as she looked round the table at the husband and wife and the three tall, well-grown children; and when the two ladies were alone in the drawing-room she broke into helpless sobbings.

"Oh, how happy you are! How I envy you! Husband, children, —all beside you. Oh, never, never let one of your girls marry a man who lives abroad. My heart is torn in two; I have no rest. I am always longing for the one who is not there. I must go back,—the major needs me; but my Peggy,—my own little girl! It is like death to leave her behind!"

Mrs Asplin put her arms round the tall figure, and rocked her gently to and fro.

"I know! I know!" she said brokenly. "I *ache* for you, dear; but I understand! I have parted with a child of my own—not for a few years, but for ever, till we meet again in God's heaven. I'll help you every way I can. I'll watch her night and day; I'll coddle her when she's ill; I'll try to make her a good woman. I'll *love* her, dear, and she shall be my own special charge. I'll be a second mother to her."

"You dear, good woman! God bless your kind heart!" said Mrs Saville brokenly. "I can't help breaking down, but indeed I have much to be thankful for. I can't tell you what a relief it is to feel that she is in this house. The principals of that school at Brighton were all that is good and excellent, but they did not understand my Peggy." The tears were still in her eyes, but she broke into a flickering smile at the last word. "My children have such spirits! I am afraid they really do give more trouble than other boys and girls, but they are not really naughty. They are truthful and generous, and wonderfully warm-hearted. I never needed to punish Peg when she was a little girl; it was enough to show that she had grieved me. She never did the same thing again after that;

but—oh, dear me!—the ingenuity of that child in finding fresh fields for mischief! Dear Mrs Asplin, I am afraid she will try your patience. You must be sure to keep a list of all the breakages and accidents, and charge them to our account. Peggy is an expensive little person. You know what Arthur was."

"Bless him—yes! I had hardly a tumbler left in the house," said Mrs Asplin, with gusto. "But I don't grieve myself about a few breakages. I have had too much to do with schoolboys for that!—And now give me all the directions you can about this precious little maid, while we have the room to ourselves."

For the next hour there the two ladies sat in conclave about Miss Peggy's mental, moral, and physical welfare. Mrs Asplin had a book in her hand, in which from time to time she jotted down notes of a curious and inconsequent character. "Pay attention to private reading. Gas-fire in her bedroom for chilly weather. See dentist in Christmas holidays. Query: gold plate over eye-tooth? Boots to order, Beavan and Company, Oxford Street. Cod-liver oil in winter. Careless about changing shoes. Damp brings on throat. Aconite and belladonna." So on, and so on. There seemed no end to the warnings and instructions of this anxious mother; but when all was settled as far as possible, the ladies adjourned into the schoolroom to join the young people at their tea, so that Mrs Saville might be able to picture her daughter's surroundings when separated from her by those weary thousands of miles.

"What a bright, cheery room!" she said smilingly, as she took her seat at the table, and her eyes wandered round as if striving to print the scene in her memory. How many times, as she lay panting beneath the swing of the punkah, she would recall that cool English room, with its vista of garden through the windows, the long table in the centre, the little figure with the pale face and plaited hair, seated midway between the top and bottom! Oh! the moments of longing—of wild, unbearable longing—when she would feel that she must break loose from her prison-house and fly away,—that not the length of the earth itself could keep her back, that she would be willing to give up life itself just to hold Peggy in her arms for five minutes, to kiss the sweet lips, to meet the glance of the loving eyes—

But this would never do! Had she not vowed to be cheerful? The young folks were looking at her with troubled glances. She roused herself, and said briskly—

"I see you make this a playroom as well as a study. Somebody has been wood-carving over there, and you have one of those dwarf billiard-tables. I want to give a present to this room—something that will be a pleasure and occupation to you all; but I can't make up my mind what would be best. Can you give me a few suggestions? Is there anything that you need, or that you have fancied you might like?"

"It's very kind of you," said Esther warmly; and echoes of "Very kind!" came from every side of the table, while boys and girls stared at each other in puzzled consideration. Maxwell longed to suggest a joiner's bench, but refrained out of consideration for the girls' feelings. Mellicent's eager face, however, was too eloquent to escape attention, and Mrs Saville smiled at her in an encouraging manner.

"Well, dear, what is it? Don't be afraid. I mean something really nice and handsome; not just a little thing. Tell me what you thought?"

"A—a new violin!" cried Mellicent eagerly. "Mine is so old and squeaky, and my teacher said I needed a new one badly. A new violin would be nicest of all."

Mrs Saville looked round the table, caught an expressive grimace going the round of three boyish faces, and raised her eyebrows inquiringly.

"Yes? Whatever you like best, of course. It is all the same to me. But would the violin be a pleasure to all? What about the boys?"

"They would hear me play! The pieces would sound nicer. They would like to hear them."

"Ahem!" coughed Maxwell loudly; and at that there was a universal shriek of merriment. Peggy's clear "Ho! ho!" rang out above the rest, and her mother looked at her with sparkling eyes. Yes, yes, yes; the child was happy! She had settled down already into the cheery, wholesome life of the vicarage, and was in her element among these merry boys and girls! She hugged the thought to her heart, finding in it her truest comfort. The laughter lasted several minutes, and broke out intermittently from time to time as that eloquent cough recurred to memory, but after all it was Mellicent who was the one to give the best suggestion.

"Well then, a—a what-do-you-call-it!" she cried. "A thing-um-me-bob! One of those three-legged things for taking photographs! The boys look so silly sometimes, rolling about together in the garden, and we have often and often said, 'Don't you wish we could take their photographs? They *would* look such frights!' We could have ever so much fun with a what-do-you-call-it?"

"Ah, that's something like!" "Good business." "Oh, wouldn't it be sweet!" came the quick exclamations; and Mrs Saville looked most pleased and excited of all.

"A camera!" she cried. "What a charming idea! Then you would be able to take photographs of Peggy and the whole household, and send them out for me to see. How delightful! That is a happy thought, Mellicent. I am so grateful to you for thinking of it, dear. I'll buy a really good large one, and all the necessary materials, and send them down at once. Do any of you know how to set to work?"

"I do, Mrs Saville," Oswald said. "I had a small camera of my own, but it got smashed some years ago. I can show them how to begin, and we will take lots of photographs of Peggy for you, in groups and by herself. They mayn't be very good at first, but you will be interested to see her in different positions. We will take her walking, and bicycling, and sitting in the garden, and every way we can think of—"

"And whenever she has a new dress or hat, so that you may know what they are like," added Mellicent anxiously. "Are her hats going to be the same as ours, or is she to choose them for herself?"

"She may choose them for herself, subject, of course, to your mother's refraining influence. If she were to develop a fondness for scarlet feathers, for instance, I think Mrs Asplin should interfere; but Peggy has good taste. I don't think she will go far wrong," said the girl's mother, looking at her fondly; and the little white face quivered before it broke into its sunny, answering smile.

Three times that evening, after Mrs Saville had left, did her companions surprise the glitter of tears in Peggy's eyes; but there was a dignified reserve about her manner which forbade outspoken sympathy. Even when she was discovered to be quietly crying behind her book, when Maxwell flipped it mischievously out of her hands,—even then did Peggy preserve her wonderful self-possession. The tears were trickling down her cheeks, and her poor little nose was red and swollen, but she looked up at Maxwell without a quiver, and it was he who stood gaping before her, aghast and miserable.

"Oh, I say! I'm fearfully sorry!"

"So am I," said Peggy severely. "It was rude, and not at all funny. And it injures the book. I have always been taught to reverence books, and treat them as dear and valued companions. Pick it up, please. Thank you. Don't do it again." She hitched herself round in her chair, and settled down once more to her reading, while Maxwell slunk back to his seat. When Peggy was offended she invariably fell back upon Mariquita's grandiose manner, and the sting of her sharp little tongue left her victims dumb and smarting.

Chapter Six.

A New Friendship.

A week after this, Mrs Saville came to pay her farewell visit before sailing for India. Mother and daughter went out for a walk in the morning, and retired to the drawing-room together for the afternoon. There was much that they wanted to say to each other, yet for the most part they were silent, Peggy sitting with her head on her mother's shoulder, andMrs Saville's arms clasped tightly round her. Every now and then she stroked the smooth brown head, and sometimes Peggy raised her lips and kissed the cheek which leant against her own, but the sentences came at long intervals.

"If I were ill, mother—a long illness—would you come?"

"On wings, darling! As fast as boat and train could bring me."

"And if you were ill?"

"I should send for you, if it were within the bounds of possibility—I promise that! You must write often, Peggy—long, long letters. Tell me all you do, and feel, and think. You will be almost a woman when we meet again. Don't grow up a stranger to me, darling."

"Every week, mother! I'll write something each day, and then it will be like a diary. I'll tell you every bit of my life..."

"Be a good girl, Peggy. Do all you can for Mrs Asplin, who is so kind to you. She will give you what money you need, and if at any time you should want more than your ordinary allowance, for presents or any special purpose, just tell her about it, and she will understand. You can have anything in reason; I want you to be happy. Don't fret, dearie. I shall be with father, and the time will pass. In three years I shall be back again, and then, Peg, then, how happy we shall be! Only three years."

Peggy shivered, and was silent. Three years seem an endless space when one is young. She shut her eyes, and pondered drearily upon all that would happen before the time of separation was passed. She would be seventeen, nearly eighteen—a young lady who wore dresses down at her ankles, and did up her hair. This was the last time, the very, very last time when she would be a child in her mother's arms. The new relationship might be nearer, sweeter, but it could never be the same, and the very sound of the words "the last time" sends a pang to the heart.

Half an hour later the carriage drove up to the door. Mr and Mrs Asplin came into the room to say a few words offarewell, and then left Peggy to see her mother off. There were no words spoken on the way, and so quietly did they move that Robert had no suspicion that anyone was near, as he took off his shoes in the cloak-room opening off the hall. He tossed his cap on to a nail, picked up his book, and was just about to sally forth, when the sound of a woman's voice sent a chill through his veins. The tone of the voice was low, almost a whisper, yet he had never in his life heard anything so thrilling as its intense and yearning tenderness. "Oh, my Peggy!" it said. "My little Peggy!" And then, as in reply, came a low moaning sound, a feeble bleat like that of a little lamb torn from its mother's side. Robert charged back into the cloak-room, and kicked savagely at the boots and shoes which were scattered about the floor, his lips pressed together, and his brows meeting in a straight black line across his forehead. Another minute, and the carriage rolled away. He peeped out of the door in time to see a little figure fly out into the rain, and walking slowly towards the schoolroom came face to face with Mrs Asplin.

"Gone?" she inquired sadly. "Well, I'm thankful it is over. Poor little dear, where is she? Flown up to her room, I suppose. We'll leave her alone until tea-time. It will be the truest kindness."

"Yes," said Robert vaguely. He was afraid that the good lady would not be so willing to leave Peggy undisturbed if she knew her real whereabouts, and was determined to say nothing to undeceive her. He felt sure that the girl had hidden herself in the summer-house at the bottom of the garden, and a nice, damp, mouldy retreat it would be this afternoon, with the rain driving in through the open window, and the creepers dripping on the walls. Just the place in which to sit and break your heart, and catch rheumatic fever with the greatest possible ease. And yet Robert said no word of warning to Mrs Asplin. He had an inward conviction that if anyone were to go to the rescue, that person should be himself, and that he, more than anyone else, would be able to comfort Peggy in her affliction. He sauntered up and down the hall until the coast was clear, then dashed once more into the cloak-room, took an Inverness coat from a nail, a pair of goloshes from the floor, and sped rapidly down the garden- path. In less than two minutes he had reached the summer- house, and was peeping cautiously in at the door. Yes; he was right. There sat Peggy, with her arms stretched out before her on the rickety table, her shoulders heaving with long, gasping sobs. Her fingers clenched and unclenched themselves spasmodically, and the smooth little head rolled to and fro in an abandonment of grief. Robert stood looking on in silent misery. He had a boy's natural hatred of tears, and his first impulse was to turn tail, go back to the house, and send someone to take his place; but even as he hesitated he shivered in the chilly damp, and remembered the principal reason of his coming. He stepped forward and dropped the cloak over the bent shoulders, whereupon Peggy started up and turned a scared white face upon him.

"Who, who—Oh! it is you! What do you want?"

"Nothing. I saw you come out, and thought you would be cold. I brought you out my coat."

"I don't want it; I am quite warm. I came here to be alone."

"I know; I'm not going to bother. Mrs Asplin thinks you are in your room, and I didn't tell her that I'd seen you go out. But it's damp. If you catch cold, your mother will be sorry."

Peggy looked at him thoughtfully, and there was a glimmer of gratitude in her poor tear-stained eyes.

"Yes; I p–p–romised to be careful. You are very kind, but I can't think of anything to-night. I am too miserably wretched."

"I know; I've been through it. I was sent away to a boarding-school when I was a little kid of eight, and I howled myself to sleep every night for weeks. It is worse for you, because you are older, but you will be happy enough in this place when you get settled. Mrs Asplin is a brick, and we have no end of fun. It is ever so much better than being at school; and, I say, you mustn't mind what Mellicent said the other night. She's a little muff, always saying the wrong thing. We were only chaffing when we said you were to be our fag. We never really meant to bully you."

"You c–couldn't if you t–tried," stammered Peggy brokenly, but with a flash of her old spirit which delighted her hearer.

"No; of course not. You can stand up for yourself; I know that very well. But look here: I'll make a compact, if you will. Let us be friends. I'll stick to you and help you when you need it, and you stick to me. The other girls have their brother to look after them, but if you want anything done, if anyone is cheeky to you, and you want him kicked, for instance, just come to me, and I'll do it for you. It's all nonsense about being a fag, but there are lots of things you could do for me if you would, and I'd be awfully grateful. We might be partners, and help one another—"

Robert stopped in some embarrassment, and Peggy stared fixedly at him, her pale face peeping out from the folds of the Inverness coat. She had stopped crying, though the tears still trembled on her eyelashes, and her chin quivered in uncertain fashion. Her eyes dwelt on the broad forehead, the overhanging brows, the square, massive chin, and brightened with a flash of approval.

"You are a nice boy," she said slowly. "I like you! You don't really need my help, but you thought it would cheer me to feel that I was wanted. Yes; I'll be your partner, and I'll be of real use to you yet. You'll find that out, Robert Darcy, before you have done with me."

"All right, so much the better. I hope you will; but you know you can't expect to have your own way all the time. I'm the senior partner, and you will have to do what I tell you. Now I say it's damp in this hole, and you ought to come back to the house at once. It's enough to kill you to sit in this draught."

"I'd rather like to be killed. I'm tired of life. I shouldn't mind dying a bit."

"Humph!" said Robert shortly. "Jolly cheerful news that would be for your poor mother when she arrived at the end of her journey! Don't be so selfish. Now then, up you get! Come along to the house."

"I wo—" Peggy began, then suddenly softened, and glanced apologetically into his face. "Yes, I will, because you ask me. Smuggle me up to my room, Robert, and don't, don't, if you love me, let Mellicent come near me! I couldn't stand her chatter to-night!"

"She will have to fight her way over my dead body," said Robert firmly; and Peggy's sweet little laugh quavered out on the air.

"Nice boy!" she repeated heartily. "Nice boy; I do like you!"

Chapter Seven.

Amateur Photographers.

Peggy looked very sad and wan after her mother's departure, but her companions soon discovered that anything like outspoken sympathy was unwelcome. The redder her eyes, the more erect and dignified was her demeanour; if her lips trembled when she spoke, the more grandiose and formidable became her conversation, for Peggy's love of long words and high-sounding expressions was fully recognised by this time, and caused much amusement in the family.

A few days after Mrs Saville sailed, a welcome diversion arrived in the shape of the promised camera. The Parcels Delivery van drove up to the door, and two large cases were delivered, one of which was found to contain the camera itself, the tripod and a portable dark room, while the other held such a collection of plates, printing-frames, and chemicals as delighted the eyes of the beholders. It was the gift of one who possessed not only a deep purse, but a most true and thoughtful kindness, for, when young people are concerned, two-thirds of the enjoyment of any present is derived from the possibility of being able to put it to immediate use. As it was a holiday afternoon, it was unanimously agreed to take two groups and develop them straightway.

"Professional photographers are so dilatory," said Peggy severely; "and indeed I have noticed that amateurs are even worse. I have twice been photographed by friends, and they have solemnly promised to send me a copy within a few days. I have waited, consumed by curiosity, and, my dears, it has been months before it has arrived! Now we will make a rule to finish off our groups at once, and not keep people waiting until all the interest has died away. There's no excuse for such dilatory behaviour!"

"There is some work to do, remember, Peggy. You can't get a photograph by simply taking off and putting on the cap; you must have a certain amount of time and fine weather. I haven't had much experience, but I remember thinking that photographs were jolly cheap, considering all the trouble they cost, and wondering how the fellows could do them at the price. There's the developing, and washing, and printing, and toning,—half a dozen processes before you are finished."

Peggy smiled in a patient, forbearing manner.

"They don't get any less, do they, by putting them off? Procrastination will never lighten labour. Come, put the camera up for us, like a good boy, and we'll show you how to do it." She waved her hand towards the brown canvas bag, and the six young people immediately seized different portions of the tripod and camera, and set to work to put them together. The girls tugged and pulled at the sliding legs, which were too new and stiff to work with ease; Maxwell turned the screws which moved the bellows, and tried in vain to understand their working; Robert peered through the lenses, and Oswald alternately raved, chided, and jeered at their efforts. With so many cooks at work, it took an unconscionable time to get ready, and even when the camera was perched securely on its spidery legs, it still remained to choose the site of the picture, and to pose the victims. After much wandering about the garden, it was finally decided that the schoolroom window would be an appropriate background for a first effort; but a heated argument followed before the second question could be decided.

"I vote that we stand in couples, arm-on-arm,—like this!" said Mellicent, sidling up to her beloved brother, and gazing into his face in a sentimental manner, which had the effect of making him stride away as fast as he could walk, muttering indignant protests beneath his breath.

Then Esther came forward with her suggestion.

"I'll hold a book as if I were reading aloud, and you can all sit round in easy, natural positions, and look as if you were listening. I think that would make a charming picture."

"Idiotic, I call it! 'Scene from the Goodchild family; mamma reading aloud to the little ones.' Couldn't possibly look easy and natural under the circumstances; should feel too miserable. Try again, my dear. You must think of something better than that."

It was impossible to please those three fastidious boys. One suggestion after another was made, only to be waved aside with lordly contempt, until at last the girls gave up any say in the matter, and left Oswald to arrange the group in a manner highly satisfactory to himself and his two friends, however displeasing to the more artistic members of the party. Three girls in front, two boys behind, all standing stiff as pokers; with solemn faces, and hair ruffled by constant peepings beneath the black cloth. Peggy in the middle, with her eyebrows more peaked than ever, and an expression of resigned martyrdom on her small, pale face; Mellicent, large and placid, on the left; Esther on the right, scowling at nothing, and, over their shoulders, the two boys' heads, handsome Max and frowning Robert.

"There," cried Oswald, "that's what I call a sensible arrangement! If you take a photograph, *take* a photograph, and don't try to do a pastoral play at the same time. Keep still a moment, and I will see if it is focused all right. I can see you pulling faces, Peggy! It's not at all becoming. Now then, I'll put in the plate—that's the way!—one—two—three—and I shall take you. Stea-dy?"

Instantly Mellicent burst into giggles of laughter, and threw up her hands to her face, to be roughly seized from behind and shaken into order.

"Be quiet, you silly thing! Didn't you hear him say steady? What are you trying to do?"

"She has spoiled this plate, anyhow," said Oswald icily. "I'll try the other, and if she can't keep still this time she had better run away and laugh by herself at the other end of thegarden. Baby!"

"Not a ba—" began Mellicent indignantly; but she was immediately punched into order, and stood with her mouth wide open, waiting to finish her protest so soon as the ordeal was over.

Peggy forestalled her, however, with an eager plea to be allowed to take the third picture herself.

"I want to have one of Oswald to send to mother, for we are not complete without him, and I know it would please her to think I had taken it myself," she urged; and permission was readily granted, as everyone felt that she had a special claim in the matter. Oswald therefore put in new plates, gave instructions as to how the shutters were to be worked, and retired to take up an elegant position in the centre of the group.

"Are you read-ee?" cried Peggy, in professional sing-song; then she put her head on one side and stared at the group with twinkling eyes. "Hee, hee! How silly you look! Everyone has a new expression for the occasion! Your own mothers would not recognise you! That's better. Keep that smile going for another moment, and—how long must I keep off the cap, did you say?"

Oswald hesitated.

"Well, it varies. You have to use your own judgment. It depends upon—lots of things! You might try one second for the first, and two for the next, then one of them is bound to be right."

"And one a failure! If I were going to depend on my judgment, I'd have a better one than that!" cried Peggy scornfully. "Ready! A little more cheerful, if you please— Christmas is coming! That's *one*. Be so good as to remain in your positions, ladies and gentlemen, and I'll try another." The second shutter was pulled out, the cap removed, and the group broke up with sighs of relief, exhausted with the strain of cultivating company smiles for a whole two minutes on end. Max stayed to help the girls to fold up the camera, while Oswald darted into the house to prepare the dark room for the development of the plates.

When he came out, ten minutes later on, it was a pleasant surprise to discover Miss Mellicent holding a plate in her hand and taking sly peeps inside the shutter, just "to see how it looked." He stormed and raved, while Mellicent looked like a martyr, wished to know how a teeny little light like that could possibly hurt anything, and seemed incapable of understanding that if one flash of sunlight could make a picture, it could also destroy it with equal swiftness. Oswald was forced to comfort himself with the reflection that there were still three plates uninjured; and, when all was ready, the six operators squeezed themselves in the dark room, to watch the process of development, indulging the while in the most flowery expectations.

"If it is very good, let me send it to an illustrated paper. Oh, do!" said Mellicent, with a gush. "I have often seen groups of people in them. 'The thing-a-me-bob touring company,' and stupid old cricketers, and things like that. We should be far more interesting."

"It will make a nice present for mother, enlarged and mounted," said Peggy thoughtfully. "I shall keep an album of my own, and mount every single picture we take. If there are any failures, I shall put them in too, for they will make it all the more amusing. Photograph albums are horribly uninteresting as a rule, but mine shall be quite different. There shall be nothing stiff and prim about it; the photographs shall be dotted about in all sorts of positions, and underneath each I shall put in—ah—conversational annotations." Her tongue lingered over the words with triumphant enjoyment. "Conversational annotations, describing the circumstances under which it was taken, and anything about it which is worth remembering... What are you going to do with those bottles?"

Oswald ruffled his hair in embarrassment. To pose as an instructor in an art, when one is in doubt about its very rudiments, is a position which has its drawbacks.

"I don't—quite—know. The stupid fellow has written instructions on all the other labels, and none on these except simply 'Developer Number 1' and 'Developer Number 2'; I think the only difference is that one is rather stronger than the other. I'll put some of the Number 2 in a dish, and see what happens; I believe that's the right way—in fact, I'm sure it is. You pour it over the plate and jog it about, and in two or three minutes the picture ought to begin to appear. Like this!"

Five eager faces peered over his shoulders, rosy red in the light of the lamp; five pairs of lips uttered a simultaneous "Oh!" of surprise; five cries of dismay followed in instant echo. It was the tragedy of a second. Even as Oswald poured the fluid over the plate, a picture flashed before their eyes, each one saw and recognised some fleeting feature; and, in the very moment of triumph, lo, darkness, as of night, a sheet of useless, blackened glass!

"What about the conversational annotations?" asked Robert slily; but he was interrupted by a storm of indignant queries, levied at the head of the poor operator, who tried in vain to carry off his mistake with a jaunty air. Now that he came to think of it, he believed you *did* mix the two developers together! Just at the moment he had forgotten the proportions, but he would go outside and look it up in the book; and he beat a hasty retreat, glad to escape from the scene of his failure. It was rather a disconcerting beginning; but hope revived once more when Oswald returned, primed with information from the *Photographic Manual*, and Peggy's plates were taken from their case and put into the bath. This time the result was slow in coming. Five minutes went by, and no signs of a picture—ten minutes, a quarter of an hour.

"It's a good thing to develop slowly; you get the details better," said Oswald, in so professional a manner that he was instantly reinstated in public confidence; but when twenty minutes had passed, he looked perturbed, and thought he would use a little more of the hastener. The bath was strengthened and strengthened, but still no signs of a picture. The plate was put away in disgust, and the second one tried with a like result. So far as it was possible to judge, there was nothing to be developed on the plate.

"A nice photographer you are, I must say! What are you playing at now?" asked Max, in scornful impatience; and Oswald turned severely to Peggy—

"Which shutter did you draw out? The one nearest to yourself?"

"Yes, I did—of course I did!"

"You drew out the nearest to you, and the farthest away from the lens?"

"Precisely—I told you so!" and Peggy bridled with an air of virtue.

"Then no wonder nothing has come out! You have drawn out the wrong shutter each time, and the plates have never been exposed. They are wasted! That's fivepence simply *thrown* away, to say nothing of the chemicals!"

His air of aggrieved virtue; Peggy's little face staring at him, aghast with horror; the thought of four plates being used and leaving not a vestige of a result, were all too funny to be resisted. Mellicent went off into irrepressible giggles; Max gave a loud "Ha, ha!" and once again a mischievous whisper sounded in Peggy's ear—

"Good for you, Mariquita! What about the 'conversational annotations'?"

Chapter Eight.

Peggy shows herself in her True Colours.

The photographic fever burnt fiercely for the next few weeks. Every spare hour was devoted to the camera, and there was not a person in the house, from the vicar himself to the boy who came in to clean boots and knives, who had not been pressed to repeated sittings. There were no more blank plates, but there were some double ones which had been twice exposed, and showed such a kaleidoscopic jumble of heads and legs as was as good as any professional puzzle; but, besides these, there were a number of groups where the likenesses were quite recognisable, though scarcely flattering enough to be pleasant to the originals. There was quite a scene in the dining-room on the evening when Oswald came down in triumph and handed round the proofs of the first presentable group, over which he had been busy all the afternoon.

"Oh, oh, oh! I'm an old woman, and I never knew it!" cried Mrs Asplin, staring in dismay at the haggard-looking female who sat in the middle of the group, with heavy, black shadows on cheeks and temple. The vicar cast a surreptitious glance in the glass above the sideboard, and tried to straighten his bent shoulders, while Mellicent's cheeks grew scarlet with agitation, and the tears were in her voice, as she cried—

"I look like a p–p–pig! It's not a bit like! A nasty, horrid, fat, puffy pig!"

"I don't care about appearances; but mine is not in the least like," Esther said severely. "I am sure no one could recognise it; I look seventy-eight at the very least."

Robert flicked the paper across the table with a contemptuous "Bah!" and Max laughed in his easy, jolly manner, and said—

"Now I know how I shall look when my brain softens! I'm glad I've seen it; it will be a lesson to me to take things easily, and not over-study."

"But look at the leaves of the ivy," protested Oswald, in aggrieved self-vindication, "each one quite clear and distinct from the others; it's really an uncommonly good plate. The detail is perfect. Look at that little bunch of flowers at the corner of the bed!" All in vain, however, did he point out the excellences of his work. The victims refused to look at the little bunch of flowers. Each one was occupied with staring at his own portrait; the Asplin family sighing and protesting, and Peggy placidly poking a pin through the eyes of the various sitters, and holding the paper to the light to view the effect. It was a little trying to the feelings of one who had taken immense pains over his work, and had given up a bicycle ride to sit for a whole afternoon in a chilly pantry, dabbling in cold water, and watching over the various processes. Oswald was ruffled, and showed it more plainly than was altogether courteous.

"I'm sorry you're not pleased," he said coldly. "I aim at truthfulness, you see, and that is what you don't get from a professional photograph. It's no good wasting time, simply to get oneself disliked. I'll go in for Nature, and leave the portrait business to somebody else. The girls can try! They think they can do everything!"

Peggy looked at Esther, and Esther looked at Peggy. They did not say a word, but a flash of understanding passed from the brown eyes to the grey, which meant that they were on their mettle. They were not going to defend themselves, but henceforth it was a case of die or produce a good photograph, and so oblige Oswald to alter his tone of scornful incredulity.

For the next week the camera was the one engrossing thought. Every minute that could be spared was devoted to experiments, so that Fräulein complained that lessons were suffering in consequence. The hearts of her pupils were not in their work, she declared; it would be a good thing if a rule could be made that no more photographs were to be taken until the Christmas holidays. She looked very fierce and formidable as she spoke, but soft-hearted Mrs Asplin put in a plea for forgiveness.

"Ah, well, then, have patience for a few days longer," she begged. "They are just children with a new toy; let them have as much of it as they will at first, and they will tire of their own accord, and settle down to work as well as ever. We can control their actions, but not their thoughts; and I'm afraid if I forbade photography at present, you would find them no more interested in lessons. I fancy there is something especially engrossing on hand this week, and we might as well let them have it out."

Even Mrs Asplin, however, hardly realised the thoroughness with which the girls were setting to work to achieve their end. They held a committee meeting on Esther's bed, sitting perched together in attitudes of inelegant comfort, with arms encircling their knees, and chins resting on the clasped hands, wherein it was proposed and seconded that Peggy, the artistic, should pose and take the sitters, while Esther, the accurate, should undertake the after-processes.

"And what am I to do?" cried Mellicent plaintively; and her elders smiled upon her with patronising encouragement.

"You shall wash up all the trays and glasses, and put them neatly away."

"You shall carry the heavy things, dear, and stand to me for your back hair. I think I could make a really good effect with your back hair." Peggy put her head on one side and stared at the flaxen mane in speculative fashion. "A long muslin gown—a wreath of flowers—a bunch of lilies in your hands! If you weren't so fat, you would do splendiforously for Ophelia. I might manage it, perhaps, if I took you from the back, with your head turned over your shoulder, so as to show only the profile. Like that! Don't move now, but let me see how you look." She took Mellicent's head between her hands as she spoke, wagged it to and fro, as if it belonged to a marionette, and then gave a frog-like leap to a farther corner of the bed to study the effect. "A little more to the right. Chin higher! Look at the ceiling. Yes-es—I can do it. I see how it can be done."

It turned out, indeed, that Peggy had a genius for designing and posing pretty, graceful pictures. With a few yards of muslin and a basket, or such odds and ends of rubbish as horrified Esther's tidy soul to behold, she achieved marvels in the way of fancy costumes, and transformed the placid Mellicent into a dozen different characters: Ophelia, crowned with flowers; Marguerite, pulling the petals of a daisy; Hebe, bearing a basket of fruit on her head, and many other fanciful impersonations, were improvised and taken before the week was over. She went about the work in her usual eager, engrossed, happy-go-lucky fashion, sticking pins by the dozen into Mellicent's flesh in the ardour of arrangement, and often making a really charming picture, only to spoil it at the last moment by a careless movement, which altered the position of the camera, and so omitted such important details as the head of the sitter, or left her squeezed into one corner of the picture, like a sparrow on the house-top.

Out of a dozen photographs, three, however, were really remarkable successes; as pretty pictures as one could wish to see, and, moreover, exceedingly good likenesses of the bonnie little subject. Esther's part of the work was performed with her usual conscientious care; and when the last prints were mounted, the partners gazed at them with rapture and pride. They were exhibited at the dinner-table the same evening amid a scene of riotous excitement. The vicar glowed with pleasure; Mrs Asplin called out, "Oh, my baby! Bless her heart!" and whisked away two tears of motherly pride. Oswald was silent and subdued; and even Robert said, "Humph—it's not so bad," a concession which turned the girls' heads by its wonderful magnanimity.

Their triumph was almost sweeter than they had expected; but, truth to tell, they had had too much of photography during the last week, and Mrs Asplin's prophecy came true, inasmuch as it now ceased to become an occupation of absorbing interest, and assumed its rightful place as an amusement to be enjoyed now and then, as opportunity afforded.

Chapter Nine.

The Honourable Rosalind.

By the beginning of October Peggy had quite settled down in her new home, and had established her right to be Arthur Saville's sister by convulsing the quiet household with her tricks and capers. She was affectionate, obedient, and strictly truthful; her prim little face, grandiose expressions, and merry ways, made her a favourite with everyone in the house, from the vicar, who loved to converse with her in language even more high-flown than her own, to the old North-country cook, who confided in the housemaid that she "fair–ly did love that little thing," and manoeuvred to have apple charlotte for dinner as often as possible, because the "little thing" had praised her prowess in that direction, and commended the charlotte as a "delicious confection." Mrs Asplin was specially tender over the girl who had been left in her charge, and, in return, Peggy was all that was sweet and affectionate, vowed that she could never do enough to repay such kindness, and immediately fell into a fresh pickle, and half frightened the life out of her companions by her hairbreadth escapes. Her careless, happy-go-lucky ways seemed all the more curious because of the almost Quaker- like neatness of her appearance. Mellicent was often untidy, and even Esther had moments of dishevelment, but Peggy was a dainty little person, whose hair was always smooth, whose dress well brushed and natty. Her artistic sense was too keen to allow of any shortcoming in this respect; but she seemed blessed with a capacity of acting before she thought, which had many disastrous consequences. She was by no means a robust girl, and Mrs Asplin fussed over her little ailments like an old mother-hen with a delicate nursling. One prescription after another was unearthed for her benefit, until the washstand in her room looked like a small chemist's shop. An array of doctor's tinctures, gargles, and tonics, stood on one side, while on the other were a number of home-made concoctions in disused wine-bottles, such as a paregoric cough-mixture, and a cooling draught to be taken the first thing in the morning, which last pretended to be lemonade, but in reality contained a number of medicinal powders. "Take it up tenderly, treat it with care!" was Peggy's motto with respect to this last-named medicine, for she had discovered that by judicious handling it was possible to enjoy a really tasty beverage, and to leave the sediment untouched at the bottom of the bottle!

Esther and Mellicent were almost equally well supplied by their anxious mother, but their bottles behaved in a well- regulated fashion, and never took upon themselves to play tricks, while those in Peggy's room seemed infected by the spirit of the owner, and amused themselves with seeing how much mischief they could accomplish. A bottle of ammonia had been provided as a cure for bites of gnats and flies; Peggy flicked a towel more hastily than usual, and down it fell, the contents streaming over the wood, and splashing on to the wardrobe near at hand, with the consequence that every sign of polish was removed, and replaced by white unsightly stains. The glass stopper of a smelling-salts bottle became fixed in its socket, and, being anointed with oil and placed before the fire to melt, popped out suddenly with a noise as of a cannon shot, aimed accurately for the centre of the mirror, and smashed it into a dozen pieces. The "safety ink-pot," out of which she indited her letters to her mother, came unfastened of its own accord and rolled up and down the clean white toilet cover. This, at least, was the impression left by Peggy's innocent protestations, while the gas and soap seemed equally obstinate—the one refusing to be lowered when she left the room, and the other insisting upon melting itself to pieces in her morning bath!

"Mrs Saville was right—Peggy is a most expensive person!" cried Mrs Asplin in dismay, when the bills for repairs came in; but when the vicar suggested the advisability of a reproof, she said, "Oh, poor child; she is so lonely—I haven't the heart to scold her;" and Peggy continued to detail accounts of her latest misfortune with an air of exaggerated melancholy, which barely concealed the underlying satisfaction. It required a philosophic mind to be able to take damages to personal property in so amiable a fashion; but occasionally Peggy's pickles took an irresistibly comical character. The story was preserved in the archives of the family of one evening when the three girls had been sent upstairs to wash their abundant locks and dry them thoroughly before retiring to bed. A fire was kindled in the old nursery, which was now used as a sewing-room, and Mrs Asplin, who understood nothing if it was not the art of making young folks happy, had promised a supper of roast apples and cream when the drying process was finished.

Esther and Mellicent were squatted on the hearth, in their blue dressing-gowns, when in tripped Peggy, fresh as a rose, in a long robe of furry white, tied round the waist with a pink cord. One bath-towel was round her shoulders, and a smaller one extended in her hands, with the aid of which she proceeded to perform a fancy dance, calling out instructions to herself the while, in imitation of the dancing-school mistress. "To the right—two—three! To the left—two—three! Spring! Pirouette! Atti–tude!" She stood poised on one foot, towel waving above her head, damp hair dripping down her back, while Esther and Mellicent shrieked with laughter, and drummed applause with heel and toe. Then she flopped down on the centre of the hearth, and there was an instantaneous exclamation of dismay.

"Phew! What a funny smell! Phew! Phew! Whatever can it be?"

"I smelt it too. Peggy, what have you been doing? It's simply awful!"

"Hair-wash, I suppose, or the soap—I noticed it myself. It will pass off," said Peggy easily; but at that moment Mrs Asplin entered the room, sniffed the air, and cried loudly—

"Bless me, what's this? A regular Apothecaries' Hall! Paregoric! It smells as if someone had been drinking quarts of paregoric! Peggy, child, your throat is not sore again?"

"Not at all, thank you. Quite well. I have taken no medicine to-day."

"But it is you, Peggy—it really is!" Mellicent declared. "There was no smell at all before you came into the room. I noticed it as soon as the door was opened, and when you came and sat down beside us—whew! simply fearful!"

"I have taken *no* medicine to-day," repeated Peggy firmly. Then she started, as if with a sudden thought, lifted a lock of hair, sniffed at it daintily, and dropped it again with an air of conviction. "Ah, I comprehend! There seems to have been a slight misunderstanding. I have mistaken the bottles. I imagined that I was using the mixture you gave me, but—"

"She has washed her hair in cough-mixture! Oh, oh, oh! She has mixed paregoric and treacle with the water! Oh, what will I do! what will I do! This child will be the death of me!" Mrs Asplin put her hand to her side, and laughed until the tears ran down her cheeks, while Mellicent rolled about on the floor, and Esther's quiet "He, he, he!" filled up the intervals between the bursts of merriment.

Peggy was marched off to have her hair re-washed and rinsed, and came back ten minutes later, proudly complacent, to seat herself in the most comfortable stool and eat roast apple with elegant enjoyment. She was evidently quite ready to enlarge upon her latest feat, but the sisters had exhausted the subject during her absence, and had, moreover, a piece of news to communicate which was of even greater interest.

"Oh, Peggy, what y'think?" cried Mellicent, running her words into each other in breathless fashion, as her habit was when excited; "I've got something beautiful to tell you. S'afternoon Bob got a letter from his mother to say that they were all coming down next week to stay at the Larches for the winter. They come almost every year, and have shooting-parties, and come to church and sit in the big square pew, where you can just see their heads over the side. They look so funny, sitting in a row without their bodies. Last year there was a young lady with them who wore a big grey hat—the loveliest hat you ever saw—with roses under the brim, and stick-up things all glittering with jewels, and she got married at Christmas. I saw her photograph in a magazine, and knew her again in a moment. I used to stare at her, and once she smiled back at me. She looked sweet when she smiled. Lady Darcy always comes to call on mother, and she and father go there to dinner ever so many times, and we are asked to play with Rosalind—the Honourable Rosalind. I expect they will ask you to go too. Isn't it exciting?"

"I can bear it," said Peggy coldly. "If I try very hard, I think I can support the strain."

The Larches, the country house of Lord Darcy, had already been pointed out to her notice; but the information that the family was coming down for the yearly visit was unwelcome to her, for a double reason. She feared, in the first place, lest it should mean a separation from Bob, who was her faithful companion, and fulfilled his promise of friendship in a silent, undemonstrative fashion, much to her fancy. In the second place, she was conscious of a rankling feeling of jealousy towards the young lady who was distinguished by the name of the Honourable Rosalind, and who seemed to occupy an exalted position in the estimation of the vicar's daughters. Her name was frequently introduced into conversation, and always in the most laudatory fashion. When a heroine was of a superlatively fascinating description, she was "Just like Rosalind"; when an article of dress was unusually fine and dainty, it would "do for Rosalind." Rosalind was spoken ofwith bated breath, as if she were a princess in a fairy tale, rather than an ordinary flesh-and-blood damsel. And Peggy did not like it; she did not like it at all, for, in her own quiet way, she was accustomed to queen it among her associates, and could ill brook the idea of a rival. She had not been happy at school, but she had been complacently conscious that of all the thirty girls she was the most discussed, the most observed, and also, among the pupils themselves, the most beloved. At the vicarage she was an easy first. When the three girls went out walking, she was always in the middle, with Esther and Mellicent hanging on an arm at either side. Robert was her sworn vassal, and Max and Oswald her respectful and, on the whole, obedient servants. Altogether, the prospect of playing second fiddle to this strange girl was by no means pleasant. Peggy tilted her chin, and spoke in a cool, cynical tone.

"What is she like, this wonderful Rosalind? Bob does not seem to think her extraordinary. I cannot imagine a 'Miss Robert' being very beautiful, and as she is his sister, I suppose they are alike."

Instantly there arose a duet of protests.

"Not in the least. Not a single bit. Rosalind is lovely! Blue eyes, golden hair—"

"Down past her waist—"

"The sweetest little hands—"

"A real diamond ring—"

"Pink cheeks—"

"Drives a pony-carriage, with long-tailed ponies—"

"Speaks French all day long with her governess—jabber, jabber, jabber, as quick as that—just like a native—"

"Plays the violin—"

"Has a lovely little sitting-room of her own, simply crammed with the most exquisite presents and books, and goes travelling abroad to France and Italy and hot places in winter. Lord and Lady Darcy simply worship her, and so does everyone, for she is as beautiful as a picture. Don't you think it would be lovely to have a lord and lady for your father and mother?"

Peggy sniffed the air in scornful superiority.

"I am very glad I've not! Titles are so ostentatious! Vulgar, I call them! The very best families will have nothing to do with them. My father's people were all at the Crusades, and the Wars of the Roses, and the Field of the Cloth of Gold. There is no older family in England, and they are called 'Fighting Savilles,' because they are always in the front of every battle, winning honours and distinctions. I expect they have been offered titles over and over again, but they would not have them. They refused them with scorn, and so would I if one were offered to me. Nothing would induce me to accept it!"

Esther rolled her eyes in a comical, sideway fashion, and gave a little chuckle of unbelief; but Mellicent looked quite depressed by this reception of her grand news, and said anxiously—

"But, Peggy, think of it! The Honourable Mariquita! It would be too lovely! Wouldn't you feel proud writing it in visitors' books, and seeing it printed in newspapers when you grow up? 'The Honourable Mariquita wore a robe of white satin, trimmed with gold!'"

"Peggy Saville is good enough for me, thank you," said that young lady, with a sudden access of humility. "I have no wish to have my clothes discussed in the public prints. But if you are invited to the Larches to play with your Rosalind, pray don't consider me! I can stay at home alone. I don't mind being dull. I can turn my time to good account. Not for the world would I interfere with your pleasure?"

"But P–P–Peggy, dar–ling Peggy, we would not leave you alone!" Mellicent's eyes were wide with horror, she stretched out entreating hands towards the unresponsive figure. To see Peggy cross and snappish like—any other ordinary mortal was an extraordinary event, and quite alarming to her placid mind. "They will ask you, too, dear! I am sure they will—we will all be asked together!" she cried; but Peggy tossed her head, refusing to be conciliated.

"I shall have a previous engagement. I am not at all sure that they are the sort of people I ought to know," she said. "My parents are so exclusive! They might not approve of the acquaintance!"

Chapter Ten.

Ambitions!

Although Fräulein had charge over the girls' education, Mr Asplin reserved to himself the right of superintending their studies and dictating their particular direction. He was so accustomed to training boys for a definite end that he had no patience with the ordinary aimless routine of a girl's school course, and in the case of his daughters had carefully provided for their different abilities and tastes. Esther was a born student, a clear-headed, hard-thinking girl, who took a delight in wrestling with Latin verbs and in solving problems in Euclid, while she had little or no artistic faculty. He put her through much the same course as his own boys, gave her half an hour's private lesson on unoccupied afternoons, and cut down the two hours' practising on the piano to a bare thirty minutes. Esther had pleaded to give up music altogether, on the ground that she had neither love nor skill for this accomplishment, but to this the vicar would not agree.

"You have already spent much time over it, and have passed the worst of the drudgery; it would be folly to lose all you have learnt," he said. "You may not wish to perform in public, but there are many other ways in which your music may be useful. In time to come you would be sorry if you could not read an accompaniment to a song, play bright airs to amuse children, or hymn tunes to help in a service. Half an hour a day will keep up what you have learned, and so much time you must manage to spare."

With Mellicent the case was almost exactly opposite. It was a waste of time trying to teach her mathematics, she had not sufficient brain power to grasp them, and if she succeeded in learning a proposition by heart like a parrot, it was only to collapse into helpless tears and protestations when the letters were altered, and, as it seemed to her, the whole argument changed thereby.

Fräulein protested that it was impossible to teach Mellicent to reason; but the vicar was loath to give up his pet theory that girls should receive the same hard mental training as their brothers. He declared that if the girl were weak in this direction, it was all the more necessary that she should be trained, and volunteered to take her in hand for half an hour daily, to see what could be done. Fräulein accepted this offer with a chuckle of satisfaction, and the vicar went on with the lessons several weeks, patiently plodding over the same ground without making the least impression on poor Mellicent's brain, until there came one happy never-to-be-forgotten morning when Algebra and Euclid went spinning up to the ceiling, and he jumped from the table with a roar of helpless laughter.

"Oh, baby! baby! this is past all bearing! We might try for a century, and never get any further. I cannot waste any more time." Then, seeing the large tears gathering, he framed the pretty face in his hands, and looked at it with a tender smile. "Never mind, darling! there are better things in this world than being clever and learned. You will be our little house-daughter; help mother with her work, and play and sing to father when he is tired in the evening. Work hard at your music, learn how to manage a house, to sew and mend and cook, and you will have nothing to regret. A woman who can make a home, has done more than many scholars."

So it came to pass that Mellicent added the violin to her accomplishments, and was despatched to her own room to practise exercises, while her elder sister wrestled with problems and equations.

When Peggy Saville arrived, here was a fresh problem, for Fräulein reported that the good child could not add five and six together without tapping them over on her finger; was as ignorant of geography as a little heathen, and had so little ear for music that she could not sing "Rule Britannia" without branching off into "God save the Queen." But when it came to poetry!—Fräulein held up her hands in admiration. It was absolutely no effort to that child to remember, her eyes seemed to flash down the page, and the lines were her own, and as she repeated them her face shone, and her voice thrilled with such passionate delight that Esther and Mellicent had been known to shed tears at the sound of words which had fallen dead and lifeless from their own lips. And at composition, how original she was! What a relief it was to find so great a contrast to other children! When it was the life of a great man which should be written, Esther and Mellicent began their essays as ninety-nine out of a hundred schoolgirls would do, with a flat and obvious statement of birth, birthplace, and parentage; but Peggy disdained such commonplace methods, and dashed headlong into the heart of her subject with a high-flown sentiment, or a stirring assertion which at once arrested the reader's interest. And it was the same with whatever she wrote; she had the power of investing the dullest subject with charm and brightness. Fräulein could not say too much of Peggy's powers in this direction, and the vicar's eye brightened as he listened. He asked eagerly to be allowed to see the girl's manuscript book, and summoned his wife from pastry-making in the kitchen to hear the three or four essays which it contained.

"What do you think of those for a girl of fourteen? There's a pupil for you! If she were only a boy! Such dash—such spirit —such a gift of words! Do you notice her adjectives? Exaggerated, no doubt, and over-abundant, but so apt, so true, so strong! That child can write: she has the gift. She ought to turn out an author of no mean rank."

"Oh, dear me! I hope not. I hope she will marry a nice, kind man who will be good to her, and have too much to do looking after her children to waste her time writing stories," cried Mrs Asplin, who adored a good novel when she could get hold of one, but harboured a prejudice against all women- authors as strong-minded creatures, who lived in lodgings, and sported short hair, inky fingers, and a pen behind the ear. Mariquita Saville was surely destined for a happier fate. "When a woman can live her *own* romance, why need she trouble her head about inventing others?"

Her husband looked at her with a quizzical smile.

"Even the happiest life is not all romance, dear. It sometimes seems unbearably prosaic, and then it is a relief to lose oneself in fiction. You can't deny that! I seem to have a remembrance of seeing someone I know seated in a big chair before this very fire devouring a novel and a Newton pippin together on more Saturday afternoons than I could number."

"Tuts!" said his wife, and blushed a rosy red, which made her look ridiculously young and pretty. Saturday afternoon was her holiday-time of the week, and she had not yet outgrown her schoolgirl love of eating apples as an accompaniment to an interesting book; but how aggravating to be reminded of her weakness just at this moment of all others! "What an inconvenient memory you have!" she said complainingly. "Can't a poor body indulge in a little innocent recreation without having it brought up against her in argument ever afterwards? And I thought we were talking about Peggy! What is at the bottom of this excitement? I know you have some plan in your head."

"I mean to see that she reads good books, and only books that will help, and not hinder, her progress. The rest will come in time. She must learn before she can teach, have some experience of her own before she can imagine the experiences of others; but writing is Peggy's gift, and she has been put in my charge. I must try to give her the right training."

From that time forward Mr Asplin studied Peggy with a special interest, and a few evenings later a conversation took place among the young people which confirmed him in his conclusion as to her possibilities. Lessons were over for the day, and girls and boys were amusing themselves in the drawing-room, while Mr Asplin read the *Spectator*, and his wife knitted stockings by the fire. Mellicent was embroidering a prospective Christmas present, an occupation which engaged her leisure hours from March to December; Esther was reading, and Peggy was supposed to be writing a letter, but was, in reality, talking incessantly, with her elbows planted on the table, and her face supported on her clasped hands. She wore a bright pink frock, which gave a tinge of colour to the pale face, her hair was unbound from the tight pigtail and tied with a ribbon on the nape of her neck, from which it fell in smooth heavy waves to her waist. It was one of the moments when her companions realised with surprise that Peggy could look astonishingly pretty upon occasion; and Oswald, from the sofa, and Max and Bob, from the opposite side of the table, listened to her words with all the more attention on that account.

She was discussing the heroine of a book which they had been reading in turns, pointing out the inconsistencies in her behaviour, and expatiating on the superior manner in which she—Mariquita—would have behaved, had positions been reversed. Then the boys had described their own imaginary conduct under the trying circumstances, drawing forth peals of derisive laughter from the feminine audience; and the question had finally drifted from "What would you do?" to "What would you be?" with the result that each one was eager to expatiate on his own pet schemes and ambitions.

"I should like to come out first in all England in the Local Examinations, get my degree of M.A., and be a teacher in a large High School," said Esther solemnly. "At Christmas and Easter I would come home and see my friends, and in summer-time I'd go abroad and travel, and rub up my languages. Of course, what I should like best would be to be headmistress of Girton, but I could not expect that to come for a good many years. I must be content to work my way up, and I shall be quite happy wherever I am, so long as I am teaching."

"Poor old Esther! and she will wear spectacles, and black alpaca dresses, and woollen mittens on her hands! Can't I see her!" cried Max, throwing back his head with one of the cheery bursts of laughter which brought his mother's eyes upon him with a flash of adoring pride. "Now there's none of that overweening ambition about me. I could bear up if I never saw an improving book again. What *I* would like would be for some benevolent old millionaire to take a fancy to me, and adopt me as his heir. I feel cut out to be a country gentleman, and march about in gaiters and knickerbockers, looking after the property, don't you know, and interviewing my tenants. I'd be strict with them, but kind at the same time; look into all their grievances, and put them right whenever I could. I'd make it a model place before I'd done with it, and all the people would adore me. That's my ambition, and a very good one it is too; I defy anyone to have a better."

"I should like to marry a very rich man with a big moustache, and a beautiful house in London with a fireplace in the hall," cried Mellicent fervently. "I should have carriages and horses, and a diamond necklace and three children: Valentine Roy—that should be the boy—and Hildegarde and Ermyntrude, the girls, and they should have golden hair like Rosalind, and blue eyes, and never wear anything but white, and big silk sashes. I'd have a housekeeper to look after the dinners and things, and a governess for the children, and never do anything myself except give orders and go out to parties. I'd be the happiest woman that ever lived."

Lazy Oswald smiled in complacent fashion.

"And the fattest! Dearie me, wouldn't you be a tub! I don't know that I have any special ambition. I mean to get my degree if I can, and then persuade the governor to send mea tour round the world. I like moving about, and change and excitement, and travelling is good fun if you avoid the fag, and provide yourself with introductions to the right people. I know a fellow who went off for a year, and had no end of a time; people put him up at their houses, and got up balls and dinners for his benefit, and he never had to rough it a bit. I could put in a year or two in that way uncommonly well."

Rob had been wriggling on his chair and scowling in his wild-bear fashion all the while Oswald was speaking, and at the conclusion he relieved his feelings by kicking out recklessly beneath the table, with the result that Peggy sat up suddenly with a "My foot, my friend! Curb your enthusiasm!" which made him laugh, despite his annoyance.

"But it's such bosh!" he cried scornfully. "It makes me sick to hear a fellow talk such nonsense. Balls and dinners—faugh! If that's your idea of happiness, why not settle down in London and be done with it! That's the place for you! I'd give my ears to go round the world, but I wouldn't thank you to go with a dress suit and a valet; I'd want to rough it, to get right out of the track of civilisation and taste a new life; to live with the Bedouin in their tents as some of those artist fellows have done, or make friends with a tribe of savages. Magnificent! I'd keep a notebook with an account of all I did, and all the strange plants and flowers and insects I came across, and write a book when I came home. I'd a lot rather rough it in Africa than lounge about Piccadilly in a frock coat and tall hat." Robert sighed at the hard prospect which lay before him as the son of a noble house, then looked across the table with a smile: "And what says the fair Mariquita? What *rôle* in life is she going to patronise when she comes to years of discretion?"

Peggy nibbled the end of her pen and stared into space.

"I've not quite decided," she said slowly. "I should like to be either an author or an orator, but I'm not sure which. I think, on the whole, an orator, because then you could watch the effect of your words. It is not possible, of course, but what I should like best would be to be the Archbishop of Canterbury, or some great dignitary of the Church. Oh, just imagine it! To stand up in the pulpit and see the dim cathedral before one, and the faces of the people looking up, white and solemn.—I'd stand waiting until the roll of the organ died away, and there was a great silence; then I would look at them, and say to myself—'A thousand people, two thousand people, and for half an hour they are in my power. I can make them think as I will, see as I will, feel as I will. They are mine! I am their leader.'—I cannot imagine anything in the world more splendid than that! I should choose to be the most wonderful orator that was ever known, and people would come from all over the world to hear me, and I would say beautiful things in beautiful words, and see the answer in their faces, and meet the flash in the eyes looking up into mine. Oh-h! if it could only—only be true; but it can't, you see. I am a girl, and if I try to do anything in public I am as nervous as a rabbit, and can only squeak, squeak, squeak in a tiny little voice that would not reach across the room. I had to recite at a prize-giving at school once, and, my dears, it was a lamentable failure! I was only audible to the first three rows, and when it was over I simply sat down and howled, and my knees shook. Oh dear, the very recollection unpowers me! So I think, on the whole, I shall be an authoress, and let my pen be my sceptre. From my quiet fireside," cried Peggy, with a sudden assumption of the Mariquita manner, and a swing of the arms which upset a vase of chrysanthemums, and sent a stream of water flowing over the table—"from my quiet fireside I will sway the hearts of men—"

"My plush cloth! Oh, bad girl—my new plush cloth! You dreadful Peggy, what will I do with you?" Mrs Asplin rushed forward to mop with her handkerchief and lift the dripping flowers to a place of safety, while Peggy rolled up her eyes with an expression of roguish impenitence.

"Dear Mrs Asplin, it was not I, it was that authoress. She was evolving her plots... Pity the eccentricities of the great!"

Chapter Eleven.

A Shakespeare Reading.

Esther was preparing for the Cambridge Local Examination at Christmas, and making a special study of *The Merchant of Venice*, as the play chosen for the year.

Fräulein explained the notes, and expatiated on the Venice of the past and the manners and customs of its inhabitants; but it was Mr Asplin who had the brilliant idea of holding a Shakespeare reading which should make the play live in the imagination of the young people, as no amount of study could do. The suggestion was made one day at dinner, and was received with acclamation by everyone present.

"Oh, how lovely, father! It will help me ever so much!" said Esther. "And Peggy must be Portia."

"I'd like to be that funny little man Launcelot—what do you call it?—only I know I couldn't do it," said Mellicent humbly. "I'll be the servants and people who come in and give messages. But, of course, Peggy must be Portia."

"Peggy shall be Portia, and I'll be the Jew, and snarl at her across the court," said Rob, with an assurance which was not at all appreciated by his companions.

"I've rather a fancy to try Shylock myself," Max declared. "Oswald would make a capital Bassanio, and you could manage Antonio all right if you tried, for he has not so much to do. Let me see: Peggy—Portia; Esther—Nerissa; Mellicent —Jessica (she's so like a Jewess, you see!); you and Oswald —Bassanio and Antonio; Shylock—my noble self. Father and mother to help out with the smaller characters. There you are! A capital cast, and everyone satisfied. I'm game to be Shylock, but I can't do the sentimental business. You two fellows will have to take them, and we'll divide the smallerfry among us."

"Indeed we will do nothing of the kind. I'm not going to take Bassanio; I couldn't do it, and I won't try. I'll have a shot at

Shylock if you like, but I can't do anything else. The cast is all wrong, except so far as Peggy is concerned. Of course she is Portia."

"Proposed, seconded, and carried unanimously that Peggy is Portia!" said Mr Asplin, smiling across the table at that young lady, who tried to look modest and unconcerned, but was plainly aglow with satisfaction. "For Shylock, as the character seems so much in demand, we had better draw lots. I will write the names on slips of paper, and you must all agree to take what comes, and make the best of it. I will fill in the gaps, and I am sure mother will help all she can—"

"Lemonade in the intervals, and coffee for those who prefer it, with some of my very best company cake," said Mrs Asplin briskly. "It will be quite an excitement. I should rather like to be Shylock myself, and defy Peggy and her decree; but I'll give it up to the boys, and make myself generally useful. Why couldn't we begin to-night?"

"Oh, Mrs Asplin, no! It will take me days to get up my part! And the costumes—consider the costumes!" cried Peggy anxiously. And her hostess raised her hands in surprise.

"The costumes! Are you going to dress up? I never thought of that!"

"Surely that is unnecessary, Peggy! You can read the play without changing your clothes!" echoed the vicar; but, from the chorus of disclaimer which greeted his words, it appeared that the young people could do nothing of the sort.

Max wanted to know how a fellow could possibly "talk Shylock" in a white tie and an evening jacket. Oswald thought it equally ridiculous to pose as an Italian lover in English clothing; and Peggy turned up her eyes and said she could not really abandon herself to her part if her costume were inappropriate. Even Esther, the sober-minded, sided with the rest, so the vicar laughed and gave way, only too pleased to sanction anything which helped the object which he had at heart.

"Dress up by all means, if it pleases you. It will be interesting to see the result. But, of course, I must be absolved from any experiments of the kind."

"Oh, of course! And mother, too, if she likes, though I should love to see her made-up as Shylock! You must not see or ask about our dresses until the night arrives. They must be a secret. You will lend us all your fineries, mother—won't you?"

"Bless your heart, yes! But I haven't got any!" said Mrs Asplin, in her funny Irish way. "They were all worn out long, long ago." She gave a little sigh for the memory of the days when she had a wardrobe full of pretty things and a dozen shimmery silk dresses hanging on the pegs, and then flashed a loving smile at her husband, in case he might think that she regretted their loss. "If there is anything about the rooms that would do, you are welcome to use it," she added, glancing vaguely at the sideboard and dumb waiter, while the boys laughed loudly at the idea of finding any "properties" in the shabby old dining-room.

Peggy, however, returned thanks in the most gracious manner, and sat wrapt in thought for the rest of the evening, gazing darkly around from time to time, and scribbling notes on sheets of note-paper.

Short of playing Shylock, which in the end fell to Maxwell's share, it seemed as if all the responsibility of the performance fell on Peggy's shoulders. She was stage manager, selecting appropriate pieces of furniture from the different rooms and piling them together behind the screen in the study, whence they could be produced at a moment's notice, to give some idea of the different scenes. She coached Esther and Mellicent in their parts, designed and superintended the making of the costumes, and gave the finishing touches to each actor in turn when the night of the "Dramatic Reading" arrived.

"Taking one consideration with another," as Max remarked, "the costumes were really masterpieces of art."

To attire two young gentlemen as Italian cavaliers, and a third as a bearded Jew, with no materials at hand beyond the ordinary furnishings of a house, is a task which calls for no small amount of ingenuity, yet this is exactly what Peggy had done.

Antonio and Bassanio looked really uncommonly fine specimens, with cycling knickerbockers, opera cloaks slung over their shoulders, and flannel shirts pouched loosely over silk sashes, and ornamented with frills of lace at wrists and neck. Darkened eyebrows gave them a handsome and distinguished air, and old straw hats and feathers sat jauntily on their tow wigs.

The vicar sat in the arm-chair by the fire, Shakespeare in hand, waiting to fill in the odd parts with his wife's help, and simultaneous cries of astonishment and admiration greeted the appearance of the two actors at the beginning of the first scene.

"It's wonderful! Did I ever see such children? What in the world have they got on their heads? Milly's old leghorn, I declare, and my pink feathers. My old pink feathers! Deary me! I'd forgotten all about them. I've never worn them since the year that—"

"'In sooth, I know not why I am so sad,'" quoth the wearer of the feathers, scowling darkly at the frivolous prattler, who straightway hid her head behind her book, and read Salanio's first speech in a tone of meek apology.

There was a great deal of confusion about the first scene, for four people had to read the parts of six, and one of the number was so much occupied with gazing at the costumes of the actors that she invariably lost her place, and had to be called to order by significant coughs and glances. By this time it generally happened that the vicar had made up his mind to come to the rescue, and both husband and wife would begin to read at the same moment, to their own amusement, and to the disgust of the two lads, who felt uncomfortable in their borrowed plumes, and keenly sensitive about their precious dignity. Antonio mumbled his last speech in undignified haste, and followed Bassanio out of the room, prepared to echo his statement that this sort of thing was "tomfoolery," and that he wasn't going to make an idiot of himself any longer to please Peggy Saville, or any other girl in the world. But the words died on his lips, for outside, in the hall, stood Peggy herself, or rather Portia, and such a Portia as made him fairly blink with amazement! Amidst the bustle of the last few days Portia's own costume had been kept a secret, so that the details came as a surprise to the other members of the party. Nerissa stood by her side, clad in a flowing costume, the component parts of which included a dressing-gown, an antimacassar, and a flowered chintz curtain; but, despite the nature of the materials, the colouring was charming, and frizzled hair, flushed cheeks, and sparkling eyes, transformed the sober Esther into a very personable attendant on the lady of Belmont. There was nothing of the dressing-gown character about Portia's own attire, however. Its magnificence took away the breath of the beholders. The little witch had combed her hair to the top of her head, and arranged it in a coil, which gave height and dignity to her figure. A string of pearls was twisted in and out among the dark tresses; her white silk frock was mysteriously lengthened and ornamented by two large diamond-shaped pieces of satin encrusted with gold, one placed at the bottom of the skirt, and the other hanging loosely from the square-cut neck of the bodice. Long yellow silk sleeves fell over the bare arms and reached the ground; and from the shoulders hung a train of golden-hued plush, lined with a paler shade of yellow. Bassanio and Gratiano stood aghast, and Portia simpered at them sweetly in the intervals between dispensing stage directions to the boot boy, who was clad in his best suit for the occasion, and sent to and fro to change the arrangement of the scenery. He wheeled the sofa into the centre of the room, piled it up with blue cushions, and retired to make way for the two ladies, who were already edging in at the door.

A gasp of astonishment greeted their appearance, but when Peggy dragged her heavy train across the room, threw herself against the cushions in an attitude calculated to show off all the splendour of her attire, when she leant her pearl-decked head upon her hand, turned her eyes to the ceiling, and said, with a sigh as natural and easy as if they were her own words which she was using, and not those of the immortal Shakespeare himself, "'By my troth, Nerissa, my little body is a-weary of this great world!'"—then the vicar broke into a loud "Hear! hear!" of delight, and Mrs Asplin seized the poker and banged uproarious applause upon the fender. For the first few minutes amazement and admiration held her dumb; but as the girls moved to and fro, and the details of their costumes became more apparent, she began to utter spasmodic cries of recognition, somewhat trying to the composure of the actors.

Portia's description of her lovers was interrupted by a cry of, "My table centres! The Turkish squares I bought at the Exhibition, and have never used! Wherever did they find them?" while a little later came another cry, as the identity of the plush train made itself known, "My *portière* from the drawing-room door! My beautiful *portière*—with the nice new lining! Oh dear, dear! it's dragging about all over the dirty carpet! Don't sit on it, dear! For pity's sake, don't git on it!"

"Mother!" cried Esther, in a deep tone of remonstrance; but Portia was unconscious of interruption. The other actors held their books in their hands, and, for the most part, read their speeches; but Peggy trusted entirely to memory, and sighed and yawned over the denunciation of her lovers, with evident satisfaction to herself as well as to the beholders. Nerissa read her part "conscientiously," as the newspapers would say, punctuating her sentences in exemplary fashion, and laying the emphasis upon the right words as directed by the stage manageress; but, such is the contrariness of things, that, with all her efforts, the effect was stiff and stifled, while Peggy drawled through her sentences, or gabbled them over at break-neck speed, used no emphasis at all, or half a dozen running, at her own sweet will, and was so truly Portia that the vicar wondered dreamily if he should have to interview the Duke of Morocco in his study, and Mrs Asplin sighed unconsciously, and told herself that the child was too young to be troubled with lovers. She must not dream of accepting any one of them for years to come!

At the end of the scene, however, anxiety about her beloved *portière* overpowered everything else in the mind of the vicar's wife, and she rushed after the actors to call out eager instructions. "Hang it up at once—there's good children. If you put it down on a chair, Peggy will sit on it as sure as fate! And oh! my table centres! Put them back in the drawer if you love me! Wrap them up in the tissue paper as you found them!"

"Mother, you are a terrible person! Go back, there's a dear, and do keep quiet!" cried a muffled voice from behind the dining-room door, as Shylock dodged back to escape observation; and Mrs Asplin retreated hastily, aghast at the sight of a hairy monster, in whom she failed to recognise a trace of her beloved son and heir. Shylock's make-up was, in truth, the triumph of the evening. The handsome lad had been transformed into a bent, misshapen old man, and anything more ugly, frowsy, and generally unattractive than he now appeared it would be impossible to imagine. A cushion gave a hump to his shoulders, and over this he wore an aged purple dressing-gown, which had once belonged to the vicar. The dressing-gown was an obvious refuge; but who but Peggy Saville would have thought of the trimming, which was the making of the shaggy, unkempt look so much desired? Peggy had sat with her hands clasped on her lap, and her head on one side, staring at the gown when it was held out for her approval two days before, then had suddenly risen, and rushed two steps at a time upstairs to the topmost landing, a wide, scantily furnished space which served for a playground on wet afternoons. An oilcloth covered the floor, a table stood in a corner, and before each of the six doors was an aged wool rug, maroon as to colouring, with piebald patches here and there where the skin of the lining showed through the scanty tufts. Peggy gave a whoop of triumph, tucked one after the other beneath her arm, and went flying down again, dropping a mat here and there, tripping over it, and nearly falling from top to bottom of the stairs. Hairbreadth escapes were, however, so much a part of her daily existence that she went on her way unperturbed, and carried her bundle into the study, where the girls sniffed derisively, and the boys begged to know what she intended to do with all that rubbish.

"'They that have no invention should be hanged,'" quoted Peggy, unperturbed. "Give me a packet of pins, and I'll soon show you what I am going to do. Dear, dear, dear, I don't know what you would do without me! You are singularly bereft of imagination."

She tossed her pigtail over her shoulder, armed herself with the largest pins she could find, and set to work to fasten the mats down the front of the gown, and round the hem at the bottom, so that the wool hung in shaggy ends over the feet. The skins were thick, the heads of the pins pressed painfully into her fingers, but she groaned and worked away until the border was arranged for stitching, and could be tried on to show the effect.

"Perfectly splendid!" was the verdict of the beholders. And so the matter of Shylock's gown was settled; but his beard still remained to be provided, and was by no means an easy problem to solve.

"Tow!" suggested Mellicent; but the idea was hooted by all the others. The idea of Shylock as a blonde was too ridiculous to be tolerated. False hair was not to be bought in a small village, and Maxwell's youthful face boasted as yet only the faintest shadow of a moustache.

The question was left over for consideration, and an inspiration came the same afternoon, when Robert hurled one of the roller-like cushions of the sofa at Oswald's head, and Oswald, in catching it, tore loose a portion of the covering.

"Now you've done it!" he cried. "The room will be covered with feathers, and then you will say it was my fault! We shall have to fasten the stupid thing up somehow or other!" He peered through the opening as he spoke, and his face changed. "It's not feathers—it's horsehair! Here's a find! What about that wig for Shylock?"

Esther was dubious.

"It would take a great deal of horsehair to make a wig. It would spoil the cushion if the horsehair were taken away; it would spoil the sofa if the cushion were small; it would spoil the room if the sofa—"

Peggy interrupted with a shriek of laughter. "Oh, oh, oh! It's like the 'House that Jack built'! How long do you intend to go on like that? Nonsense, my dear! It would be perfectly easy to take out what we want, and put it back afterwards. I'll promise to do it myself and sew it up tightly, though, if you desire my opinion, I think the cushion would be improved by letting in a little air. You might as well lean your head on a brick. Max, you are a made man! You shall have a beautiful, crinkly black wig, and a beard to match! We will sew them to your turban, and fasten them with black elastic. It will never show, and I'll finish off the joins after you are dressed. You'll see?"

"You can do as you like! I'm in your hands!" said Max easily; and when the night of the reading arrived, and he was attired in wig and gown, Peggy seated him in a chair and tucked a towel under his chin with an air of business. She had a number of small accessories on a table near at hand, and Max was first instructed to stick pieces of black plaster over alternate teeth, so that he might appear to possess only a few isolated fangs, and then made to lie back in his chair, while his dresser stood over him with a glue-brush in one hand and a bunch of loose horsehair in the other.

"Shut your eyes!" she cried loudly. And before he could say "Jack Robinson" a tuft of the wiry stuff covered his eyebrow. "Keep your face still!" And, to his horror, the gum was daubed from the borders of the beard, halfway up to his eyes, and little prickly ends of hair were held in Peggy's palm and pressed against his cheeks until they were firmly attached.

This, indeed, was more than he had bargained for! He jerked back his head, and began a loud-voiced protest, only to be interrupted by shrieks of excitement.

"Oh, oh, oh! It's beautiful—beautiful! What a fright! What a delicious fright! No one would know you! You look an old hairy monster who would gobble up half a dozen Christians. Do look at yourself!"

Peggy felt the pride of an artist in the result of her efforts, and Max was hardly less delighted than herself as he stood before the glass, gazing at his hairy cheeks and leering horribly, to admire his toothless gums. If the result were so hideous as to astonish even those who had watched the process of his make-up, what wonder that the effect upon Shylock's fond parents was of a stupefying nature!

Horror kept Mrs Asplin silent until the middle of the scene between Shylock and Antonio when the bond is signed, and then her agitation could no longer be controlled, and Shylock's little speeches were interrupted by entreaties to take that horrid stuff off his teeth, to use plenty of hot water in washing his face, and to be sure to anoint it plentifully with cold cream after doing so.

An ordinary lad would have lost his temper at these interruptions; but Max adored his mother, and could never take anything she did in a wrong spirit. Anger being therefore impossible, the only other resource was to laugh, which, in Peggy's opinion, was even worse than the former. A Shylock who chuckled between his speeches, and gave a good-humoured "Ha! ha!" just before uttering his bitterest invective, was a ridiculous parody of the character, with whom it would be impossible to act. It would be hard indeed if all her carefully rehearsed speeches lost their effect, and the famous trial scene were made into a farce through these untimely interruptions!

The second part of the play went more smoothly, however, as the audience settled down to a more attentive hearing, and the actors became less self-conscious and embarrassed. If four out of the six were sticks, who never for a moment approached the verge of the natural, Portia and Shylock did nobly, and, when the reading was over and the young people gathered round the fire in the drawing-room, it was unanimously agreed that they had acquired a more intimate knowledge of the play by this one evening's representation than by weeks of ordinary study.

"I feel so much more intimate with it!" said Esther. "It seems to have made it alive, instead of just something I have read in a book. It was a delightful thought, father, and I am grateful to you for proposing it. I wish I could do all my lessons in the same way."

"I've not enjoyed myself so much for ages. You just did beautifully, all of you, and the dresses were a sight to behold. As for Peggy, she's a witch, and could make up costumes on a desert island, if she were put to it! But I don't know what is going to happen to my poor, dear boy's face. Oswald, what is he doing? Isn't he coming to have some lemonade and cake?" asked Mrs Asplin anxiously. And Oswald chuckled in a heartless fashion.

"Pride must abide. He would be Shylock, whether we liked it or not, so let him take the consequences. He is fighting it out with cold cream in the bathroom, and some of the horsehair sticks like fun. I'll go up and tell him we have eaten all the cake. He was getting savage when I came down, and it will sweeten his temper!"

Chapter Twelve.

Peggy in Trouble.

As Peggy sat writing in the study one afternoon, a shaggy head came peering round the door, and Robert's voice said eagerly—"Mariquita! A word in your ear! Could you come out and take a turn round the garden for half an hour before tea, or are you too busy?"

"Not at all. I am entirely at your disposal," said Peggy elegantly; and the young people made their way to the cloak-room, swung on coats and sailor hats, and sallied out into the fresh autumn air.

"Mariquita," said Robert then, using once more the name by which he chose to address Peggy in their confidential confabs, "Mariquita, I am in difficulties! There is a microscope advertised in *Science* this week, that is the very thing I have been pining for for the last six years. I must *get* it, or die; but the question is—*how*? You see before you a penniless man." He looked at Peggy as he spoke, and met her small, demure smile.

"My dear and honourable sir—"

"Yes, yes, I know; drop that, Mariquita! Don't take for granted, like Mellicent, that because a man has a title he must necessarily be a millionaire. Everything is comparative! My father is rich compared to the vicar, but he is really hard-up for a man in his position. He gets almost no rent for his land nowadays, and I am the third son. I haven't as much pocket-money in a month as Oswald gets through in a week. Now that microscope costs twenty pounds, and if I were to ask the governor for it, he wouldn't give it to me, but he would sigh and look wretched at being obliged to refuse. He's a kind-hearted fellow, you know, who doesn't like to say 'No,' and I hate to worry him. Still—that microscope! I must have it. By hook or by crook, I must have it. I've set my mind on that."

"I'm sure I hope you will, though for my part you must not expect me to look through it. I like things to be pretty, and when you see them through a microscope they generally look hideous. I saw my own hand once—ugh!" Peggy shuddered. "Twenty pounds! Well, I can only say that my whole worldly wealth is at your disposal. Draw on me for anything you like—up to seven-and-six! That's all the money I have till the beginning of the month."

"Thanks!—I didn't intend to borrow; I have a better idea than that. I was reading a magazine the other day, and came upon a list of prize competitions. The first prize offered was thirty pounds, and I'm going to win that prize! The microscope costs only twenty pounds, but the extra ten would come in usefully for—I'll tell you about that later on! The *Piccadilly Magazine* is very respectable and all that sort of thing; but the governor is one of the good, old-fashioned, conservative fellows, who would be horrified if he saw my name figuring in it. I'm bound to consider his feelings, but all the same I'm going to win that prize. It says in the rules—I've read them through carefully—that you can ask your friends to help you, so that there would be nothing unfair about going into partnership with someone else. What I was going to suggest was that you and I should collaborate. I'd rather work with you than with any of the others, and I think we could manage it rather well between us. Our contribution should be sent in in your name; that is to say, if you wouldn't object to seeing yourself in print."

"I should love it. I'm proud of my name; and it would be a new sensation." But Peggy spoke in absent-minded fashion, as if her thoughts were running on another subject. Rob had used a word which was unfamiliar in her ears, a big word, a word with a delightful intellectual roll, and she had not the remotest idea of its meaning. Collaborate! Beautiful! Not for worlds would she confess her ignorance, yet the opportunity could not be thrown away. She must secure the treasure, and add it to her mental store. She put her head on one side, and said pensively—

"I shall be most happy to er—er—In what other words can I express 'collaborate,' Rob? I object to repetition?"

"Go shags!" returned Robert briefly. "I would do the biggest part of the work, of course—that's only fair, because I want two-thirds of the money—but you could do what you liked, and have ten pounds for your share. Ten pounds would come in very usefully for Christmas."

"Rather! I'd get mother and father lovely presents, and Mrs Asplin too; and buy books for Esther, and a little gold ring for Mellicent—it's her idea of happiness to have a gold ring. I'll help you with pleasure, Rob, and I'm sure we shall get the prize. What have we to do? Compose some poetry?"

"Goodness, no! Fancy me making up poetry! It's to make up a calendar. There are subjects given for each month—sorrow, love, obedience, resignation—that sort of thing, and you have to give a quotation for each day. It will take some time, but we ought to stand a good chance. You are fond of reading, and know no end of poetry, and where I have a pull is in knowing French and German *so* well. I can give them some fine translations from the Latin and Greek too, for the matter of that, and put the authors' names underneath. That will impress the judges, and make 'em decide in our favour. I've been working at it only three days, and I've got over fifty quotations already. We must keep note-books in our pockets, and jot down any ideas that occur to us during the day, and go over them together at night. You will know a lot, I'm sure."

"'Sorrow and silence are strong,
    and patient endurance is godlike,
Therefore accomplish thy labour of love,

till the heart is made godlike.'"

quoted Peggy with an air; and Rob nodded approval.

"That's it! That's the style! Something with a bit of a sermon in it to keep 'em up to the mark for the day. Bravo, Mariquita! you'll do it splendidly. That's settled, then. We shall have to work hard, for there is only a month before it must be sent off, and we must finish in good time. When you leave things to the last, something is bound to come in the way. It will take an age to write out three hundred and sixty-five extracts."

"It will indeed, for they must be very nicely done," said Peggy fastidiously. "Of course it is most important that the extracts themselves should be good, but it matters almost as much that they should look neat and attractive. Appearances go such a long way." And when Robert demurred, and stated his opinion that the judges would not trouble their heads about looks, she stuck firmly to her point.

"Oh, won't they, though! Just imagine how you would feel if you were in their position, and had to look over scores of ugly, uninteresting manuscripts. You would be bored to death, and, after plodding conscientiously through a few dozen, you would get so mixed up that you would hardly be able to distinguish one from another. Then suddenly— suddenly,"—Peggy clasped her hands with one of her favourite dramatic gestures—"you would see before you a dainty little volume, prettily written, easy to read, easy to hold, nice to look at, and do you mean to say that your heart wouldn't give a jump, and that you would not take a fancy to the writer from that very moment? Of course you would; and so, if you please, I am going to look after the decorative department, and see what can be done. I must give my mind to it—Oh! I'll tell you what would be just the thing. When I was in the library one day lately I saw some sweet little note- books with pale green leaves and gilt edges. I'll count the pages, and buy enough to make up three hundred and sixty- five, and twelve extra, so as to put one plain sheet between each month. Then we must have a cover. Two pieces of cardboard would do, with gilt edges, and a motto in Old

English letters—'*The months in circling-orbit fly*.' Have I read that somewhere, or did I make it up? It sounds very well. Well, what next?" Peggy was growing quite excited, and the restless hands were waving about at a great rate. "Oh, the pages! We shall have to put the date at the top of each. I could do that in gold ink, and make a pretty little skriggle—er —'*arabesque*' I should say, underneath, to give it a finish. Then I'd hand them on to you to write the extracts in your tiny little writing. Rob, it will be splendid! Do you really think we shall get the prize?"

"I *mean* to get it! We have a good library here, and plenty of time, if we like to use it. I'm going to get up at six every morning. I shan't fail for want of trying, and if I miss this I'll win something else. My mind is made up! I'm going to buy that microscope!" Robert tossed his head and looked ferocious, while Peggy peered in his rugged face, and, womanlike, admired him the more for his determination.

They lingered in the garden discussing details, planning out the work, and arranging as to the different books to be overlooked until the tea hour was passed, and Mrs Asplin came to the door and called to them to come in.

"And nothing on your feet but your thin slippers? Oh, you Peggy!" she exclaimed in despair. "Now you will have a cold, and ten to one it will fly to your throat. I shall have to line you a penny every time you cross the doorstep without changing your shoes. Summer is over, remember. You can't be too careful in these raw, damp days. Run upstairs this minute and change your stockings."

Peggy looked meek, and went to her room at once to obey orders; but the mischief was done—she shivered, and could not get warm, her head ached, and her eyes felt heavy. Mrs Asplin looked anxiously at her in the drawing-room after dinner, and finally called her to her side.

"Peggy, come here! Aren't you well? Let me feel your hand. Child, it's like a coal! You are in a fever. Why didn't you tell me at once?"

"Because I—really, it's nothing, Mrs Asplin! Don't be worried.

I don't know why I feel so hot. I was shivering only a minute ago."

"Go straight upstairs and take a dose of ammoniated quinine. Turn on the fire in your room. Max! Robert! Oswald! Esther! Mellicent! will everyone please look after Peggy in the future, and see that she does not run out in her slippers!" cried Mrs Asplin in a despairing voice; and Peggy bolted out of the door, in haste to escape before more reproaches could be hurled at her head.

But an alarm of a more serious nature than a threatened cold was to take place before the evening was over. The young people answered briefly, Mrs Asplin turned back to her book, and silence settled down upon the occupants of the drawing-room. It was half-past eight, the servants had carried away the dinner things, and were enjoying their evening's rest in the kitchen. The vicar was nodding in his easy-chair, the house was so quiet that the tick of the old grandfather clock in the hall could be heard through the half-opened door. Then suddenly came the sound of flying footsteps, the door burst open, and in rushed Peggy once more,—but such a Peggy, such an apparition of fear, suffering, and terror as brought a cry of consternation from every lip. Her eyes were starting from her head, her face was contorted in spasmodic gaspings for breath, her arms sawed the air like the sails of a windmill, and she flew round and round the room in a wild, unheeding rush.

"Peggy, my child! my child! what is the matter? Oh, Austin—oh! What shall we do?" cried Mrs Asplin, trying to catch hold of the flying arms, only to be waved off with frenzied energy. Mellicent dissolved into tears and retreated behind the sofa, under the impression that Peggy had suddenly taken leave of her senses, and practical Esther rushed upstairs to search for a clue to the mystery among the medicine bellies on Peggy's table. She was absent only for a few minutes; but it seemed like an hour to the watchers, for Peggy's face grew more and more agonised, she seemed on the verge of suffocation, and could neither speak nor endure anyone to approach within yards of her mad career. Presently, however, she began to falter, to draw her breath in longer gasps, and as she did so there emerged from her lips a series of loud whooping sounds, like the crowing of a cock, or the noise made by a child in the convulsions of whooping-cough. The air was making its way to the lungs after the temporary stoppage, and the result would have been comical if any of the hearers had been in a mood for jesting, which, in good truth, they were not.

"Thank Heaven! She will be better now. Open the window and leave her alone. Don't try to make her speak. What in the world has the child been doing?" cried the vicar wonderingly; and at that moment Esther entered, bearing in her hand the explanation of the mystery—a bottle labelled "Spirits of Ammonia," and a tumbler about an eighth full of a white milky-looking fluid.

"They were in the front of the table. The other things had not been moved. I believe she has never looked at the labels, but seized the first bottle that came to her hand—this dreadfully strong ammonia which you gave her for the gnat bites when she first came."

A groan of assent came from the sofa on which Peggy lay, choking no longer, but ghastly white, and drawing her breath in painful gasps. Mrs Asplin sniffed at the contents of the tumbler, only to jerk back her head with watery eyes and reddened lips.

"No wonder that the child was nearly choked! The marvel is that she had ever regained her breath after such a mistake. Her throat must be raw!" She hurried out of the room to concoct a soothing draught, at which Peggy supped at intervals during the evening, croaking out a hoarse, "Better, thank you!" in reply to inquiries, and looking so small and pathetic in her nest of cushions that the hearts of the beholders softened at the sight. Before bedtime, however, she revived considerably, and, her elastic spirits coming to her aid, entertained the listeners with a husky but dramatic account of her proceedings. How she had not troubled to turn the gas full up, and had just seized the bottle, tilted some of the contents into a tumbler in which there was a small portion of water, without troubling to measure it out, and gulped it down without delay. Her description of the feelings which ensued was a really clever piece of word-painting, but behind the pretence of horror at her own carelessness there rang a hardly concealed note of pride, as though, in thus risking her life, she had done something quite clever and distinguished.

Mrs Asplin exhausted herself in "Ohs!" and "Ahs!" of sympathy, and had nothing harsher to say than—

"Well now, dearie, you'll be more careful another time, won't you?" But the vicar's long face grew longer than ever as he listened, and the lines deepened in his forehead. Peggy was inexperienced in danger-signals, but Esther and Mellicent recognised the well-known signs, and were at no loss to understand the meaning of that quiet, "A word with you in the study, Mariquita, if you please!" with which he rose from the breakfast-table next morning.

Peggy's throat was still sore, and she fondly imagined that anxiety on its behalf was the cause of the summons, but she was speedily undeceived, for the vicar motioned towards a chair, and said, in short grave sentences, as his manner was when annoyed—

"I wish to speak to you about the event of last night; I am afraid that you hardly realise the matter in its true light. I was not at all pleased with the manner in which you gave your explanation. You appeared to imagine that you had done something clever and amusing. I take a very different view. You showed a reprehensible carelessness in trifling with medicines in the dark; it might have caused you your life, or, at best, a serious injury. As it was, you brought pain upon yourself, and gave us all a serious alarm. I see nothing amusing in such behaviour, but consider it stupid, and careless to an almost criminal extent."

Peggy stood motionless, eyes cast down, hands clasped before her—a picture of injured innocence. She did not say a word in self-defence, but her feelings were so plainly written on her face that the vicar's eyes flashed with impatience.

"Well, what have you to say?"

Peggy sighed in dolorous fashion.

"I am sorry; I know it was careless. I am always doing things like that. So is Arthur. So was father when he was a boy. It's in the family. It's unfortunate, but—"

"Mariquita," said the vicar sternly, "you are *not* sorry! If I had seen that you were penitent, I should not have spoken, for you would have been sufficiently punished by your own sufferings, but you are not sorry; you are, on the whole, rather proud of the escapade! Look into your own heart and see if it is not so?"

He paused, looking at her with grave, expectant eyes, but there was no sign of conviction upon the set face. The eyes were still lowered, the lips drooped with an expression of patient endurance. There was silence in the room while Peggy studied the carpet, and the vicar gazed at her downcast face. A moment before he had been on the verge of anger, but the sternness melted away in that silence, and gave place to an anxious tenderness. Here was a little human soul committed to his care—how could he help? how best guide and train? The long, grave face grew beautiful in that moment with the expression which it wore every Sunday as he gazed around the church at the beginning of the sermon, noting this one and that, having a swift realisation of their needs and failings, and breathing a prayer to God that He would give to his lips the right word, to his heart the right thought, to meet the needs of his people. Evidently, sternness and outspoken blame was not the best way to touch the girl before him. He must try another mode.

"Peggy," he said quietly, "do you think you realise what a heavy responsibility we laid upon ourselves when we undertook the care of you for these three years? If any accident happened to you beneath our roof, have you ever imagined what would be our misery and remorse at sending the news to your parents? About their feelings I do not speak; you can realise them for yourself. We safeguard you with every precaution in our power; we pray morning and night that you may be preserved in safety; is it too much to ask that you will do your part by showing more forethought, and by exercising some little care in the daily duties of life? I ask it for our sakes as well as your own."

A pink flush spread over Peggy's cheeks; she gulped nervously and raised her eyes to the vicar's face. Twice her lips opened as if to speak, but the natural reserve, which made it agony to her to express her deepest feelings, closed them again before a word had been spoken. The question was not answered, but a little hand shot out and nestled in Mr Asplin's with a spasmodic grip which was full ofeloquence.

"Yes, dear, I know you will! I know you will!" he said, answering the unspoken promise, and looking down at her with one of his sweet, kindly smiles. "It will be a comfort to my wife as well as myself. She is very nervous about you. She was upstairs three times in the night, to satisfy herself that you were well after your fright, and is too tired herself to come downstairs this morning. She is always bright and cheery, but she is not very strong. You would be sorry to make her ill."

No answer, only another grip of the hand, and a sudden straightening of the lips, as if they were pressed together to avoid an involuntary trembling. There is something especially touching in the sight of restrained emotion; and as the vicar thought of his own two daughters, his heart was very tender over the girl whose parents were separated from her by six thousand miles of land and sea.

"Well now, dear, I have said my say, and that is an end of it. I don't like finding fault, but my dear wife has thrown that duty on my shoulders by being too tender-hearted to say a word of blame even when it is needed. Her method works very well, as a rule, but there are occasions when it would be criminal to withhold a just reprimand." The vicar stopped short, and a spasm of laughter crossed his face. Peggy's fingers had twitched within his own as he spoke those last two words, and her eyes had dilated with interest. He knew as well as if he had been told that she was gloating over the new expression, and mentally noting it for future use. Nothing, however, could have been sweeter or more natural than the manner in which she sidled against him, and murmured—

"Thank you so much. I am sorry! I will truly try;" and he watched her out of the room with a smile of tender amusement.

"A nice child—a good child—feels deeply. I can rely upon her to do her best."

Robert was hanging about in the passage, ready, as usual, to fulfil his vows of support, and Peggy slid her hand through his arm and sauntered slowly with him towards the schoolroom. Like the two girls, he had been at no loss to understand the reason of the call to the study, and would fain have expressed his sympathy, but Peggy stopped him with uplifted finger.

"No, no—he was perfectly right. You must not blame him. I have been guilty of reprehensible carelessness, and merited a reprimand!"

Chapter Thirteen.

Jealous Thoughts.

Peggy felt weak and shaken for some days after her fright, and was thankful to stay quietly indoors and busy herself with her new task. The gas-fire could be turned on in her room whenever she desired, and at every spare moment she ran upstairs, locked her door behind her, and began to write. Robert insisted that the work should be kept secret, and that not a word should be said about the competition downstairs, for he was sensitive about the remarks of his companions, and anxious to keep a possible failure to himself. All the work had to be done upstairs, therefore, and the frequent absence of the partners from the schoolroom, though much regretted, did not seem at all inexplicable to the others. It was understood that Peggy and Robert had some interest in common; but as winter advanced this was no unusual occurrence in a house where Christmas was a carnival, and surprises of an elaborate nature were planned by every member of the household. It was taken for granted that the work had some connection with Christmas, and inquiries were discreetly avoided.

With an old calendar before her as a model for the lettering, Peggy did her work neatly and well, and the gilt "arabesques" had an artistic flourish which was quite professional. When Robert was shown the first half-dozen sheets he whistled with surprise, and exclaimed, "Good old Mariquita!" a burst of approval before which Peggy glowed with delight. It had been agreed that, after printing the first ten days of January, Peggy should go on to the first ten of February, and so on throughout the year, so that Rob should be able to use what quotations had already been found under each heading, and should not be detained until the whole thirty or thirty-one had been chosen.

The partners were most fastidious in their selection at the beginning of their work; but when half the time had passed, and not one-third of the necessary number of quotations had been found, alarm seized upon the camp, and it was realised that a little more latitude must be shown.

"We shall have to use up all the old ones which we struck off the list," said Rob disconsolately. "I'm sorry; but I never realised before that three hundred and sixty-five was such an outrageously large number. And we shall have to get books of extracts, and read them through from beginning to end. Nearly two hundred more to find; a hundred and fifty, say, when we have used up those old ones! It will take us all our time!"

"I'll get up at six every morning and read by my fire," said Peggy firmly. "If it's necessary, I'll get up at five, and if I can't find bits to suit all the stupid old things, I'll—I'll write some myself! There! Why shouldn't I? I often make up things in my head, and you wouldn't believe how fine they are. I think of them days afterwards, and ask myself, 'Now where did I read that?' and then it comes back to me. 'Dear me; I made it up myself!' If we get very short, Rob, there wouldn't be any harm in writing a few sentences and signing them 'Saville,' would there?"

"Not if they were good enough," said Rob, trying to suppress the laugh which would have hurt Peggy's feelings, and looking with twinkling eyes at the little figure by his side, so comically unprofessional, with her lace collar, dainty little feet, and pigtail of dark brown hair.

"You mustn't get up too early in the morning and overtire yourself. I can't allow that!" he added firmly. "You have looked like a little white ghost the last few days, and your face is about the size of my hand. You must get some colour into your cheeks before the holidays, or that beloved Arthur will think we have been ill-treating you when he comes down."

Peggy gave a sharp sigh, and relapsed into silence. It was the rarest thing in the world to hear her allude to any of her own people. When a letter arrived, and Mrs Asplin asked questions concerning father, mother, or brother, she answered readily enough, but she never offered information, or voluntarily carried on the conversation. Friends less sympathetic might have imagined that she was so happy in her new home that she had no care beyond it, but no one in the vicarage made that mistake. When the Indian letter was handed to her across the breakfast-table, the flush of delight on the pale cheeks brought a reflected smile to every face, and more than one pair of eyes watched her tenderly as she sat hugging the precious letter, waiting until the moment should come when she could rush upstairs and devour its contents in her own room. Once it had happened that mail day had arrived and brought no letter, and that had been a melancholy occasion. Mrs Asplin had looked at one envelope after another, had read the addresses twice, thrice, even four times over, before she summoned courage to tell of its absence.

"There is no letter for you to-day, Peggy!" Her voice was full of commiseration as she spoke, but Peggy sat in silence, her face stiffened, her head thrown back with an assumption of calm indifference. "There must have been some delay in the mail. You will have two letters next week, dearie, instead of one."

"Probably," said Peggy. Mellicent was staring at her with big, round eyes; the vicar peered over the rim of his spectacles; Esther passed the marmalade with eager solicitude; her friends were all full of sympathy, but there was a "Touch-me-if-you-dare!" atmosphere about Peggy that day which silenced the words on their lips. It was evident that she preferred to be left alone, and though her eyes were red when she came down to lunch, she held her chin so high, and joined in the conversation with such an elegant flow of language, that no one dare comment on the fact. Two days later the letter arrived, and all was sunshine again; but, in spite of her cheery spirits, her friends realised that Peggy's heart was not in the vicarage, and that there were moments when the loneliness of her position pressed on her, and when she longed intensely for someone of her very own, whose place could not be taken by even the kindest of friends.

Like most undemonstrative people, Peggy dearly loved to be appreciated, and to receive marks of favour from those around. Half the zest with which she entered into her new labour was owing to the fact that Robert had chosen her from all the rest to be his partner. She was aglow with satisfaction in this fact, and with pleasure in the work itself, and the only cloud which darkened her horizon at the present moment was caused by those incidental references to the fair Rosalind which fell so often from her companions' lips.

"Everything," said Peggy impatiently to herself, "everything ends in Rosalind! Whatever we are talking about, that stupid girl's name is bound to be introduced! I asked Mellicent if she would have a scone at tea this afternoon, and she said something about Rosalind in reply—Rosalind liked scones, or she didn't like scones, or some ridiculous nonsense of the sort! Who wants to know what Rosalind likes? I don't! I'm sick of the name! And Mrs Asplin is as silly as the rest! The girls must have new dresses because Rosalind is coming, and they will be asked to tea at the Larches! If their green dresses are good enough for us, why won't they do for Rosalind, I should like to know? Rob is the only sensible one. I asked him if she were really such a marvellous creature, and he said she was an affected goose! He ought to know better than anyone else! Curls indeed! One would think it was something extraordinary to have curls! My hair would curl too, if I chose to make it, but I don't; I prefer to have it straight! If she is the 'Honourable Rosalind,' I am Mariquita Saville, and I'm not going to be patronised by anybody—so there!" and Peggy tossed her head, and glared at the reflection in the glass in a lofty and scornful manner, as though it were the offending party who had had the audacity to assume superiority.

Robert was one with Peggy in hoping that his people would not leave town until such time as the calendar should be despatched on its travels, for when they were installed at the Larches he was expected to be at home each week from Saturday until Monday, and the loss of that long holiday afternoon would interfere seriously with the work on hand. He had seen so little of his people for the last few years, that he would be expected to be sociable during the short time that he was with them, and could hardly shut himself up in his room for hours at a time. Despair then settled down upon both partners, when a letter arrived to say that the Darcy family were coming down even earlier than had been expected, and summoning Robert to join them at the earliest possible moment.

"This is awful!" cried the lad, ruffling his hair with a big, restless hand. "I know what it means—not only Saturdays off, but two or three nights during the week into the bargain! Between you and me, Mariquita, the governor is coming down here to economise, and intends to stay much longer than usual. Hector has been getting into debt again; he's the eldest, you know—the one in the Life Guards. It's a lot too bad, for he has had it all his own way so far, and when he runs up bills like this, everyone has to suffer for it. Mother hates the country for more than a few weeks at a time, and will be wretched if she is kept here all through the winter. I know how it will be: she will keep asking people down, and getting up all sorts of entertainments to relieve the dulness. It's all very well in its way, but just now when I need every minute—"

"Shall you give up trying for the prize?" asked Peggy faintly, and Rob threw back his head with emphatic disclaimer.

"I never give up a thing when I have made up my mind to do it! There are ten days still, and a great deal can be done in ten days. I'll take a couple of books upstairs with me every night, and see if I can find something fresh. There is one good thing about it, I shall have a fresh stock of books to choose from at the Larches. It is the last step that costs in this case. It was easy enough to fix off the first hundred, but the last is a teaser!"

On Saturday morning a dogcart came over to convey Robert to the Larches, and the atmosphere of the vicarage seemed charged with expectation and excitement. The Darcys had arrived; to-morrow they would appear at church; on Monday they would probably drive over with Rob and pay a call. These were all important facts in a quiet country life, and seemed to afford unlimited satisfaction to every member of the household. Peggy grew so tired of the name of Darcy that she retired to her room at eight o'clock, and was busy at work over the September batch of cards, when a knock came to the door, and she had to cover them over with the blotting- paper to admit Mellicent in her dressing-gown, with her hair arranged for the night in an extraordinary number of little plaited pigtails.

"Will you fasten the ends for me, Peggy, please?" she requested. "When I do it, the threads fall off, and the ends come loose. I want it to be specially nice for to-morrow!"

"But it will look simply awful, Mellicent, if you leave it like this. It will be frizzed out almost on a level with your head. Let me do it up in just two tight plaits; it will be far, far nicer," urged Peggy, lifting one little tail after another, and counting their number in dismay. But no, Mellicent would not be persuaded. The extra plaits were a tribute to Rosalind, a mark of attention to her on her arrival with which she would suffer no interference; and as a consequence of her stubbornness she marched to church next morning disfigured by a mop of untidy, tangled hair, instead of the usual glossy locks.

Peggy preserved a demeanour of stately calm, as she waited for the arrival of the Darcy family, but even she felt a tremor of excitement when the verger hobbled up to the square pew and stood holding the door open in his hand. The heads of the villagers turned with one consent to the doorway; only one person in the church disdained to move her position, but she heard the clatter of horses' hoofs from without, and presently the little procession passed the vicarage pew, and she could indulge her curiosity without sacrifice to pride. First of all came Lord Darcy, a thin, oldish man, with a face that looked tired and kind, and faintly amused by the amount of attention which his entrance had attracted. Then his wife, a tall, fair woman, with a beautiful profile, and an air of languid discontent, who floated past with rustling silken skirts, leaving an impression of elegance and luxury, which made Mrs Asplin sigh and Mellicent draw in her breath with a gasp of rapture. Then followed Robert with his shaggy head, scowling more fiercely than ever in his disgust at finding himself an object of attention, and last of all a girlish figure in a grey dress, with a collar of soft, fluffy chinchilla, and a velvet hat with drooping brim, beneath which could be seen a glimpse of a face pink and white as the blossoms of spring, and a mass of shining, golden hair. Peggy shut her lips with a snap, and the iron entered into her soul. It was no use pretending any longer! This was Rosalind, and she was fairer, sweeter, a hundred times more beautiful than she had ever imagined!

Chapter Fourteen.

Rosalind's Visit.

Robert did not make his appearance next morning, and his absence seemed to give fresh ground for the expectation that Lady Darcy would drive over with him in the afternoon and pay a call at the vicarage.

Mrs Asplin gathered what branches of russet leaves still remained in the garden and placed them in bowls in the drawing-room, with a few precious chrysanthemums peeping out here and there; laid out her very best tea-cloth and d'oyleys, and sent the girls upstairs to change their well-worn school dresses for something fresher and smarter.

"And you, Peggy dear—you will put on your pretty red, of course!" she said, standing still, with a bundle of branches in her arms, and looking with a kindly glance at the pale face, which had somehow lost its sunny expression during the last two days.

Peggy hesitated and pursed up her lips.

"Why 'of course,' Mrs Asplin? I never change my dress until evening. Why need I do it to-day, just because some strangers may call whom I have never seen before?"

It was the first time that the girl had objected to do what she was told, and Mrs Asplin was both surprised and hurt by the tone in which she spoke—a good deal puzzled too, for Peggy was by no means indifferent to pretty frocks, and as a rule fond of inventing excuses to wear her best clothes. Why, then, should she choose this afternoon of all others to refuse so simple a request? Just for a moment she felt tempted to make a sharp reply, and then tenderness for the girl whose mother was so far-away took the place of the passing irritation, and she determined to try a gentler method.

"There is not the slightest necessity, dear," she said quietly. "I asked only because the red dress suits you so well, and it would have been a pleasure to me to see you looking your best. But you are very nice and neat as you are. You need not change unless you like."

She turned to leave the room as she finished speaking; but before she had reached the door Peggy was by her side, holding out her hands to take possession of twigs and branches.

"Let me take them to the kitchen, please! Let me help you!" she said quickly, and just for a moment a little hand rested on her arm with a spasmodic pressure. That was all; but it was enough. There was no need of a formal apology. Mrs Asplin understood all the unspoken love and penitence which was expressed in that simple action, and beamed with her brightest smile.

"Thank you, my lassie, please do! I'm glad to avoid going near the kitchen again, for when cook once gets hold of me I can never get away. She tells me the family history of all her relatives, and indeed it's very depressing, it is," (with a relapse into her merry Irish accent), "for they are subject to the most terrible afflictions! I've had one dose of it to-day, and I don't want another!"

Peggy laughed, and carried off her bundle, lingered in the kitchen just long enough to remind the cook that "apple charlotte served with cream" was a seasonable pudding at the fall of the year, and then went upstairs to put on the red dress, and relieve her feelings by making grimaces at herself in the glass as she fastened the buttons.

At four o'clock the patter of horses' feet came from below, doors opened and shut, and there was a sound of voices in the hall. The visitors had arrived!

Peggy pressed her lips together, and bent doggedly over her writing. She had not progressed with her work as well as she had hoped during Rob's absence, for her thoughts had been running on other subjects, and she had made mistake after mistake. She must try to finish one batch at least, to show him on his return. Unless she was especially sent for, she would not go downstairs; but before ten minutes had passed, Mellicent was tapping at the door and whispering eager sentences through the keyhole.

"Peggy, quick! They've come! Rosalind's here! You're to come down! Quick! Hurry up!"

"All right, my dear, keep calm! You will have a fit if you excite yourself like this!" said Peggy coolly.

The summons had come, and could not be disregarded, and on the whole she was not sorry. The meeting was bound to take place sooner or later, and, in spite of her affectation of indifference, she was really consumed with curiosity to know what Rosalind was like. She had no intention of hurrying, however, but lingered over the arrangement of her papers until Mellicent had trotted downstairs again, and the coast was clear. Then she sauntered after her with leisurely dignity, opened the drawing-room door, and gave a swift glance round.

Lady Darcy sat talking to Mrs Asplin a few yards away, in such a position that she faced the doorway. She looked up as Peggy entered, and swept her eyes curiously over the girl's figure. She looked older than she had done from across the church the day before, and her face had a bored expression, but, if possible, she was even more elegant in her attire. It seemed quite extraordinary to see such a fine lady sitting on that well-worn sofa, instead of the sober figure of the vicar's wife.

Peggy flashed a look from one to the other—from the silk dress to the serge, from the beautiful weary face to the cheery loving smile—and came to the conclusion that, for some mysterious reason, Mrs Asplin was a happier woman than the wife of the great Lord Darcy.

The two ladies stopped talking and looked expectantly towards her.

"Come in, dear! This is our new pupil, Lady Darcy, for whom you were asking. You have heard of her—"

"From Robert. Oh yes, frequently! I was especially anxious to see Robert's little friend. How do you do, dear? Let me see! What is your funny little name? Molly—Dolly—something like that, I think—I forget for the moment?"

"Mariquita Saville!" quoth Peggy grandiloquently. She was consumed with regret that she had no second name to add to the number of syllables, but she did her best with those she possessed, rolling them out in her very best manner and with a stately condescension which made Lady Darcy smile for the first time since she entered the room.

"Oh–h!" The lips parted to show a gleam of regular white teeth. "That's it, is it? Well, I am very pleased to make your acquaintance, Mariquita. I hope we shall see a great deal of you while we are here. You must go and make friends with Rosalind—my daughter. She is longing to know you."

"Yes, go and make friends with Rosalind, Peggy dear! She was asking for you," said Mrs Asplin kindly; and as the girl walked away the two ladies exchanged smiling glances.

"Amusing! Such grand little manners! Evidently a character."

"Oh, quite! Peggy is nothing if not original. She is a dear, good girl, but quite too funny in her ways. She is really the incarnation of mischief, and keeps me on tenter-hooks from morning until night, but from her manner you would think she was a model of propriety. Nothing delights her so much as to get hold of a new word or a high-sounding phrase."

"But what a relief to have someone out of the ordinary run! There are so many bores in the world, it is quite refreshing to meet with a little originality. Dear Mrs Asplin, you really must tell me how you manage to look so happy and cheerful in this dead-alive place? I am desolate at the idea of staying here all winter. What in the world do you find to do?"

Mrs Asplin laughed.

"Indeed, that's not the trouble at all; the question is how to find time to get through the day's duties! It's a rush from morning till night, and when evening comes I am delighted to settle down in an easy-chair with a nice book to read. One has no chance of feeling dull in a house full of young people."

"Ah, you are so good and clever, you get through so much. I want to ask your help in half a dozen ways. If we are to settle down here for some months, there are so many arrangements to make. Now tell me, what would you do in this case?" The two ladies settled down to a discussion on domestic matters, while Peggy crossed the room to the corner where Rosalind Darcy sat in state, holding her court with Esther and Mellicent as attendant slaves. She wore the same grey dress in which she had appeared in church the day before, but the jacket was thrown open, and displayed a distractingly dainty blouse, all pink chiffon, and frills, and ruffles of lace. Her gloves lay in her lap, and the celebrated diamond ring flashed in the firelight as she held out her hand to meet Peggy's.

"How do you do? So glad to see you! I've heard of you often. You are the little girl who is my bwothar's fwiend." She pronounced the letter "r" as if it had been "w," and the "er" in brother as if it had been "ah," and spoke with a languid society drawl more befitting a woman of thirty than a schoolgirl of fifteen.

Peggy stood motionless and looked her over, from the crown of her hat to the tip of the little trim shoe, with an expression of icy displeasure.

"Oh dear me, no," she said quietly, "you mistake the situation. You put it the wrong way about. Your brother is the big boy whom I have allowed to become a friend of mine!"

Esther and Mellicent gasped with amazement, while Rosalind gave a trill of laughter, and threw up her pretty white hands.

"She's wexed!" she cried. "She's wexed, because I called her little! I'm wewwy sowwy, but I weally can't help it, don't you know. It's the twuth! You are a whole head smaller than I am." She threw back her chin, and looked over Peggy's head with a smile of triumph. "There, look at that, and I'm not a year older. I call you wewwy small indeed for your age."

"I'm thankful to hear it! I admire small women," said Peggy promptly, seating herself on a corner of the window-seat, and staring critically at the tall figure of the visitor. She would have been delighted if she could have persuaded herself that her height was awkward and ungainly, but such an effort was beyond imagination. Rosalind was startlingly and wonderfully pretty; she had never seen anyone in real life who was in the least like her. Her eyes were a deep, dark blue, with curling dark lashes, her face was a delicate oval, and the pink and white colouring, and flowing golden locks, gave her the appearance of a princess in a fairy tale rather than an ordinary flesh-and-blood maiden. Peggy looked from her to Mellicent, who was considered quite a beauty among her companions, and, oh dear me! how plain, and fat, and prosaic she appeared when viewed side by side with this radiant vision! Esther stood the comparison better, for, though her long face had no pretensions to beauty, it was thoughtful and interesting in expression. There was no question which was most charming to look at; but if it had come to choice of a companion, an intelligent observer would certainly have decided in favour of the vicar's daughter. Esther's face was particularly grave at this moment, and her eyes met Peggy's with a reproachful glance. What was the matter with the girl this afternoon? Why did she take up everything that Rosalind said in that hasty, cantankerous manner? Here was an annoying thing—to have just given an enthusiastic account of the brightness and amicability of a new companion, and then to have that companion come into the room only to make snappish remarks, and look as cross and ill-natured as a bear! She turned in an apologetic fashion to Rosalind, and tried to resume the conversation at the point where it had been interrupted by Peggy's entrance.

"And I was saying, we have ever so many new things to show you—presents, you know, and things of that kind. The last is the nicest of all: a really good big camera with which we can take proper photographs. Mrs Saville—Peggy's mother—gave it to us before she left. It was a present to the schoolroom, so it belongs equally to us all, and we have such fun with it. We are beginning to do some good things now, but at first they were too funny for anything. There is one of father where his boots are twice as large as his head, and another of mother where her face has run, and is about a yard long, and yet it is so like her! We laughed till we cried over it, and father has locked it away in his desk. He says he will keep it to look at when he is low-spirited."

Rosalind gave a shrug to her shapely shoulders.

"It would not cheer me up to see a cawicature of myself! I don't think I shall sit to you for my portrait, if that is the sort of thing you do, but you shall show me all your failures. It will amuse me. You will have to come up and see me vewwy often this winter, for I shall be so dull. We have been abroad for the last four years, and England seems so dark and dweawy. Last winter we were at Cairo. We lived in a big hotel, and there was something going on almost every night. I was not out, of course, but I was allowed to go into the room for an hour after dinner, and to dance with the gentlemen in mother's set. And we went up the Nile in a steamer, and dwove about every afternoon, paying calls, and shopping in the bazaars. It never rains in Cairo, and the sun is always shining. It seems so wonderful! Just like a place in a fairy tale." She looked at Peggy as she spoke, and that young person smiled with an air of elegant condescension.

"It would do so to you. Naturally it would. When one has been born in the East, and lived there the greater part of one's life, it seems natural enough, but the trippers from England who just come out for a few months' visit are always astonished. It used to amuse us so much to hear their remarks!"

Rosalind stared, and flushed with displeasure. She was accustomed to have her remarks treated with respect, and the tone of superiority was a new and unpleasing experience.

"You were born in the East?"

"Certainly I was!"

"Where, may I ask?"

"In India—in Calcutta, where my father's regiment was stationed."

"You lived there till you were quite big? You can remember all about it?"

"All I want to remember. There was a great deal that I choose to forget. I don't care for India. England is more congenial to my feelings."

"And can you speak the language? Did you learn Hindostanee

while you were there?"

"Naturally. Of course I did."

A gasp of amazement came from the two girls in the window, for a knowledge of Hindostanee had never been included in the list of Peggy's accomplishments, and she was not accustomed to hide her light under a bushel. They gazed at her with widened eyes, and Rosalind scented scepticism in the air, and cried quickly—

"Say something, then. If you can speak, say something now, and let us hear you."

"Pardon me!" said Peggy, simpering. "As a matter of fact, I was sent home because I was learning to speak too well. The language of the natives is not considered suitable for English children of tender age. I must ask you to be so kind as to excuse me. I should be sorry to shock your sensibilities."

Rosalind drew her brows together and stared steadily in the speaker's face. Like many beautiful people, she was not over-gifted with a sense of humour, and therefore Peggy's grandiose manner and high-sounding words failed to amuse her as they did most strangers. She felt only annoyed and puzzled, dimly conscious that she was being laughed at, and that this girl with the small face and the peaked eyebrows was trying to patronise her—Rosalind Darcy—instead of following the vicar's daughters in adoring her from a respectful distance, as of course it was her duty to do. She had been anxious to meet the Peggy Saville of whom her brother had spoken so enthusiastically, for it was a new thing to hear Rob praise a girl, but it was evident that Peggy on her side was by no means eager to make her acquaintance. It was an extraordinary discovery, and most disconcerting to the feelings of one who was accustomed to be treated as a person of supreme importance. Rosalind could hardly speak for mortification, and it was an immense relief when the door opened, and Max and Oswald hurried forward to greet her. Then indeed she was in her element, beaming with smiles, and indulging a dozen pretty little tricks of manner for the benefit of their admiring eyes. Max took possession of the chair by her side, his face lighted up with pleasure and admiration. He was too thoroughly natural and healthy a lad to be much troubled with sentiment, but ever since one winter morning five years before, when Rosalind had first appeared in the little country church, she had been his ideal of all that was womanly and beautiful. At every meeting he discovered fresh charms, and to-day was no exception to the rule. She was taller, fairer, more elegant. In *some* mysterious manner she seemed to have grown older than he, so that, though he was in reality three years her senior, he was still a boy, while she was almost a young lady.

Mrs Asplin looked across the room, and a little anxious furrow showed in her forehead. Maxwell's admiration for Rosalind was already an old story, and as she saw his eager face and sparkling eyes, a pang of fear came into his mother's heart. If the Darcys were constantly coming down to the Larches, it was only natural to suppose that this admiration would increase, and it would never do for Max to fall in love with Rosalind! The vicar's son would be no match for Lord Darcy's daughter; it would only mean a heartache for the poor lad, a clouded horizon just when life should be the brightest. For a moment a prevision of trouble filled her heart, then she waved it away in her cheery, hopeful fashion—

"Why, what a goose I am! They are only children. Time enough to worry my head about love affairs in half a dozen years to come. The lad would be a Stoic if he didn't admire her. I don't see how he could help it!"

"Rosalind is lovelier than ever, Lady Darcy, if that is possible!" she said aloud, and her companion's face brightened with pleasure.

"Oh, do you think so?" she cried eagerly. "I am so glad to hear it, for this growing stage is so trying. I was afraid she might outgrow her strength and lose her complexion, but so far I don't think it has suffered. I am very careful of her diet, and my maid understands all the new skin treatments. So much depends on a girl's complexion. I notice your youngest daughter has a very good colour. May I ask what you use?"

"Soap and water, fresh air, good plain food,—those are the only cosmetics we use in this house," said Mrs Asplin, laughing outright at the idea of Mellicent's healthy bloom being the result of "skin treatment." "I am afraid I have too much to do looking after the necessities of life for my girls, Lady Darcy, to worry myself about their complexions."

"Oh yes. Well, I'm sure they both look charming; but Rosalind will go much into society, and of course,"—She checked herself before the sentence was finished; but Mrs Asplin was quick enough to understand the imputation that the complexions of a vicar's daughters were but of small account, but that it was a very different matter when the Honourable Rosalind Darcy was concerned. She understood, but she was neither hurt nor annoyed by the inferences, only a little sad and very, very pitiful. She knew the story of the speaker's life, and the reason why she looked forward to Rosalind's entrance into society with such ambition. Lady Darcy had been the daughter of poor but well-born parents, and had married the widower, Lord Darcy, not because she loved him or had any motherly feeling for his two orphan boys, but simply and solely for a title and establishment, and a purse full of money. Given these, she had fondly imagined that she was going to be perfectly happy. No more screwing and scraping to keep up appearances; no more living in dulness and obscurity; she would be Lady Darcy, the beautiful young wife of a famous man. So, with no thought in her heart but for her own worldly advancement, Beatrice Fairfax stood before God's altar and vowed to love, honour, and obey a man for whom she had no scrap of affection, and whom she would have laughed to scorn if he had been poor and friendless. She married him, but the life which followed was not by any means all that she had expected. Lord Darcy had heavy money losses, which obliged him to curtail expenses almost immediately after his wedding; her own health broke down, and it was a knife in her heart to know that her boy was only the third son, and that the two big, handsome lads at Eton would inherit the lion's share of their father's property. Hector, the Lifeguardsman, and Oscar, the Dragoon, were for ever running into debt and making fresh demands on her husband's purse. She and her children had to suffer for their extravagances; while Robert, her only son, was growing up a shy, awkward lad, who hated society, and asked nothing better than to be left in the country alone with his frogs and his beetles. Ambition after ambition had failed her, until now all her hopes were centred in Rosalind, the beautiful daughter, in whom she saw a reproduction of herself in the days of her girlhood. She had had a dull and obscure youth; Rosalind should be the belle of society. Her own marriage had been a disappointment; Rosalind should make a brilliant alliance. She had failed to gain the prize for which she had worked; she would live again in Rosalind's triumphs, and in them find fullest satisfaction.

So Lady Darcy gloated over every detail of her daughter's beauty, and thought day and night of her hair, her complexion, her figure, striving still to satisfy her poor tired soul with promises of future success, and never dreaming for a moment that the prize which seemed to elude her grasp had been gained long ago by the vicar's wife, with her old- fashioned dress and work-worn hands. But Mrs Asplin knew, and thanked God in her heart for the sweetness and peace of her dear, shabby home; for the husband who loved her, and the children whom they were training to be good servants for Him in the world Yes, and for that other child too, who had been taken away at the very dawn of his manhood, and who, they believed, was doing still better work in the unseen world.

Until Lady Darcy discovered that the only true happiness rose from something deeper than worldly success, there was nothing in store for her but fresh disappointments and heart-hunger; while as for Rosalind, the unfortunate child of such a mother—Mrs Asplin looked at the girl as she sat leaning back in her chair, craning her throat, and showing off all her little airs and graces for the benefit of the two admiring schoolboys, gratified vanity and self-love showing on every line of her face.

"It seems almost cruel to say so," she sighed to herself, "but it would be the best thing that could happen to the child if she were to lose some of her beauty before she grew up. Such a face as that is a terrible temptation to vanity." But Mrs Asplin did not guess how soon these unspoken words would come back to her memory, or what bitter cause she would have to regret their fulfilment.

Chapter Fifteen.

A Pink Luncheon.

For the next week conversation was more strictly centred on Rosalind than ever, and the gloomy expression deepened on Peggy's face. She was, in truth, working too hard for her strength, for, as each day passed, the necessity of hurrying on with the calendar became more apparent; and as Robert was no longer master of his own time, she was obliged to come to his aid in writing out the selected quotations.

At every spare moment of the day she was locked in her room, scribbling away for dear life or searching for appropriate extracts, and, as a consequence, her brain refused to rest when she wished it to do so. She tossed wakefully on her pillow, and was often most inclined for sleep when six o'clock struck, and she dragged herself up, a white- cheeked, weary little mortal, to sit blinking over the fire, wishing feebly that it was time to go to bed again, instead of getting up to face the long, long day.

Robert was not more observant than most boys of his age, and Peggy would have worked herself to death before she had complained to him. She was proud to feel that he depended on her more than ever, that without her help he could not possibly have finished his task, while his words of gratitude helped to comfort a heart which was feeling sore and empty.

In truth, these last few weeks had been harder for Peggy than those immediately following her mother's departure. Then each one in the house had vied with the other in trying to comfort her, whereas now, without any intention of unkindness, her companions often appeared to be neglectful.

When Rosalind was present Esther hung on one arm and Mellicent on the other, without so much as a glance over the shoulder to see if Peggy were following. Instead of a constant

"Peggy, what would you like?"

"What does Peggy say?" her opinion was never even asked, while Rosalind's lightest word was treated as law.

It would have been hard for any girl under the circumstances, but it was doubly hard when that girl was so dependent on her friends, and so sensitive and reserved in disposition as Peggy Saville. She would not deign to complain or to ask for signs of affection which were not voluntarily given, but her merry ways disappeared, and she became so silent and subdued that she was hardly recognisable as the audacious Peggy of a few weeks earlier.

"Peggy's so grumpy," Mellicent complained to her mother. "She never laughs now, nor makes jokes, nor flies about as she used to do! She's just as glum and mum as can be, and she never sits with us! She is always in her bedroom with the door locked, so that we can't get in! She's there now! I think she might stay with us sometimes! It's mean, always running away!"

Mrs Asplin drew her brows together and looked worried. She had not been satisfied about Peggy lately, and this news did not tend to reassure her. Her kind heart could not endure that anyone beneath her roof should be ill or unhappy, and the girl had looked both during the last few days. She went upstairs at once and tapped at the door, when Peggy's voice was raised in impatient answer.

"I can't come! Go away! I'm engaged!"

"But I want to speak to you, dear! Please let me in!" she replied in her clear, pleasant tones; whereupon there was a hasty scamper inside, and the door was thrown open.

"Oh–h! I didn't know it was you; I thought it was one of the girls. I'm sorry I kept you waiting."

Mrs Asplin gave a glance around. The gas-fire was lit, but the chair beside it stood stiffly in the corner, and the cushion was uncrushed. Evidently, the girl had not been sitting there. The work-basket was in its accustomed place, and there were no cottons or silks lying about—Peggy had not been sewing at Christmas presents, as she had half hoped to find her. A towel was thrown over the writing-table, and a piece of blotting-paper lay on the floor. A chair was pushed to one side, as if it had been lately used. That looked as if she had been writing letters.

"Peggy dear, what are you doing all by yourself in this chilly room?"

"I'm busy, Mrs Asplin. I lit the fire as soon as I came in."

"But a room does not get warm in five minutes. I don't want you to catch cold and be laid up with a sore throat. Can't you bring your writing downstairs and do it beside the others?"

"I would rather not. I can get on so much better by myself."

"Are you writing to India—to your mother?"

"N–no, not just now."

"Then really, dear, you must come downstairs! This won't do! Your mother wished you to have a fire in your room, so that you might be able to sit here when you wanted to be alone, but she never meant you to make it a habit, or to spend all your spare time alone. It isn't healthy to use a room night and day, and to burn so much gas, and it isn't sociable, Peggy dear. Mellicent has just been complaining that you are hardly ever with them nowadays. Come along, like a good girl; put the writing away and amuse yourself downstairs. You have done enough work for one day. You don't do me credit with those white cheeks."

Peggy stood with her eyes fixed on the carpet without uttering a word. It would have been the easiest thing in the world to say, "Oh, do let me stay upstairs as much as I like for a day or two longer. I have a piece of work on hand which I am anxious to finish. It is a secret, but I hope to tell you all about it soon, and I am sure you will be pleased." If she had done so, she knew perfectly well how hearty and pleasant would have been Mrs Asplin's consent; but there are some states of mind in which it is a positive pleasure to be a martyr, and to feel oneself misunderstood, and this was just the mood in which Peggy found herself at present. She heard Mrs Asplin sigh, as if with anxiety and disappointment, as she left the room, and shrugged her shoulders in wilful indifference.

"She thinks I like sitting shivering here! I slave, and slave, from morning till night, and then people think I am sulky! I am not working for myself. I don't want the wretched old ten pounds; I could have ten pounds to-morrow if I needed it. Mother said I could. I am working to help Rob, and now I shall have to sit up later, and get up earlier than ever, as I mayn't work during the day. Mellicent said I was never with them, did she! I don't see that it matters whether I am there or not! They don't want me; nobody wants me, now that Rosalind has come! I hate Rosalind—nasty, smirking, conceited thing!" and Peggy jerked the towel off the writing- table and flicked it violently to and fro in the air, just as a little relief to her overcharged feelings.

She was crossing the hall with unwilling steps when the postman's knock sounded at the door, and three letters in long, narrow envelopes fell to the ground. Each envelope was of a pale pink tint, with a crest and monogram in white relief; one was addressed to the Misses Asplin, another to Oswald Elliston, and a third to Miss Mariquita Saville.

"Invitations!" cried Peggy, with a caper of delight. "Invitations! How scrumptious!" Her face clouded for a moment as the sight of the letters "R.D." suggested the sender of the letters; but the natural girlish delight in an unexpected festivity was stronger even than her prejudices, and it was the old, bright Peggy who bounced into the schoolroom holding up the three letters, and crying gleefully, "*Quis, Quis*, something nice for somebody! An invitation!"

"*Ego, Ego*!" came the eager replies, and the envelopes were seized and torn open in breathless haste.

"From Rosalind! Oh, how funny! 'Requests the pleasure—company—to a pink luncheon.' What in the world is a 'pink luncheon'?—'on Tuesday next, the 20th inst.'"

"A p-p-pink luncheon? How wewwy stwange!" echoed Mellicent, who had been suddenly affected with an incapacity to pronounce the letter "r" since the arrival of Rosalind Darcy on the scene—a peculiarity which happened regularly every autumn, and passed off again with the advent of spring. "How can a luncheon possibly be pink?"

"That's more than I can tell you, my dear! Ask Rob. What does it mean, Rob?" asked Peggy curiously; and Robert scowled, and shook back his shock of hair.

"Some American fad, I believe. The idea is to have everything of one colour—flowers, drapery, and food, china—everything that is on the table. It's a fag and an awful handicap, for you can't have half the things you want. But let us be modern or die—that's the motto nowadays. Mother is always trying to get hold of new-fangled notions."

"'Peggy Saville requests the pleasure of Jane Smith's company to a magenta supper.'—'Peggy Saville requests the pleasure of Mr Jones's company to a purple tea.' It's a splendid idea! I like it immensely," said Peggy, pursing her lips, and staring in the fire in meditative fashion. "Pink—pink
—what can we eat that is pink? P-prawns, p-pickles, p-p-pomegranates, P-aysandu tongues (you would call those pink, wouldn't you—pinky red?) Humph! I don't think it sounds very nice. Perhaps they dye the things with cochineal. I think I shall have a sensible brown and green meal before I go, and then I can nibble elegantly at the pinkies. Would it be considered a delicate mark of attention if I wore a pink frock?"

"Certainly it would. Wear that nice one that you put on in the evenings. Rosalind will be in pink from head to foot, you may depend on it," said Robert confidently; whereupon Mellicent rushed headlong from the room to find her mother, and plead eagerly that summer crepon dresses of the desired tint should be brought forth from their hiding-place and freshened up for the occasion. To accede to this request meant an extra call upon time already fully occupied, but mothers have a way of not grudging trouble where their children are concerned. Mrs Asplin said, "Yes, darling, of course I will!" and set to work with such goodwill that all three girls sported pink dresses beneath their ulsters when they set off to partake of the mysterious luncheon, a few days later.

Rosalind came to the bedroom to receive them, and looked

on from an arm-chair, while Lady Darcy's maid helped the visitors to take off their wraps. She herself looked like a rose in her dainty pink draperies, and Peggy had an impression that she was not altogether pleased to see that her guests were as appropriately dressed as herself. She eyed them up and down, and made remarks to the maid in that fluent French of hers which was so unintelligible to the schoolgirls' ears. The maid smirked and pursed up her lips, and then, meeting Peggy's steady gaze, dropped her eyes in confusion. Peggy knew, as well as if she had understood every word, that the remarks exchanged between mistress and maid had been of a depreciatory nature, not as concerned her own attire—that was as perfect in its way as Rosalind's own—but with reference to the home-made dresses of the vicar's daughters, which seemed to have suddenly become clumsy and shapeless when viewed in the mirrors of this elegant bedroom. She was in arms at once on her friends' behalf, and when Peggy's dignity was hurt she was a formidable person to tackle. In this instance she fixed her eyes first on the maid, and then on Rosalind herself with a steady, disapproving stare which was not a little disconcerting.

"I am sorry," she said, "but we really don't know French well enough to follow your conversation! You were talking about us, I think. Perhaps you would be kind enough to repeat your remarks in English?"

"Oh-h, it doesn't matter! It was nothing at all important!" Rosalind flushed, and had the grace to look a trifle ashamed of her own ill-breeding, but she did not by any means appreciate the reproof. The girls had not been ten minutes in the house, and already that aggravating Peggy Saville had succeeded in making her feel humiliated and uncomfortable. The same thing happened whenever they met. The respect and awe and adoring admiration which she was accustomed to receive from other girls of her own age seemed altogether wanting in Peggy's case; and yet, strange to say, the very fact that she refused to fall down and worship invested Peggy with a peculiar importance in Rosalind's eyes. She longed to overcome her prejudices and add her name to the list of her adorers, and to this end she considered her tastes in a way which would never have occurred to her in connection with Mrs Asplin's daughters. In planning the pink luncheon Peggy had been continually in her mind, and it is doubtful whether she would have taken the trouble to arrange so difficult an entertainment had not the party from the vicarage included that important personage, Miss Mariquita Saville.

From the bedroom the girls adjourned to the morning-room, where Lady Darcy sat waiting; but almost as soon as they had exchanged greetings, the gong sounded to announce luncheon, and they walked across the hall aglow with expectation.

The table looked exquisite, and the guests stood still in the doorway and gasped with admiration. The weather outside was grey and murky, but tall standard lamps were placed here and there, and the light which streamed from beneath the pink silk shades gave an air of warmth and comfort to the room. Down the centre of the table lay a slip of looking-glass, on which graceful long-necked swans seemed to float to and fro, while troughs filled with soft pink blossoms formed a bordering. Garlands of pink flowers fell from the chandelier and were attached to the silver candelabra, in which pink candles burned with clear and steady flare. Glass, china, ornaments, were all of the same dainty colour, and beside each plate was a dainty little buttonhole nosegay, with a coral-headed pin, all ready to be attached to the dress or coat of the owner.

"It's—it's beautiful!" cried Mellicent ecstatically; while Peggy's beauty-loving eye turned from one detail to another with delighted approbation. "Really," she said to herself in astonishment, "I couldn't have done it better myself! It's quite admirable!" and as Rosalind's face peered inquiringly at her beneath the canopy of flowers, she nodded her head, and smiled generous approval.

"Beautiful! Charming! I congratulate you! Did you design it and arrange everything yourself?"

"Mother and I made it up between us. We didn't do the actual work, but we told the servants what to do, and saw that it was all right. The flowers and bonbons are easy enough to manage; it's the things to eat that are the greatest trouble."

"It seems to be too horribly prosaic to eat anything at such a table, except crumpled rose-leaves, like the princess in the fairy tale," said Peggy gushingly; but at this Mellicent gave an exclamation of dismay, and the three big lads turned their eyes simultaneously towards the soup tureen, as if anxious to assure themselves that they were not to be put off with such ethereal rations.

The soup was pink. "Tomato!" murmured Peggy to herself, as she raised the first creamy spoonful to her lips. The fish was covered with thick pink sauce; tiny little cutlets lurked behind ruffles of pink paper; pink baskets held chicken soufflés; moulds of pink cream and whipped-up syllabubs were handed round in turns, and looked so tempting that Mellicent helped herself at once, and nearly shed tears of mortification on finding that they were followed by distracting pink ices, which were carried away again before she could possibly finish what was on her plate. Then came dessert-plates and finger-glasses, in which crystallised rose-leaves floated in the scented water, as if in fulfilment of Peggy's suggestion of an hour before, and the young people sat in great contentment, eating rosy apples, bananas pared and dipped in pink sugar, or helping themselves to the delicious bonbons which were strewed about the table.

While they were thus occupied the door opened, and Lord Darcy came into the room. He had not appeared before, and he shook hands with the visitors in turn, and then stood at the head of the table looking about him with a slow, kindly smile. Peggy watched him from her seat, and thought what a nice face he had, and wondered at the indifferent manner in which he was received by his wife and daughter. Lady Darcy leant back in her chair and played with her fruit, the sleeves of her pink silk tea-gown falling back from her white arms. Rosalind whispered to Max, and neither of them troubled to cast so much as a glance of welcome at the new-comer. Peggy thought of her own father, the gallant soldier out in India, of the joy and pride with which his comings and goings were watched; of Mr Asplin in the vicarage, with his wife running to meet him, and Mellicent resting her curly bead on his shoulder; and the figure of the old lord standing unnoticed at the head of his own table assumed a pathetic interest. It seemed, however, as if Lord Darcy were accustomed to be overlooked, for he showed no signs of annoyance; on the contrary, his face brightened, and he looked at the pretty scene with sparkling eyes. The room was full of a soft rosy glow, the shimmer of silver and crystal was reflected in the sheet of mirror, and beneath the garlands of flowers the young faces of the guests glowed with pleasure and excitement. He looked from one to the other—handsome Max, dandy Oswald, Robert with his look of strength and decision; then to the girls—Esther, gravely smiling; wide-eyed Mellicent; Peggy, with her eloquent, sparkling eyes; Rosalind, a queen of beauty among them all; finally to the head of the table, where sat his wife.

"I must congratulate you, dear," he said heartily. "It is the prettiest sight I have seen for a long time. You have arranged admirably, but that's no new thing; you always do. I don't know where you get your ideas. These wreaths—eh? I've never seen anything like them before. What made you think of fastening them up there?"

"I have had them like that several times before, but you never notice a thing until its novelty is over, and I am tired to death of seeing it," said his wife, with a frown and an impatient curve of the lip, as if she had received a rebuke instead of a compliment.

Peggy stared at her plate, felt Robert shuffle on his chair by her side, and realised that he was as embarrassed and unhappy as herself. The beautiful room with its luxurious appointments seemed to have suddenly become oppressive and cheerless, for in it was the spirit of discontent and discord between those who should have been most in harmony. Esther was shocked, Mellicent frightened, the boys looked awkward and uncomfortable. No one ventured to break the silence, and there was quite a long pause before Lady Darcy spoke again in quick, irritable tones.

"Have you arranged to get away with me on Thursday, as I asked you?"

"My dear, I cannot. I explained before. I am extremely sorry, but I have made appointments which I cannot break. I could take you next week if you would wait."

"I can't wait. I told you I had to go to the dentist's. Do you wish me to linger on in agony for another week? And I have written to Mrs Bouverie that I will be at her 'At Home' on Saturday. My appointments are, at least, as binding as yours. It isn't often that I ask you to take me anywhere, but when it is a matter of health I do think you might show a little consideration."

Lord Darcy drew his brows together and bit his moustache. Peggy recalled Robert's description of the "governor looking wretched" when he found himself compelled to refuse a favour, and did not wonder that the lad was ready to deny himself a pleasure rather than see that expression on his father's face. The twinkling light had died out of his eyes, and he looked old and sad and haggard, far more in need of physical remedies than his wife, whose "agony" had been so well concealed during the last two hours as to give her the appearance of a person in very comfortable health. Rosalind alone looked absolutely unruffled, and lay back in her chair nibbling at her bonbon, as though such scenes were of too frequent occurrence between her parents to be deserving of attention.

"If you have made up your mind to go to-morrow, and cannot go alone, you must take Robert with you, Beatrice, for I cannot leave. It is only for four days, and Mr Asplin will no doubt excuse him, if you write and explain the circumstances."

Lord Darcy left the room, and Robert and Peggy exchanged agonised glances. Go away for nearly a week, when before two days were over the calendar must be sent to London, and there still remained real hard work before it was finished! Peggy sat dazed and miserable, seeing the painful effort of the last month brought to naught, Robert's ambition defeated, and her own help of no avail. That one glance had shown the lad's face flushed with emotion; but when his mother spoke to him in fretful tones, bidding him be ready next morning when she should call in the carriage on her way to the station, he answered at once with polite acquiescence—

"Very well, mater, I won't keep you waiting. I shall be ready by half-past ten if you want me."

Chapter Sixteen.

An Unexpected Visitor.

Lady Darcy left the young people by themselves after luncheon, and, as was only natural, conversation at once turned on the proposed visit to London. Peggy was too much perturbed to speak, but Mellicent put the very inquiry which she most wished answered, being never troubled with bashfulness in asking questions.

"Has your mother's tooth been hurting her very much, Rosalind?"

"Tooth! what tooth? Oh, I think she did have a little twinge one night; but it's not the dentist whom she is really going to see. That's only an excuse. She really wants to go to some parties," said Rosalind lightly; whereat her brother scowled at her under heavy brows.

"What business have you to say that? What can you know about it, pray? If mother says she is in pain, it is not for you to contradict, and make up your own explanations. Leave her to manage her own affairs—"

He spoke rapidly, but Rosalind only shrugged her shoulders, and whispered something in Max's ear, at which he smiled and nodded his head, evidently taking her part against her brother, to Peggy's intense indignation.

No words were exchanged between the partners on the subject of the calendar until they were once more at home; when Robert took advantage of the first quiet opportunity, and came up to Peggy with a face of set determination.

"Mariquita!" he said, "*I—am—not—going—to give in*! If you

stick to me, we can still manage to get the calendar off in time. There are twenty more quotations to be found. I'll sit up to-night and fix them off, and go on writing as long as I can keep awake, but I can't take a dozen books up to town with me, so I must leave it to you to finish up. I'll mark the passages I choose, write the full address on a piece of paper, and leave everything ready for you to make up the parcel. All you will have to do will be to write the remaining cards, and to see that it is sent off on Friday. Five o'clock will be time enough, but if you can get it off in the morning, so much the better. You think you can manage as much as that?"

"Oh yes! I'd do anything rather than give up now. It would be too grudging. I am not afraid of a little more work."

"You have done more than your share already. I am mad about it, but it can't be helped. I couldn't refuse to go with the mater, and I wouldn't if I could. She is really not at all strong, and does not like the life down here. It will do her good to have a few days' change."

Peggy looked at him steadily. She did not speak, but her eyes grew soft and shining, and there was something at once so sweet, so kindly, and so gentle in her expression that Rob exclaimed in surprise—

"I say, Peggy, you—you do look pretty! I never saw you look like that before—what have you been doing to yourself?"

"Doing!" Peggy straightened herself at that, in offended dignity. "Doing, indeed! What do you mean? Don't you think I am pretty as a rule?"

"Never thought about it," returned Robert carelessly. "You are Peggy—that's enough for me. A nice state I should be in to-day if it were not for you! You are the jolliest little brick I ever met, and if I get this prize it will be far more your doing than my own."

Well, that was good hearing! Peggy held her head high for the rest of that evening, and felt as if nothing would have power to depress her for the future. But, alas, when the pendulum is at its highest it begins to swing downwards. Peggy's heart sank as she watched Robert drive away from the door the next morning, and it went on sinking more and more during the next twenty-four hours, as she realised the responsibility which weighed upon her shoulders. When she came down to breakfast on Friday morning the calendar was finished and ready to be made up for the post, but her head was splitting with pain as the result of the long hours' work stolen from sleep, and a dead weight of depression had settled on her spirits. It seemed of a sudden that all this work and effort was waste of time; that the chances of being successful were infinitesimally small; that even if it were gained, the prize was of little value; that if Robert's absence for four days made such a difference in the life at the vicarage, it would become altogether unbearable when he said good-bye at the beginning of the year and went up to Oxford; that she was a desperately unfortunate little unit, thrust into the midst of a family which was complete in itself, and had only a kindly toleration to offer to a stranger; that, in all probability, there would shortly be a war in India, when her father would be killed, her mother die of a broken heart, and Arthur be called out to join the ranks of the recruits. She conjured up a touching picture of herself, swathed in crape, bidding good- bye to her brother at the railway station, and watching the scarlet coat disappear in the distance, as the train steamed away. It was all most miserable and picturesque, and outside the fog gathered, and the rain poured down in a fine, persistent drizzle. It was one of those typical November days when it seems as if the earth itself is in the blues, and that it becomes everyone living on its surface to follow its example.

When afternoon came Peggy curled herself in an arm-chair in the corner of the study, and stared gloomily at the fire. It was four o'clock. In another hour the postman would call for the letters, and she would deliver the precious packet into his hands. She had made it up in the dinner-hour, with some faint idea of carrying it to the village; but she was tired, the rain poured, and Rob had said that the afternoon post would do. She had given up the idea of going out, and taken a nap instead on the top of her bed. And now it was four o'clock. Mellicent called out that she was dying for tea-time to come; it had seemed such a long, long day; they really ought to have tea earlier on these dreary, murky afternoons. "*I want my tea*!" she chanted, in shrill, penetrating tones, and instantly the refrain was taken up by the other voices, and repeated over and over again with ever-increasing volume, until the mistress of the house rushed in to discover the reason of the clamour.

"Bless your hearts, you shall have it at once!" she cried. "I'll ring and have it brought in, and ransack my cupboards to see what treats I can give you. Poor dears, it *is* dull for you sitting indoors all day long. We must think of some bright, exciting games for this evening." No sooner said than done; she did not wait until Mary appeared, but bustled off to meet her, to enlist the cook's sympathy, and put out the promised delicacies, and when the table was set she returned to the room and seated herself, smilingly, in Esther's place.

"I am going to stay with you this afternoon," she said brightly. "Draw up your chairs, dears, and let us be jovial. There is no credit in being happy when the sun is shining, as dear old Mark Tapley would have said; but it will really be praiseworthy if we succeed in being festive this afternoon. Come, Peggy, dearie!"

Peggy turned her dreary little face and stared at the table. From outside came the sound of the opening and shutting of the door, of footsteps in the hall. She glanced at the clock, wondering if it could possibly be the postman already, found it was only ten minutes past four, and dismissed the supposition with a sigh. "I don't—think—I want—" she was beginning slowly, when, of a sudden, there came a tremendous rat-tat-tat on the schoolroom door; the handle was not turned, but burst open; a blast of chilly air blew into the room, and in the doorway stood a tall, handsome youth, with square shoulders, a gracefully poised head, and Peggy Saville's eave-like brows above his dancing eyes.

"Oh, what a surprise!" came the cry in loud laughing tones. "How do you do, everybody? Just thought I would step in as I was passing, and have a cup of tea, don't you know."

"My boy! My boy! Oh, how good to see you!" cried Mrs Asplin rapturously. Mellicent gurgled with surprise, and Peggy stood up by her chair and stretched out both arms like a child to its mother.

"Arthur!—oh—Arthur!" she gasped, and there was a pathos, a longing, an almost incredulous rapture in her voice which made the tears start in Mrs Asplin's eyes, and brought a cloud of anxiety over the new-comer's face.

"Why, Peg!" he cried. "My little Peg! Is something wrong, dear? You look as melancholy as—"

"Peggy has not been like herself for the last few weeks. I think she has had an attack of homesickness and longing for her own people. I'm so glad you've come. You will do her more good than a dozen tonics. Bless the boy; how big he is! And how did you manage to get away, dear, and how long can you stay? Tell me all about it. I am consumed with curiosity —"

"I can stay till Monday or Tuesday, if you can put me up; and I came away because I—I suppose I am not quite up to the mark. My head bothers me. It aches, and I see black specks floating before my eyes. The doctor advised me to knock off for a few days, and I thought I would rather come here than anywhere."

"I should think so, indeed. Of course we can put you up—proud and pleased to do so. Well, this is a pleasant surprise for a dull November day! You couldn't have had a better one if you had had a hundred wishes, could you, Peggy? You won't feel melancholy any longer?"

"I'm just enraptured! Saturday, Sunday, Monday—three whole days and two halves, as good as four days—almost a week! It's too delicious—too utterly delicious to realise!"

Peggy drew deep sighs of happiness, and hung on to Arthur's arm in an abandonment of tenderness which showed her in a new light to her companions. She would not loosen her grasp for a moment, and even when seated at the table kept her fingers tightly locked round his arm, as though afraid that he might escape.

As for Arthur himself, he was in the wildest spirits. He was as handsome a young soldier as one could wish to see, and his likeness to Peggy seemed only to make him more attractive in the eyes of the beholders.

"Hurrah!" he cried cheerily. "Hurrah, for a good old vicarage tea! Scones? that's the style! Mary made them, I hope, and put in lots of currants. Raspberry jam! I say, mater, do you remember that solemn waitress you had, who told you that the jam was done again, and when you exclaimed in horror, said, 'Yes, 'um, it's not a bit of good buying raspberry jam. *They like it*!' Ha, ha, ha! I've often thought of that! That looks uncommonly good cake you have over there. Thank you, I think I will! Begin with cake, and work steadily back to bread and butter—that's the style, isn't it, Peggums? Esther, I looks towards you! Mellicent, you are as thin as ever, I see. You should really do something for it. There are regular hollows in your cheeks."

"Nasty, horrid thing! You are always teasing! How would you like it if you were struck fat yourself?" cried Mellicent, aggrieved. But, in spite of herself, her chubby cheeks dimpled with smiles as Arthur rolled his eyes at her across the table, for there was something irresistibly fascinating about this young fellow, and it was like old times to see him seated at the tea-table and to listen to his merry rattling voice.

"The dominie must grant a general holiday to-morrow," he declared, "and we will do something fine to celebrate the occasion. We'll have out this wonderful camera in the morning and take some groups. You and I must be taken together, Peggy, to send out to the parents. You promised to send me copies of all the things you took, but you are as false in that respect as the whole race of amateur photographers. They are grand hands at promising, but they never, by any chance—Hallo! What's that? My cup over? Awfully sorry, mater, really! I'll put a penny in the missionary- box. Was it a clean cloth?"

"Oh, my dear boy, don't apologise! I should not have felt that it was really you if you had not knocked your cup over! To see the table-cloth swimming with tea all round convinces me that it is Arthur himself, and nobody else! Tut, tut! What does a table-cloth matter?" And Mrs Asplin beamed upon her favourite as if she were really rather delighted than otherwise at his exploit.

It was a merry, not to say noisy, meal which followed. Peggy's lost spirits had come back with the first glimpse of Arthur's face; and her quips and cranks were so irresistibly droll that three separate times over Mellicent choked over her tea, and had to be relieved with vigorous pounding on the back, while even Esther shook with laughter, and the boys became positively uproarious.

Then Mr Asplin came in, and Arthur was carefully concealed behind the window-curtains, while he was asked whom he would most like to see if the choice were given him. In provoking manner he mentioned at once a brother in Australia, and, when informed that relatives were not on the list, recollected an old college chum who was out in the Mauritius.

"Oh dear, what a stupid man!" cried his wife in despair. "We don't mean the friends of your youth, dear! Think of the last few years and of your young friends! Now, if you could choose, whom would you—"

"Arthur Saville!" said the vicar promptly, upon which Arthur made a loophole between the curtains and thrust his mischievous face through the gap, to the vicar's amazement and the uproarious delight of the onlookers. A dozen questions had to be asked and answered about studies, examinations, and health, while Peggy sat listening, beaming with happiness and pride.

It came as quite a shock to all when the vicar announced that it was time to dress for dinner, and Mrs Asplin looked at Peggy with an apologetic smile.

"We were all so charmed to see Arthur that I'm afraid we have been selfish and engrossed too much of his attention. You two will be longing for a cosy little chat to yourselves. If you run upstairs now, Peggy, and hurry through your dressing, there will be a little time before dinner, and you could have this room to yourselves."

"Yes, run along, Peg! It won't take me ten minutes to get into my clothes, and I'll be here waiting for you!" cried Arthur eagerly. And Peggy went flying two steps at a time upstairs to her own room.

The gas was lit; the can of hot water stood in the basin, the towel neatly folded over the top; the hands of the little red clock pointed to six o'clock, and the faint chime met her ear as she entered.

Peggy stood still in the doorway, an icy chill crept through her veins, her hands grasped the lintel, and her eyes grew wide and blank with horror. There, on the writing-table lay a brown paper parcel—the precious parcel which contained the calendar which had been the object of such painful work and anxiety!

Chapter Seventeen.

Peggy is lost.

Arthur Saville waited in vain by the schoolroom fire, for his sister did not join him. And when he entered the dining-room in response to the summons of the gong, she had not yet made her appearance.

Mrs Asplin looked at him with uplifted brows.

"Where is Peggy?"

"I don't know. I haven't seen her since she went upstairs. The little wretch can't have hurried very much."

"She hasn't been with you, then! Never mind, there is plenty of time to come. She must be making a special toilet for your benefit."

But when the first course was nearly over and the girl had not yet appeared, Mrs Asplin grew impatient, and despatched the servant to hasten her movements.

"Just tell her that we have been at table for nearly ten minutes. Ask if she will be long."

Mary left the room, was absent a short time, and came back with an extraordinary statement.

"Miss Peggy is not in her room, ma'am."

"Not in her room! Then she must have come downstairs. Perhaps she didn't hear the gong. Just look in the schoolroom, Mary, and in the other rooms too, and tell her to come at once."

Another few minutes passed, and back again came Mary, looking flushed and mysterious.

"I can't see Miss Peggy anywhere, ma'am. She has not come downstairs."

"You have looked in the drawing-room—Mr Asplin's study?"

"Yes, ma'am."

"Did you go upstairs again?"

"No, ma'am. I had looked there before."

"Esther dear, you go!" cried Mrs Asplin quickly. "Bring her down at once! What in the world is the child doing? It's most extraordinary!"

"She's not given to playing games of hide-and-seek just at dinner-time, is she?" asked Arthur, laughing. "I am never surprised at anything Peggy does. She has some little prank on hand, depend upon it, and will turn up in good time. It's her own fault if she misses her dinner."

"But it's so extraordinary! To-night of all nights, when you have just arrived! I wish the child would come!" replied Mrs Asplin, craning her neck forward to listen to the cries of "Peggy! Peggy!" which came from the upper storey.

The door stood open, and everyone ceased talking to follow Esther's footsteps to and fro, to count the opening and shutting of doors—one, two, three, four, five—to look apprehensively at each other as the messenger returned—alone!

"Mother, she is not there! I've looked everywhere—in every corner—and she has not changed her dress, nor washed, nor anything. The room looks exactly as if she had never gone in; but she did, for we all followed her upstairs. I looked over the wardrobe, and all her dresses are there, and the can of hot water is untouched, and the gas left full up."

"Oh dear, what can have happened?" Mrs Asplin pushed back her chair and stood up, looking anxious and puzzled. "I cannot rest until she is found! I must look myself! Go on with dinner, all of you; I won't be long. Where can the child be hiding herself?"

"Don't worry, mater!" said Arthur kindly. "It's very tiresome of Peggy to disappear at such an inopportune moment, but no harm can have happened to her, you know. It's impossible! As I said before, she has probably some wild prank in her head of which this is a part. I'll give her a lecture when I catch her for spoiling dinner like this, and such an uncommonly good dinner too!" And Arthur smiled in cheery fashion, and tried his best to keep up the failing spirits of the company by chatting away while his hostess was out of the room, as if nothing had happened which was the least unusual or alarming.

When Mrs Asplin returned, however, after a lengthened absence, there was a simultaneous rising from the table to listen to her report.

"She is not in the house! Jane began at the top and I began at the bottom, and we searched every hole and corner. I have looked in the very cupboards and wardrobes! I even searched the cistern-room, but she is not to be found. I don't know what to do next. It seems impossible that she can have disappeared—yet where can she be?"

"Have you looked in the cloak-room to see if any of her outdoor things are missing?"

"I went in, but I never thought of looking at her clothes. Outdoor? What on earth should take the child out at this hour in the dark and rain?"

"I can't tell you that, dear, but we must think of every possibility. Esther, you know best what Peggy had in the cloak-room—see if anything is missing. Mellicent, run upstairs and find if any hats or jackets have been taken from their places. If she is not in the house, she must have gone out. It was most thoughtless and foolish to go without asking permission, and at such an hour; but, as Arthur says, there is not much chance of any harm befalling her. Try not to work yourself up into a state of anxiety, dear; we shall soon find your truant for you. Well, Esther, what is it?"

"Her mackintosh has gone, father, and her red tam-o'-shanter, and her snow-shoes. Her peg is next to mine, and there is nothing on it but her check golf cape."

"She has gone out, then! What can it mean?—to-night of all nights, when she was so happy, when Arthur had just arrived, when she promised to be downstairs in ten minutes—"

"It is most extraordinary! It must have been something of great importance, one would say. Does anyone know if Peggy had any special interest on hand at present? Was there any gift which she wished to buy? It does not happen to be anyone's birthday to-morrow, does it? Yours, Arthur, for instance? No? The birthday of a school-friend, then? She might suddenly have remembered such an occasion, and rushed out to post a letter—"

"But there is no post until to-morrow morning, so she would gain no time by doing that. The postman called at five o'clock, and the letters were on the hall-table waiting for him as usual. I do not know of any work that she had on hand, but the girls have complained that she has spent all her spare time in her room lately, and when I spoke to her about it she said she was writing—"

"Perhaps she is writing a book," suggested Mellicent thoughtfully. "She says she is going to be an authoress when she grows up. I think Robert knew what she was doing. They were always talking together and looking over books, and I heard him say to her, 'Bring me all you have finished, to look over.' I said something to her about printing some photographs for Christmas cards, and she said she could do nothing until after the nineteenth."

"The nineteenth!" echoed the vicar sharply. "That is to-day. We gather from that, then, that Peggy had been busy with work, either by herself or in conjunction with Robert, which had to be completed by to-day. Nobody has the least idea of what nature it was? No? Then I shall go to Robert's room and see if there is anything lying about which can give me a clue."

"I'll go with you, sir," said Arthur, who was beginning to look a little anxious and uneasy, as the moments passed by and brought no sign of his sister; but, alas, the scattered papers on Rob's table gave no clue to the mystery!

When one is endeavouring to find a reason why a girl should mysteriously disappear from her home, it does not help very much to find a few slips of paper on which are written such items as "Tennyson's Poems, page 26," "Selections from British Authors, 203," "Macaulay's Essays, 97," etcetera.

Arthur and Mr Asplin looked at one another, puzzled and disappointed, and had no alternative but to return to the dining-room and confess their failure.

"Would not it be a good thing to go up to the Larches, and hear what Robert has to say on the subject?" Arthur asked; and when he was told that Robert was in London he still held to his suggestion.

"For someone else in the house may know about it," he declared. "Rob may have confided in his mother or sister. At the worst we can get his address, and telegraph to him for information, if she has not returned before we get back. She might even have gone to the Larches herself to—to see Rosalind!"

"Peggy doesn't like Rosalind. She never goes to see her if she can help it. I'm quite sure she has not gone there," said Mellicent shrewdly. "It is more likely she has gone to Fräulein's lodgings to tell her about Arthur. She is fond of Fräulein."

The suggestion was not very brilliant, but it was hailed with eagerness by the listeners as the most probable explanation yet offered.

"Then I'll tell you what we will do. I'll go off to the Larches," cried Arthur, "and one of you fellows can see Fräulein, and find out if Peggy has been there. We must try every place, likely and unlikely. It is better than sitting here doing nothing."

Max frowned and hesitated. "Or—er—or you might go to Fräulein, and I'll take the Larches! It is a long walk for you after your journey," he suggested, with a sudden access of politeness, "and there seems more probability that Fräulein may be able to help us. You could go there and back in a short time."

"Just as you like, of course. It is all the same to me," returned Arthur, in a tone which plainly intimated that it was nothing of the sort. Mrs Asplin looked from one to the other of the flushed faces, realising that even in the midst of anxiety the image of beautiful, golden-haired Rosalind had a Will-o'-the-wisp attraction for the two big lads; but her husband saw nothing of what lay behind the commonplace words, and said calmly—

"Very well, then, Max, be off with you as fast as you can go. Find out if Robert has said anything about the work which he has had on hand; find out his address in town, and, if possible, where a telegram would reach him this evening. Arthur will call at Fräulein's lodgings; and, Oswald, you might go with him so far, and walk through the village. Ask at old Mrs Gilpin's shop if Miss Saville has been there, but don't talk about it too much; we don't want to make more fuss than we can help. Keep your eyes open!"

The three lads departed without further delay; the vicar put on his coat and hat preparatory to searching the garden and the lanes in the immediate neighbourhood, and the womenkind of the household settled down to an hour of painful waiting.

Mrs Asplin lay back in her chair, with her hand to her head, now silent, now breaking out into impetuous lamentations. The fear lest any accident had happened to Peggy paralysed her with dread. Her thoughts went out to far-away India; she imagined the arrival of the ominous cablegram; pictured it carried into the house by a native servant; saw the light die out of two happy faces at the reading of the fatal words. "Oh, Peggy, Peggy!" she groaned. "Oh, the poor father—the poor mother! What will I do? What will I do? Oh, Peggy, dearie, come back I come back!"

Esther busied herself looking after a dozen little domestic arrangements, to which no one else seemed capable of attendance, and Mellicent laid her head on her mother's lap, and never ceased crying, except for one brief interval, when she darted upstairs to peep inside the old oak chest, prompted thereto by a sudden reminiscence of the bride of the "Mistletoe Bough." There was no Peggy inside the chest, however; only a few blankets, and a very strong smell of camphor; so Mellicent crept back to her footstool, and cried with redoubled energy. In the kitchen the fat old cook sat with a hand planted on either knee, and thrilled the other servants with an account of how "a cousin of me own brother-in-law, him that married our Annie, had a child as went a-missing, as fine a girl as you could wish to see from June to January. Beautiful kerly 'air, for all the world like Miss Mellicent's, and such nice ways with her! Everybody loved that child, gentle and simple. 'Beller,' 'er name was, after her mother. She went out unbeknownst, just as it might be Miss Peggy, and they searched and better searched,"—cook's hands waved up and down, and the heads of the listeners wagged in sympathy—"and never a trace could they find. 'Er father—he's a stone-mason by trade, and getting good money—he knocked off work, and his friends they knocked off too, and they searched the country far and wide. Day and night I tell you they searched, a week on end, and poor Isabeller nearly off her head with grief. I've heard my sister say as she never tasted bite nor sup the whole time, and was wasted to a shadow. Eh, poor soul, it's hard to rare up a child, and have it go out smiling and bonnie, and never see nothink of it again but its bones—for she had fallen into a lime pit, had Beller, and it was nothing but her skeleton as they brought 'ome. There was building going on around there, and she was playing near the pit—childlike—just as it might be Miss Peggy..." Soon and on. The horrors accumulated with every moment. The housemaid had heard tell of a beautiful little girl, the heiress to a big estate, who had been carried off by strolling gipsies, and never been seen again by her sorrowing relatives; while the waitress hinted darkly that the time might come when it would be a comfort to know force had been employed, for sharper than a serpent's tooth was an ungrateful child, and she always *had* said that there was something uncanny about that little Miss Saville!

The clock was striking nine o'clock when the first of the messengers came back to report his failure; he was closely followed by a second; and last of all came Max, bringing word that nothing had been seen or heard of Peggy at the Larches; that neither Lord Darcy nor Rosalind had the faintest idea of the nature of the work which had just been completed; and, further, that on this evening Robert was escorting his mother to some entertainment, so that even if sent off at once a telegram could not reach him until a late hour. Mrs Asplin turned her white face from one speaker to the other, and, when the last word was spoken, broke into a paroxysm of helpless weeping.

Chapter Eighteen.

The Secret Confessed.

"Something has happened! Something terrible has happened to the child! And she was left in our charge. We are responsible. Oh, if any harm has happened to Peggy, however, ever, ever, can I bear to live and send the news to her parents—"

"My dearest, you have done your best; you could not have been kinder or more thoughtful. No blame can attach to you. Remember that Peggy is in higher hands than yours. However far from us she may be, she can never stray out of God's keeping. It all seems very dark and mysterious, but—"

At this moment a loud rat-tat-tat sounded on the knocker, and with one accord the hearers darted into the hall, and stood panting and gasping, while Arthur threw open the door.

"Telegram, sir!" said a sharp, young voice, and the brown envelope which causes so much agitation in quiet households was thrust forward in a small cold hand. Arthur looked at the address and handed it to the vicar.

"It is for you, sir, but it cannot possibly be anything about—"

Mr Asplin tore open the envelope, glanced over the words, and broke into an exclamation of amazement. "It is! It is from Peggy herself!—'Euston Station. Returning by 10.30 train. Please meet me at twelve o'clock.—Peggy.' What in the world does it mean?" He looked round the group of anxious faces, only to see his own expression of bewilderment repeated on each in turn.

"Euston! Returning! She is in London. She is coming back from town!"

"She ran away to London, to-night when she was so happy, when Arthur had just arrived! Why? Why? Why?"

"She must have caught the seven o'clock train."

"She must have left the house almost immediately after going upstairs to dress for dinner."

"Oh, father, why should she go to London?"

"I am quite unable to tell you, my dear," replied the vicar drily. He looked at his wife's white, exhausted face, and his eyes flashed with the "A-word-with-you-in-my-study" expression, which argued ill for Miss Peggy's reception. Mrs Asplin, however, was too thankful to know of the girl's safety to have any thought for herself. She began to smile, with the tears still running down her face, and to draw long breaths of relief and satisfaction.

"It's no use trying to guess at that, Millie dear. It is enough for me to know that she is alive and well. We shall just have to try and compose ourselves in patience until we hear Peggy's own explanation. Let me see! There is nearly an hour before you need set out. What can we do to pass the time as quickly as possible?"

"Have some coffee, I should say! None of us have had too much dinner, and a little refreshment would be very welcome after all this strain," said Arthur promptly, and Mrs Asplin eagerly welcomed the suggestion.

"That's what I call a really practical proposal! Ring the bell, dear, and I will order it at once. I am sure we shall all have thankful hearts while we drink it." She looked appealingly at Mr Asplin as she spoke; but there was no answering smile on his face, and the lines down his cheeks looked deeper and grimmer than ever.

"Oh, goody, goody, goodness, aren't I glad I am not Peggy!" sighed Mellicent to herself; while Arthur Saville pursed his lips together, and thought, "Poor little Peg! She'll catch it. I've never seen the dominie look so savage. This is a nice sort of treat for a fellow who has been ordered away for rest and refreshment! I wish the next two hours were safely over."

Wishing, unfortunately, however, can never carry us over the painful crises of our lives. We have to face them as best we may, and Arthur needed all his cheery confidence to sustain him during the damp walk which followed, when the vicar tramped silently by his side, his shovel hat pulled over his eyes, his mackintosh coat flapping to and fro in the wind.

They reached the station in good time, and punctually to the minute the lights of the London express were seen in the distance. The train drew up, and among the few passengers who alighted the figure of Peggy, in her scarlet-trimmed hat, was easily distinguished. She was assisted out of the carriage by an elderly gentleman, in a big travelling coat, who stood by her side as she looked about for her friends. As Mr Asplin and Arthur approached, they only heard his hearty, "Now you are all right!" and Peggy's elegant rejoinder, "Exceedingly indebted to you for all your kindness!" Then he stepped back into the carriage, and she came forward to meet them, half shy, half smiling, "I—I am afraid that you—"

"We will defer explanations, Mariquita, if you please, until we reach home. A fly is waiting. We will return as quickly as possible," said the vicar frigidly; and the brother and sister lagged behind as he led the way out of the station, gesticulating and whispering together in furtive fashion.

"Oh, you Peggy! *Now* you have done it! No end of a row!"

"Couldn't help it! Had to go. Stick to me, Arthur, whatever you do!"

"Like a leech! We'll worry through somehow. Never say die!" Then the fly was reached, and they jolted home in silence.

Mrs Asplin and the four young folks were sitting waiting in the drawing-room, and each one turned an eager, excited face towards the doorway as Peggy entered, her cheeks white, but with shining eyes, and hair ruffled into little curls beneath the scarlet cap. Mrs Asplin would have rushed forward in welcome, but a look in her husband's face restrained her, and there was a deathlike silence in the room as he took up his position by the mantelpiece.

"Mariquita," he said slowly, "you have caused us to-night some hours of the most acute and painful anxiety which we have ever experienced. You disappeared suddenly from among us, and until ten o'clock, when your telegram arrived, we had not the faintest notion as to where you could be. The most tragic suspicions came to our minds. We have spent the evening in rushing to and fro, searching and inquiring in all directions. Mrs Asplin has had a shock from which, I fear, she will be some time in recovering. Your brother's pleasure in his visit has been spoiled. We await your explanation. I am at a loss to imagine any reason sufficiently good to excuse such behaviour; but I will say no more until I have heard what you have to say."

Peggy stood like a prisoner at the bar, with hanging head and hands clasped together. As the vicar spoke of his wife, she darted a look at Mrs Asplin, and a quiver of emotion passed over her face. When he had finished she drew a deep breath, raised her head and looked him full in the face with her bright, earnest eyes.

"I am sorry," she said slowly. "I can't tell you in words *how* sorry I am. I know it will be difficult, but I hope you will forgive me. I was thinking what I had better do while I was coming back in the train, and I decided that I ought to tell you everything, even though it is supposed to be a secret. Robert will forgive me, and it is Robert's secret as much as mine. I'll begin at the beginning. About five weeks ago Robert saw an advertisement of a prize that was offered by a magazine. You had to make up a calendar with quotations for every day in the year, and the person who sent in the best selection would get thirty pounds. Rob wanted the money very badly to buy a microscope, and he asked me to help him. I was to have ten pounds for myself if we won, but I didn't care about that. I just wanted to help Rob. I said I would take the money, because I knew if I didn't he would not let me work so hard, and I thought I would spend it in buying p-p-presents for you all at Christmas."—Peggy's voice faltered at this point, and she gulped nervously several times before she could go on with her story.—"We had to work very hard, because the time was so short. Robert had not seen the advertisement until it had been out some time. I printed the headings on the cards; that is why I sat so much in my own room. The last fortnight I have been writing every morning before six o'clock. Oh, you can't think how difficult it was to get it finished, but Robert was determined to go on; he thought our chance was very good, because he had found some beautiful extracts, and translated others, and the pages really looked pretty and dainty. The manuscript had to be in London this morning; if it missed the post last night, all our work would have been wasted, and at the last moment Lady Darcy took Rob away with her, and I was left with everything to finish. I *may* have slept a little bit the last two nights; I did lie down for an hour or two, and I *may* have had a doze, but I don't think so! I wrote the last word this morning after the breakfast-bell had rung, and I made up the parcel at twelve o'clock. I thought of going out and posting it then; of course, that is what I should have done, but,"—her voice trembled once more—"I was so tired! I thought I would give it to the postman myself, and that would do just as well. I didn't put it with the letters because I was afraid someone would see the address and ask questions, and Rob had said that I was to keep it a secret until we knew whether we had won. I left the parcel on my table. Then Arthur came! I was so happy—there was so much to talk about—we had tea—it seemed like five minutes. Everyone was amazed when we found it was time to dress, but even then I forgot all about the calendar. I only remembered that Arthur was here, and was going to stay for four days, and all the way upstairs I was saying to myself, 'I'm happy, I'm happy; oh I *am* happy!' because, you know, though you are so kind, you have many relatives belonging to you whom you love better than me, and my own people are all far-away, and sometimes I've been very lonely! I thought of nothing but Arthur, and then I opened the door of my room, and there, before my eyes, was the parcel—Rob's parcel that he had trusted to me—that I had solemnly promised to post in time—"

She stopped short, and there was a gasp of interest and commiseration among the listeners. Peggy caught it; she glanced sharply at the vicar's face, saw its sternness replaced by a momentary softness, and was quick to make the most of her opportunity. Out flew the dramatic little hand, her eyes flashed, her voice thrilled with suppressed excitement.

"It lay there before my eyes, and I stood and looked at it.—I thought of nothing, but just stood and stared. I heard you all come upstairs, and the doors shut, and Arthur's voice laughing and talking; but there was only one thing I could remember—I had forgotten Rob's parcel, and he would come back, and I should have to tell him, and see his face! I felt as if I were paralysed, and then suddenly I seized the parcel in my hands, and flew downstairs. I put on my cap and cloak and went out into the garden. I didn't know what I was going to do, but I was going to do *something*! I ran on and on, through the village, down towards the station. I knew it was too late for the post-office, but I had a sort of feeling that if I were at the station something might be done. Just as I got there a train came in, and I heard the porter call out,'London express.' I thought—No! I did not think at all—I just ran up to a carriage and took a seat, and the door banged, and away we went. The porter came and asked for my ticket, and I had a great deal of trouble to convince him that I had only come from here, and not all the way. There was an old lady in the carriage, and she told him that it was quite true, for she had seen me come in. When we went off again, she looked at me very hard, and said, 'Are you in trouble, dear?' and I said, 'Yes, I am; but oh, please don't talk to me! Do please leave me alone!' for I had begun to realise what I had done, and that I couldn't be back for hours and hours, and that you would all be anxious and unhappy. I think I was as miserable as you were when I sent off that telegram. I posted the parcel in London, and went and sat in the waiting-room. I had an hour and a half to wait, and I was wretched and nervous and horribly hungry. I had no money left except a few coppers, and I was afraid to spend them and have nothing left. It seemed like a whole day, but at last the train came in, and I saw an old gentleman with white hair standing on the platform. I took a fancy to his appearance, so I walked up to him, and bowed, and said, 'Excuse me, sir—I find myself in a dilemma! Will you allow me to travel in the same carriage as yourself?' He was most agreeable. He had travelled all over the world, and talked in the most interesting fashion, but I could not listen to his conversation. I was too unhappy. Then we arrived, and Mr Asplin called me 'M-M-Mariquita!' and w- wouldn't let you kiss me—"

Her voice broke helplessly this time, and she stood silent, with quivering lip, while sighs and sobs of sympathy echoed from every side. Mrs Asplin cast a glance at her husband, half defiant, half appealing, met a smile of assent, and rushed impetuously to Peggy's side.

"My darling! I'll kiss you now. You see we knew nothing of your trouble, dear, and we were so very, very anxious. Mr Asplin is not angry with you any longer, are you, Austin? You know now that she had no intention of grieving us, and that she is truly sorry—"

"I never thought—I never thought,"—sobbed Peggy; and the vicar gave a slow, kindly smile.

"Ah, Peggy, that is just what I complain about. You don't think, dear, and that causes all the trouble. No, I am not angry any longer. I realise that the circumstances were peculiar, and that your distress was naturally very great. At the same time, it was a most mad thing for a girl of your age to rush off by rail, alone, and at night-time, to a place like London. You say that you had only a few coppers left in your purse. Now suppose there had been no train back to-night, what would you have done? It does not bear thinking of, my dear; or that you should have waited alone in the station for so long, or thrown yourself on strangers for protection. What would your parents have said to such an escapade?"

Peggy sighed, and cast down her eyes. "I think they would have been cross too. I am sure they would have been anxious, but I know they would forgive me when I was sorry, and promised that I really and truly would try to be better and more thoughtful! They would say, 'Peggy dear, you have been sufficiently punished! Consider yourself absolved!'"

The vicar's lips twitched, and a twinkle came into his eye. "Well then, I will say the same! I am sure you have regretted your hastiness by this time, and it will be a lesson to you in the future. For Arthur's sake, as well as your own, we will say no more on the subject. It would be a pity if his visit were spoiled. Just one thing, Peggy, to show you that, after all, grown-up people are wiser than young ones, and that it is just as well to refer to them now and then, in matters of difficulty. Has it ever occurred to you that the mail went up to London by the very train in which you yourself travelled, and that by giving your parcel to the guard it could still have been put in the bag? Did that thought never occur to your wise little brain?"

Peggy made a gesture as of one heaping dust and ashes on her head. "I never did," she said, "not for a single moment! And I thought I was so clever! I am prostrate with confusion!"

Chapter Nineteen.

Rosalind's Ball.

In consideration of Arthur's presence and of the late hours and excitement of the night before, the next day was observed as a holiday in the vicarage. Mrs Asplin stayed in bed until lunch-time, the boys went for a bicycle ride, and Peggy and her brother had a delightful chat together by the schoolroom fire, when he told her more details about his own plans than he had been able to touch upon in a dozen letters.

"The preliminary examination for Sandhurst begins on the 26th this year," he explained, "and so far as I can make out I shall romp through it. I am going to take all the subjects in Class One—mathematics, Latin, French, geometrical drawing, and English composition; I'll astonish them in the last subject! Plenty of dash and go, eh, Peggy,—that's the style to fetch 'em! In Class Two you can only take two subjects, so I'm going in for chemistry and physics. I rather fancy myself in physics, and if I don't come out at the head of the list, or precious near the head, it won't be for want of trying. I have worked like a nigger these last six months; between ourselves, I thought I had worked too hard a few days ago; I felt so stupid and dizzy, and my head ached until I could hardly open my eyes. If I had not come away, I believe I should have broken down, but I'm better already, and by Tuesday I shall be as fit as a fiddle. I hope I do well, it would be so jolly to cable out the news to the old pater; and I say, Peg, I don't mean to leave Sandhurst without bringing home something to keep as a souvenir. At the end of each Christmas term a sword is presented to the cadet who passes out first in the final exam.—'The Anson Memorial Sword.' Mariquita!"—Arthur smote his breast, and struck a fierce and warlike attitude,—"that sword is mine! In the days to come, when you are old and grey-headed, you will see that rusty blade hanging over my ancestral hearth, and tell in faltering tones the story of the gallant youth who wrested it from his opponents."

"Ha, ha!" responded Peggy deeply. There was no particular meaning in the exclamation, but it seemed right and fitting in the connection, and had a smack of melodrama which was quite to her taste. "Of course you will be first, Arthur!" she added; "and, oh dear! how proud I shall be when I see you in all your uniform! I am thankful all my men relatives are soldiers, they are so much more interesting than civilians. It would break my heart to think of you as a civilian! Of course wars are somewhat disconcerting, but then one always hopes there won't be wars."

"I don't!" cried Arthur loudly. "No, no—active service for me, and plenty of it!

"'Come one, come all, this rock shall fly
From its firm base as soon as I!'

"That's my motto, and my ambition is the Victoria Cross, and I'll get that too before I'm done; you see if I don't! It's the ambition of my life, Peg. I lie awake and think of that little iron cross; I go to sleep and dream of it, and see the two words dancing before my eyes in letters of fire, 'For Valour,' 'For Valour,' 'For Valour.' Ah!"—he drew a deep breath of excitement—"I don't think there is anything in the world I should envy, if I could only gain that."

Peggy gazed at him with kindling eyes. "You are a soldier's son," she said, "and the grandson of a soldier, and the great-grandson of a soldier; it's in your blood; you can't help it—it's in my blood too, Arthur! I give you my solemn word of honour that if the French or Germans came over to invade this land, I'd—" Peggy seized the ruler and waved it in the air with a gesture of fiercest determination—"I'd fight them! There! I'd shoot at them; I'd go out and spike the guns; I'd—I'd climb on the house-tops and throw stones at them. You needn't laugh, I tell you I should be *terrible*! I feel as if I could face a whole regiment myself. The spirit—the spirit of my ancestors is in my breast, Arthur Reginald, and woe betide that enemy who tries to wrest from me my native land!" Peggy went off into a shriek of laughter, in which Arthur joined, until the sound of the merry peals reached Mrs Asplin's ears as she lay wearily on her pillow, and brought a smile to her pale face. "Bless the dears! How happy they are!" she murmured to herself; nor even suspected that it was a wholesale massacre of foreign nations which had been the cause of this gleeful outburst.

Arthur left the vicarage on Tuesday evening, seemingly much refreshed by the few days' change, though he still complained of his head, and pressed his hand over his eyes from time to time as though in pain. The parting from Peggy was more cheerful than might have been expected, for in a few more weeks Christmas would be at hand, when, as he himself expressed it, he hoped to return with blushing honours thick upon him. Peggy mentally expended her whole ten pounds in a present for the dear handsome fellow, and held her head high in the consciousness of owning a brother who was destined to be Commander-in-Chief of the British forces in the years to come.

The same evening Robert returned from his visit to London. He had heard of Peggy's escapade from his father and sister, and was by no means so grateful as that young lady had expected.

"What in all the world possessed you to play such a mad trick?" he queried bluntly. "It makes me ill to think of it. Rushing off to London on a wet, foggy night, never even waiting to inquire if there was a return train, or to count if you had enough money to see you through! Goodness only knows what might have happened! You are careless enough in an ordinary way, but I must say I gave you credit for more sense than that."

"Well, but, Rob," pleaded Peggy, aggrieved, "I don't think you need scold! I did it for you, and I thought you would be pleased."

"Did you indeed? Well, you are mightily mistaken; I wouldn't have let you do a thing like that for all the microscopes in the world. I don't care a rap for the wretched old microscope."

"Oh! oh!"

"In comparison, I mean. Of course I should have been glad to get it if it had come to me in an ordinary way, but I was not so wrapped up in the idea that I would not have been reasonable, if you had come to me quietly and explained that you had missed the post."

Peggy shook her head sagely. "You think so now, because the danger is over, and you are sure it can't happen. But I know better. I can tell you exactly what would have happened. You wouldn't have stormed or raged, it would have been better if you had, and sooner over; you would just have stood still, and—glared at me! When I'd finished speaking, you would have swallowed two or three times over, as if you were gulping down something which you dared not say, and then turned on your heel and marched out of the room. That's what you would have done, my dear and honourable sir, and you know it!"

Robert hung his head and looked self-conscious.

"Well, if I had! A fellow can't hide all he feels in the first moment of disappointment. But I should have got over it, and you know very well that I should never have brought it up against you. 'Glared!' What if I *did* glare? There is nothing very terrible in that, is there?"

"Yes, there is. I could not have borne it, when I had been trying so hard to help you. And it would not have been only the first few minutes. Every time when you were quiet and depressed, when you looked at your specimens through your little old glass and sighed, and pitched it away, as I've seen you do scores and scores of times, I should have felt that it was my fault, and been in the depths of misery. No, no, I'm sorry to the depths of my heart that I scared dear Mrs Asplin and the rest, but it is a matter of acute satisfaction to me to know that your chance has in no way been hindered by your confidence in me!" and Peggy put her head on one side, and coughed in a faint and ladylike manner, which brought the twinkle back into Robert's eyes.

"Good old Mariquita!" he cried, laughing. "'Acute satisfaction' is good, Mariquita—decidedly good! You will make your name yet in the world of letters. Well, as I said before, you are a jolly little brick, and the best partner a fellow ever had! Mind you, I tell you straight that I think you behaved badly in cutting off like that; but I'll stand by you to the others, and not let them sit upon you while I am there."

"Thanks!" said Peggy meekly. "But, oh, I beseech of you, don't bring up the subject if you can help it! I'm tired to death of it all! The kindest thing you can do is to talk hard about something else, and give them a fresh excitement to think about. Talk about—about—about Rosalind if you will; anything will do—only, for pity's sake, leave me alone, and pretend there is not such a thing in the world as a calendar!"

"Right you are!" said Robert, laughing. "I'll steer clear of the rocks! And as it happens, I have got a piece of news that will put your doings into the background at one fell swoop. Rosalind is going to give a party! The Earl and Countess of Berkhampton are coming down to the Larches the week after next, and are going to bring their two girls with them. They are great lanky things, with about as much 'go' in the pair as in one of your little fingers; but this party is to be given in their honour. The mater has asked everyone of a right age within a dozen miles around, and the house will be crammed with visitors. Your card is coming to-morrow, and I hope you will give me the honour of the first round, and as many as possible after that."

"The first, with pleasure; I won't promise any more until I see how we get on. It doesn't seem appropriate to think of your dancing, Rob; there is something too heavy and serious in your demeanour. Oswald is different; he would make a charming dancing master. Oh, it will be an excitement! Mellicent will not be able to eat or sleep for thinking of it; and poor Mrs Asplin will be running up seams on the sewing-machine, and making up ribbon bows from this day to that. I'm glad I have a dress all ready, and shan't be bothered with any trying on! You don't know what it is to stand first on one leg and then on the other, to be turned and pulled about as if you were a dummy, and have pins stuck into you as if you were a pin-cushion! I adore pretty clothes, but every time I go to the dressmaker's I vow and declare that I shall take to sacks. Tell them at dinner, do, and they will talk about it for the rest of the evening!"

Peggy's prophecy came true, for the subject of Rosalind's party became a topic of such absorbing interest as left room for little else during the next few weeks. New dresses had to be bought and made for the girls, and Peggy superintended the operations of the village dressmaker with equal satisfaction to herself and her friends.

Rosalind appeared engrossed in preparations, and two or three times a week, as the girls trudged along the muddy roads, with Fräulein lagging in the rear, the jingle of bells would come to their ears, and Rosalind's two white long-tailed ponies would come dashing past, drawing the little open carriage in which their mistress sat, half-hidden among a pile of baskets and parcels. She was always beautiful and radiant, and as she passed she would turn her head over her shoulders and look at the three mud-bespattered pedestrians with a smile of pitying condescension, which made Peggy set her teeth and draw her eyebrows together in an ominous frown.

One day she condescended to stop and speak a few words from her throne among the cushions.

"How de do? So sowwy not to have been to see you! Fwightfully busy, don't you know. We are decowating the wooms, and don't know how to finish in time. It's going to be quite charming!"

"We know! We know! Rob told us. I'm dying to see it. You should ask Peggy to help you, if you are in a hurry. She's s–imply splendid at decorations! Mother says she never knew anyone so good at it as Peggy!" cried Mellicent, with an outburst of gushing praise, in acknowledgment of which she received a thunderous frown and such a sharp pinch on the arm as penetrated through all her thick winter wrappings.

Rosalind, however, only ejaculated, "Oh, weally!" in an uninterested manner, and whipped up her ponies without taking any further notice of the suggestion; but it had taken root in her mind all the same, and she did not forget to question her brother on the first opportunity.

Mellicent Asplin had said that Peggy Saville was clever at decoration. Was it true, and would it be the least use asking her to come and help in the decorations?

Robert laughed, and wagged his head with an air of proud assurance.

Clever! Peggy? She was a witch! She could work wonders! If you set her down in an empty room, and gave her two-and-sixpence to transform it into an Alhambra, he verily believed she could do it. The way in which she had rigged up the various characters for the Shakespeare reading was nothing short of miraculous. Yes, indeed, Peggy would be worth a dozen ordinary helpers. The question was, Would she come?

"Certainly she will come. I'll send down for her at once," said Rosalind promptly, and forthwith sat down and wrote a dainty little note, not to Peggy herself, but to Mrs Asplin, stating that she had heard great accounts of Peggy Saville's skill in the art of decoration, and begging that she might be allowed to come up to the Larches to help with the final arrangements, arriving as early as possible on the day of the party, and bringing her box with her, so as to be saved the fatigue of returning home to dress. It was a prettily worded letter, and Mrs Asplin was dismayed at the manner of its reception.

"No, Peggy Saville won't!" said that young person, pursing her lips and tossing her head in her most high and mighty manner. "She won't do anything of the sort! Why should I go? Let her ask some of her own friends! I'm not her friend! I should simply loathe to go!"

"My dear Peggy! When you are asked to help! When this entertainment is given for your pleasure, and you can be of real use—"

"I never asked her to give the party! I don't care whether I go or not! She is simply making use of me for her own convenience!"

"It is not the first or only time that you have been asked, as you know well, Peggy. And sometimes you have enjoyed yourself very much. You said you would never forget the pink luncheon. In spite of all you say, you owe Rosalind thanks for some pleasant times; and now you can be of some service to her. Well, I'm not going to force you, dear. I hate unwilling workers, and if it's not in your heart to go, stay at home, and settle with your conscience as best you can."

Peggy groaned with sepulchral misery.

"Wish I hadn't got no conscience! Tiresome, presuming thing —always poking itself forward and making remarks when it isn't wanted. I suppose I shall have to go, and run about from morning till night, holding a pair of scissors, and nasty little balls of string, for Rosalind's use! Genius indeed! What's the use of talking about genius? I know very well I shall not be allowed to do anything but run about and wait upon her. It's no use staring at me, Mrs Asplin. I mean it all—every single word."

"No, you don't, Peggy! No, you don't, my little kind, warm-hearted Peggy! I know better than that! It's just that foolish tongue that is running away with you, dearie. In your heart you are pleased to do a service for a friend, and are going to put your whole strength into doing it as well and tastefully as it can be done."

"I'm not! I'm not! I'm not! I'm savage, and it's no use pretending—"

"Yes, you are! I know it! What is the good of having a special gift if one doesn't put it to good use? Ah, that's the face I like to see! I didn't recognise my Peggy with that ugly frown. I'll write and say you'll come with pleasure."

"It's to please you, then, not Rosalind!" said Peggy obstinately. But Mrs Asplin only laughed, dropped a kiss upon her cheek, and walked away to answer the invitation forthwith.

Chapter Twenty.

At the Larches.

The next morning, immediately after breakfast, Peggy went up to her own room to pack for her visit to the Larches. The long dress-box, which had been stored away ever since its arrival, was brought out, and its contents displayed to an admiring audience, consisting of Mrs Asplin, Esther, Mellicent, and Mary the housemaid.

Everything was there that the heart of girl could desire, and a mother's forethought provide for her darling's use when she was far-away. A dress of cobweb Indian muslin embroidered in silk, a fan of curling feathers, a dear little satin pocket in which to keep the lace handkerchief, rolls of ribbons, dainty white shoes, with straggly silk stockings rolled into the toes.

Peggy displayed one article after another, while Mellicent groaned and gurgled with delight; Mary exclaimed, "My, Miss Peggy, but you will be smart!" and Mrs Asplin stifled a sigh at the thought of her own inferior preparations.

Punctually at ten o'clock the carriage drove up to the door, and off Peggy drove, not altogether unwillingly, now that it had come to the pinch, for after all it *is* pleasant to be appreciated, and, when a great excitement is taking place in the neighbourhood, it is only human to wish to be in the thick of the fray.

Lady Darcy welcomed her guest with gracious kindness, and, as soon as she had taken off her hat and jacket in the dressing-room which was allotted to her use, she was taken straight away to the chief room, where the work of decoration was being carried briskly forward. The village joiner was fitting mirrors into the corners and hammering with deafening persistence, a couple of gardeners were arranging banks of flowers and palms, and Rosalind stood in the midst of a bower of greenery, covered from head to foot in a smock of blue linen, and with a pair of gardening gloves drawn over her hands.

She gave a little cry of relief and satisfaction as Peggy entered.

"Oh, Mawiquita, so glad you have come! Mother is so busy that she can't be with me at all, and these wretched bwanches pwick my fingers! Do look wound, and say how it looks! This is weally the servants' hall, you know, as we have not a pwoper ballroom, and it is so square and high that it is perfectly dweadful to decowate! A long, narrow woom is so much better!"

Peggy thought the arrangements tasteful and pretty; but she could not gush over the effect, which, in truth, was in no way original or striking. There seemed little to be done in the room itself, so she suggested an adjournment into the outer hall, which seemed to offer unique opportunities.

"That space underneath the staircase!" she cried eagerly. "Oh, Rosalind, we could make it look perfectly sweet with all the beautiful Eastern things that you have brought home from your travels! Let us make a little harem, with cushions to sit on, and hanging lamps, and Oriental curtains for drapery. We could do it while the men are finishing this room, and be ready to come back to it after lunch."

"Oh, what a sweet idea! Mawiquita, you are quite too clever!" cried Rosalind, aglow with pleasure. "Let us begin at once. It will be ever so much more intewesting than hanging about here."

She thrust her hand through Peggy's arm as she spoke, and the two girls went off on a tour through the house to select the most suitable articles for their decoration of the "harem." There was no lack of choice, for the long suite of reception-rooms was full of treasures, and Peggy stopped every few minutes to point with a small forefinger and say, "That screen, please! That table! That stool!" to the servants who had been summoned in attendance. The smaller things, such as ornaments, table-cloths, and lamps she carried herself, while Rosalind murmured sweetly, "Oh, don't twouble! You mustn't, weally! Let me help you!" and stood with her arms hanging by her side, without showing the faintest sign of giving the offered help.

As the morning passed away, Peggy found indeed that the Honourable Miss Darcy was a broken reed to lean upon in the way of assistance. She sat on a stool and looked on while the other workers hammered and pinned and stitched—so that Peggy's prophecy as to her own subordinate position was exactly reversed, and the work of supervision was given entirely into her hands.

It took nearly two hours to complete the decorations of the "harem," but when all was finished the big ugly space beneath the staircase was transformed into as charming a nook as it is possible to imagine. Pieces of brilliant flag embroidery from Cairo draped the farther wall, a screen of carved work shut out the end of the passage, gauzy curtains of gold and blue depended in festoons from the ascending staircase, and stopped just in time to leave a safe place for a hanging lamp of wrought iron and richly coloured glass. On the floor were spread valuable rugs and piles of bright silken cushions, while on an inlaid table stood a real Turkish hookah and a brass tray with the little egg-shaped cups out of which travellers in the East are accustomed to sip the strong black coffee of the natives.

Peggy lifted the ends of her apron in her hands and executed a dance of triumph on her own account when all was finished, and Rosalind said, "Weally, we have been clever! I think we may be proud of ourselves!" in amiable effusion.

The two girls went off to luncheon in a state of halcyon amiability which was new indeed in the history of their acquaintance, and Lady Darcy listened with an amused smile to their rhapsodies on the subject of the morning's work, promising faithfully not to look at anything until the right moment should arrive, and she should be summoned to gaze and admire.

By the time that the workers were ready to return to the room, the men had finished the arrangements at which they had been at work before lunch, and were beginning to tack festoons of evergreens along the walls, the dull paper of which had been covered with fluting of soft pink muslin. The effect was heavy and clumsy in the extreme, and Rosalind stamped her foot with an outburst of fretful anger.

"Stop putting up those wreaths! Stop at once! They are simply hideous! It weminds me of a penny weading in the village schoolwoom! You might as well put up 'God save the Queen' and 'A Mewwy Chwistmas' at once! Take them down this minute, Jackson! I won't have them!"

The man touched his forehead, and began pulling out the nails in half-hearted fashion.

"Very well, miss, as you wish. Seems a pity, though, not to use 'em, for it took me all yesterday to put 'em together. It's a sin to throw 'em away."

"I won't have them in the house, if they took you a week!" Rosalind replied sharply, and she turned on her heel and looked appealingly in Peggy's face. "It's a howwid failure! The woom looks so stiff and stwaight—like a pink box with nothing in it! Mother won't like it a bit. What can we do to make it better?"

Peggy scowled, pursed up her lips, pressed her hand to her forehead, and strode up and down the room, rolling her eyes from side to side, and going through all the grimaces of one in search of inspiration. Rosalind was right: unless some device were found by which the shape of the room could be disguised, the decorations must be pronounced more or less a failure. She craned her head to the ceiling, and suddenly beamed in triumph.

"I have it! The very thing! We will fasten the garlands to that middle beam, and loop up the ends at intervals all round the walls. That will break the squareness, and make the room look like a tent, with a ceiling of flowers."

"Ah-h!" cried Rosalind; and clasped her hands with a gesture of relief. "Of course! The vewy thing! We ought to have thought of it at the beginning. Get the ladder at once, Jackson, and put in a hook or wing, or something to hold the ends; and be sure that it is strong enough. What a good thing that the weaths are weady! You see, your work will not be wasted after all."

She was quite gracious in her satisfaction, and for the next two hours she and Peggy were busily occupied superintending the hanging of the evergreen wreaths and in arranging bunches of flowers to be placed at each point where the wreaths were fastened to the wall. At the end of this time, Rosalind was summoned to welcome the distinguished visitors who had arrived by the afternoon train. She invited Peggy to accompany her to the drawing-room, but in a hesitating fashion, and with a glance round the disordered room, which said, as plainly as words could do, that she would be disappointed if the invitation were accepted; and Peggy, transformed in a moment into a poker of pride and dignity, declared that she would prefer to remain where she was until all was finished.

"Well, it weally would be better, wouldn't it? I will have a tway sent in to you here, and do, Mawiquita, see that evewything is swept up and made tidy at once, for I shall bring them in to look wound diwectly after tea, and we must have the wooms tidy!"

Rosalind tripped away, and Peggy was left to herself for a lonely and troublesome hour. The tea-tray was brought in, and she was just seating herself before an impromptu table, when up came a gardener to say that one of "these 'ere wreaths seemed to hang uncommon near the gas-bracket. It didn't seem safe like." And off she went in a panic of consternation to see what could be done. There was nothing for it but to move the wreath some inches farther away, which involved moving the next also, and the next, and the next, so as to equalise the distances as much as possible; and by the time that they were settled to Peggy's satisfaction, lo, table and tray had been whisked out of sight by some busy pair of hands, and only a bare space met her eyes. This was blow number one, for, after working hard all afternoon, tea and cake come as a refreshment which one would not readily miss. She cheered herself, however, by putting dainty finishing touches here and there, seeing that the lamp was lighted in the "harem" outside, and was busy placing fairy lamps among the shrubs which were to screen the band, when a babel of voices from outside warned her that the visitors were approaching. Footsteps came nearer and nearer, and a chorus of exclamations greeted the sight of the "harem." The door stood open, Peggy waited for Rosalind's voice to call and bid her share the honours, but no summons came. She heard Lady Darcy's exclamation, and the quick, strong tones of the strange countess.

"Charming, charming; quite a stroke of genius! I never saw a more artistic little nook. What made you think of it, my dear?"

"Ha!" said Peggy to herself, and took a step forward, only to draw back in dismay, as a light laugh reached her ear, followed by Rosalind's careless—

"Oh, I don't know; I wanted to make it pwetty, don't you know; it was so dweadfully bare, and there seemed no other way."

Then there was a rustle of silk skirts, and the two ladies entered the room, followed by their respective daughters, Rosalind beautiful and radiant, and the Ladies Berkhampton with their chins poked forward, and their elbows thrust out in ungainly fashion. They paused on the threshold, and every eye travelled up to the wreath-decked ceiling. A flush of pleasure came into Lady Darcy's pale cheeks, and she listened to the countess's compliments with sparkling eyes.

"It is all the work of this clever child," she said, laying her hand fondly on Rosalind's shoulder. "I have had practically nothing to do with the decorations. This is the first time I have been in the room to-day, and I had no idea that the garlands were to be used in this way. I thought they were for the walls."

"I congratulate you, Rosalind! You are certainly very happy in your arrangements," said the countess cordially. Then she put up her eyeglass and stared inquiringly at Peggy, who stood by with her hair fastened back in its usual pigtail, and a big white apron pinned over her dress.

"She thinks I am the kitchen-maid!" said Peggy savagely to

herself; but there was little fear of such a mistake, and, the moment that Lady Darcy noticed the girl's presence, she introduced her kindly enough, if with somewhat of a condescending air.

"This is a little friend of Rosalind's who has come up to help. She is fond of this sort of work," she said; then, before any of the strangers had time to acknowledge the introduction, she added hastily, "And now I am sure you must all be tired after your journey, and will be glad to go to your rooms and rest. It is quite wicked of me to keep you standing. Let me take you upstairs at once!"

They sailed away with the same rustle of garments, the same babel of high-toned voices, and Peggy stood alone in the middle of the deserted room. No one had asked her to rest, or suggested that she might be tired; she had been overlooked and forgotten in the presence of the distinguished visitor. She was only a little girl who was "fond" of this sort of work, and, it might be supposed, was only too thankful to be allowed to help! The house sank into silence. She waited for half an hour longer, in the hope that someone would remember her presence, and then, tired, hungry, and burning with repressed anger, crept upstairs to her own little room and fell asleep upon the couch.

Chapter Twenty One.

Another Accident!

Dinner was served unusually early that evening, and was an embarrassing ordeal from which Peggy was thankful to escape.

On her way upstairs, however, Rosalind called her back with an eager petition.

"Oh, Peggy! would you mind awwanging some flowers? A big hamper has just awwived from town, and the servants are all so dweadfully busy. I must get dwessed in time to help mother to weceive, but it wouldn't matter if you were a few minutes late. Thanks so much! Awfully obliged."

She gave her thanks before an assent had been spoken, and tripped smilingly away, while Peggy went back to the big room to find a great tray full of hothouse treasures waiting to be arranged, and no availing vases in which to place them. The flowers, however, were so beautiful, and the fronds of maidenhair so green and graceful, that the work was a pleasure; she enjoyed discovering unlikely places in which to group them, and lingered so long over her arrangements that the sudden striking of the clock sent her flying upstairs in a panic of consternation. Another quarter of an hour and the vicarage party would arrive, for they had been bidden a little in advance of the rest, so that Robert might help his mother and sister in receiving their guests. Peggy tore off dress and apron, and made all the speed she could, but she was still standing in dressing-jacket and frilled white petticoat, brushing out her long waves of hair when the door opened and Esther and Mellicent entered. They had begged to be shown to Miss Saville's room, and came rustling in, smiling and beaming, with woollen caps over their heads, snow-shoes on their feet, and fleecy shawls swathed round and round their figures, and fastened with a hairpin on the left shoulder, in secure and elegant fashion. Peggy stood, brush in hand, staring at them and shaking with laughter.

"He! he! he! I hope you are warm enough! Esther looks like a sausage, and Mellicent looks like a dumpling. Come here, and I'll unwind you. You look as if you could not move an inch, hand or foot."

"It was mother," Mellicent explained. "She was so afraid we would catch cold. Oh, Peggy, you are not half dressed. You will be late! Whatever have you been doing? Have you had a nice day? Did you enjoy it? What did you have for dinner?"

Peggy waved her brush towards the door in dramatic warning.

"Rosalind's room!" she whispered. "Don't yell, my love, unless you wish every word to be overheard. This is her dressing-room, which she lent to me for the occasion, so there's only a door between us.—There, now, you are free. Oh, dear me, how you have squashed your sash! You really must remember to lift it up when you sit down. You had better stand with your back to the fire, to take out the creases."

Mellicent's face clouded for a moment, but brightened again as she caught sight of her reflection in the swing glass. Crumples or no crumples, there was no denying that blue was a becoming colour. The plump, rosy cheeks dimpled with satisfaction, and the flaxen head was twisted to and fro to survey herself in every possible position.

"Is my hair right at the back? How does the bow look? I haven't burst, have I? I thought I heard something crack in the cab. Do you think I will do?"

"Put on your slippers, and I'll tell you. Anyone would look a fright in evening dress and snow-shoes."

Peggy's answer was given with a severity which sent Mellicent waddling across the room to turn out the contents of the bag which lay on the couch, but the next moment came a squeal of consternation, and there she stood in the attitude of a tragedy queen, with staring eyes, parted lips, and two shabby black slippers grasped in either hand.

"M-m-m-my old ones!" she gasped in horror-stricken accents. "B-b-b-brought them by mistake!" It was some moments before her companions fully grasped the situation, for the new slippers had been black too, and of much the same make as those now exhibited. Mrs Asplin had had many yearnings over white shoes and stockings, all silk and satin, and tinkling diamond buckles like those which had been displayed in Peggy's dress-box. Why should not her darlings have dainty possessions like other girls? It went to her heart to think what an improvement these two articles would make in the simple costumes; then she remembered her husband's delicate health, his exhaustion at the end of the day, and the painful effort with which he nerved himself to fresh exertions, and felt a bigger pang at the thought of wasting money so hardly earned. As her custom was on such occasions, she put the whole matter before the girls, talking to them as friends, and asking their help in her decision.

"You see, darlings," she said, "I want to do my very best for you, and if it would be a real disappointment not to have these things, I'll manage it somehow, for once in a way. But it's a question whether you would have another chance of wearing them, and it seems a great deal of money to spend for just one evening, when poor dear father—"

"Oh, mother, no, don't think of it! Black ones will do perfectly well. What can it matter what sort of shoes and stockings we wear? It won't make the least difference in our enjoyment," said Esther the sensible; but Mellicent was by no means of this opinion.

"I don't know about that! I love white legs!" she sighed dolefully. "All my life long it has been my ambition to have white legs. Silk ones with little bits of lace let in down the front, like Peggy's. They're so beautiful! It doesn't seem a bit like a party to wear black stockings; only of course I know I must, for I'd hate to waste father's money. When I grow up I shall marry a rich man, and have everything I want. It's disgusting to be poor... Will they be nice black slippers, mother, with buckles on them?"

"Yes, dearie. Beauties! Great big buckles!" said Mrs Asplin lovingly; and a few days later a box had come down from London, and the slippers had been chosen out of a selection of "leading novelties"; worn with care and reverence the previous evening, "to take off the stiffness," and then after all —oh, the awfulness of it!—had been replaced by an old pair, in the bustle of departure.

The three girls stared at one another in consternation. Here was a catastrophe to happen just at the last moment, when everyone was so happy and well satisfied! The dismay on the chubby face was so pitiful that neither of Mellicent's companions could find it in her heart to speak a word of reproof. They rather set to work to propose different ways out of the difficulty.

"Get hold of Max, and coax him to go back for them!"

"He wouldn't; it's no use. It's raining like anything, and it would take him an hour to go there and come back."

"Ask Lady Darcy to send one of the servants—"

"No use, my dear. They are scampering up and down like mice, and haven't a moment to spare from their own work."

"See if Rosalind would lend me a pair!"

"Silly goose! Look at your foot. It is three times the size of hers. You will just have to wear them, I'm afraid. Give them to me, and let me see what can be done." Peggy took the slippers in her hands and studied them critically. They were certainly not new, but then they were by no means old; just respectable, middle-aged creatures, slightly rubbed on the heel and white at the toes, but with many a day of good hard wear still before them.

"Oh, come," she said reassuringly, "they are not so bad, Mellicent! With a little polish they would look quite presentable. I'll tap at the door and ask Rosalind if she has some that she can lend us. She is sure to have it. There are about fifty thousand bottles on her table."

Peggy crossed the room as she spoke, tapped on the panel, and received an immediate answer in a high complacent treble.

"Coming! Coming! I'm weady;" then the door flew open; a tiny pink silk shoe stepped daintily over

'ROSALIND! WHAT A PERFECT *ANGEL* YOU LOOK! BUT, OH! HAVE YOU GOT ANY BOOT-POLISH?'

the mat, and Rosalind stood before them in all the glory of a new Parisian dress. Three separate gasps of admiration greeted her appearance, and she stood smiling and dimpling while the girls took in the fascinating details—the satin frock of palest imaginable pink, the white chiffon over-dress which fell from shoulder to hem in graceful freedom, sprinkled over with exquisite rose—leaves—it was all wonderful—fantastic—as far removed from Peggy's muslin as from the homely crepon of the vicar's daughters.

"Rosalind! what a perfect *angel* you look!" gasped Mellicent, her own dilemma forgotten in her wholehearted admiration; but the next moment memory came back, and her expression changed to one of pitiful appeal. "But, oh, have you got any boot-polish? The most awful thing has happened. I've brought my old shoes by mistake! Look! I don't know what on earth I shall do, if you can't give me something to black the toes." She held out the shoes as she spoke, and Rosalind gave a shrill scream of laughter.

"Oh! oh! Those things! How fwightfully funny! what a fwightful joke! You will look like Cinderwella, when she wan away, and the glass slippers changed back to her dweadful old clogs. It is too scweamingly funny, I do declare!"

"Oh, never mind what you declare! Can you lend us some boot-polish—that's the question!" cried Peggy sharply. She knew Mellicent's horror of ridicule, and felt indignant with the girl who could stand by, secure in her own beauty and elegance, and have no sympathy for the misfortune of a friend. "If you have a bottle of peerless gloss, or any of those shiny things with a sponge fastened on the cork, I can make them look quite respectable, and no one will have any cause to laugh."

"Ha, ha, ha!" trilled Rosalind once more, "Peggy is cwoss! I never knew such a girl for flying into tantwums at a moment's notice! Yes, of course I'll lend you the polish. There is some in this little cupboard—there! I won't touch it, in case it soils my gloves. Shall I call Marie to put it on foryou?"

"Thank you, there's no need—I can do it! I would rather do it myself!"

"Oh—oh, isn't she cwoss! You will bweak the cork if you scwew it about like that, and then you'll never be able to get it out. Why don't you pull it pwoperly?"

"I know how to pull out a cork, thank you; I've done it before!"

Peggy shot an angry glance at her hostess, and set to work again with doubled energy. Now that Rosalind had laughed at her inability, it would be misery to fail; but the bottle had evidently lain aside for some time, and a stiff black crust had formed round the cork which made it difficult to move. Peggy pulled and tugged, while Rosalind stood watching, laughing her aggravating, patronising little laugh, and dropping a word of instruction from time to time. And then, quite suddenly, a dreadful thing happened. In the flash of an eye—so quickly and unexpectedly, that, looking back upon it, it seemed like a nightmare which could not possibly have taken place in real life—the cork jerked out in Peggy's hand, in response to a savage tug, and with it out flew an inky jet, which rose straight up in the air, separated into a multitude of tiny drops, and descended in a flood—oh, the horror of that moment!— over Rosalind's face, neck, and dress.

One moment a fairy princess, a goddess of summer, the next a figure of fun with black spots scattered thickly over cheeks and nose, a big splash on the white shoulder, and inky daubs dotted here and there between the rose-leaves. What a transformation! What a spectacle of horror! Peggy stood transfixed; Mellicent screamed in terror; and Esther ran forward, handkerchief in hand, only to be waved aside with angry vehemence. Rosalind's face was convulsed with anger; she stamped her foot and spoke at the pitch of her voice, as if she had no control over her feelings.

"Oh, oh, oh! You wicked girl! you hateful, detestable girl! You did it on purpose, because you were in a temper! You have been in a temper all the afternoon! You have spoiled my dress! I was weady to go downstairs. It is eight o'clock. In a few minutes everyone will be here, and oh, what shall I do— what shall I do! Whatever will mother say when she sees me?"

As if to give a practical answer to this inquiry, there came a sound of hasty footsteps in the corridor, the door flew open, and Lady Darcy rushed in, followed by the French maid.

"My darling, what is it? I heard your voice. Has something happened? Oh-h!" She stopped short, paralysed with consternation, while the maid wrung her hands in despair. "Rosalind, what *have* you done to yourself?"

"Nothing, nothing! It was Peggy Saville; she splashed me with her horrid boot-polish—I gave it to her for her shoes. It is on my face, my neck, in my mouth—"

"I was pulling the cork. It came out with a jerk. I didn't know; I didn't see!—"

Lady Darcy's face stiffened with an expression of icy displeasure.

"It is too annoying! Your dress spoiled at the last moment!

Inexcusable carelessness! What is to be done, Marie? I am in despair!"

The Frenchwoman shrugged her shoulders with an indignant glance in Peggy's direction.

"There is nothing to do. Put on another dress—that is all. Mademoiselle must change as quick as she can. If I sponge the spots, I spoil the whole thing at once."

"But you could cut them out, couldn't you?" cried Peggy, the picture of woe, yet miserably eager to make what amends she could. "You could cut out the spots with sharp scissors, and the holes would not show, for the chiffon is so full and loose. I—I think I could do it, if you would let me try!"

Mistress and maid exchanged a sharp, mutual glance, and the Frenchwoman nodded slowly.

"Yes, it is true; I could rearrange the folds. It will take some time, but still it can be done. It is the best plan."

"Go then, Rosalind, go with Marie; there is not a moment to spare, and for pity's sake don't cry! Your eyes will be red, and at any moment now the people may begin to arrive. I wanted you to be with me to receive your guests. It will be most awkward being without you, but there is no help for it, I suppose. The whole thing is too annoying for words!"

Lady Darcy swept out of the room, and the three girls were once more left alone; but how changed were their feelings in those few short moments! There was not the shadow of a smile between them; they looked more as if they were about to attend a funeral than a scene of festivity, and for several moments no one had the heart to speak. Peggy still held the fatal cork in her hand, and went through the work of polishing Mellicent's slippers with an air of the profoundest dejection. When they were finished she handed them over in dreary silence, and was recommencing the brushing of her hair, when something in the expression of the chubby face arrested her attention. Her eyes flashed; she faced round with a frown and a quick, "Well, what is it? What are you thinking now?"

"I—I wondered," whispered Mellicent breathlessly, "if you did do it on purpose! Did you *mean* to spoil her dress, and make her change it?"

Peggy's hands dropped to her side, her back straightened until she stood stiff and straight as a poker. Every atom of expression seemed to die out of her face. Her voice had a deadly quiet in its intonation.

"What do you think about it yourself?"

"I—I thought perhaps you did! She teased you, and you were so cross. You seemed to be standing so very near her, and you are jealous of her—and she looked so lovely! I thought perhaps you did..."

"Mellicent Asplin," said Peggy quietly, and her voice was like the east wind that blows from an icy-covered mountain, —"Mellicent Asplin, my name is Saville, and in my family we don't condescend to mean and dishonourable tricks. I may not like Rosalind, but I would have given all I have in the world sooner than this should have happened. I was trying to do you a service, but you forget that. You forget many things! I have been jealous of Rosalind, because when she arrived you and your sister forgot that I was alone and far-away from everyone belonging to me, and were so much engrossed with her that you left me alone to amuse myself as best I might. You were pleased enough to have me when no one else was there, but you left me the moment someone appeared who was richer and grander than I. I wouldn't have treated *you* like that, if our positions had been reversed. If I dislike Rosalind, it is your fault as much as hers; more than hers, for it was you who made me dread her coming!"

Peggy stopped, trembling and breathless. There was a moment's silence in the room, and then Esther spoke in a slow, meditative fashion.

"It is quite true!" she said. "We *have* left you alone, Peggy; but it is not quite so bad as you think. Really and truly we like you far the best, but—but Rosalind is such a change to us! Everything about her is so beautiful and so different, that she has always seemed the great excitement of our lives. I don't know that I'm exactly fond of her, but I want to see her, and talk to her, and hear her speak, and she is only here for a short time in the year. It was because we looked upon you as really one of ourselves that we seemed to neglect you; but it was wrong, all the same. As for your spoiling her dress on purpose, it's ridiculous to think of it. How could you say such a thing, Mellicent, when Peggy was trying to help you, too? How *could* you be so mean and horrid?"

"Oh, well, I'm sure I wish I were dead!" wailed Mellicent promptly. "Nothing but fusses and bothers, and just when I thought I was going to be so happy! If I'd had white shoes, this would never have happened. Always the same thing! When you look forward to a treat, everything is as piggy and nasty as it can be! Wish I'd never come! Wish I'd stayed at home, and let the horrid old party go to Jericho! Rosalind's crying, Peggy's cross, you are preaching! This is a nice way to enjoy yourself, I must say!"

Nothing is more hopeless than to reason with a placid person who has lapsed into a fit of ill-temper. The two elder girls realised this, and remained perfectly silent while Mellicent continued to wish for death, to lament the general misery of life, and the bad fortune which attended the wearers of black slippers. So incessant was the stream of her repinings, that it seemed as if it might have gone on for ever, had not a servant entered at last, with the information that the guests were beginning to arrive, and that Lady Darcy would be glad to see the young ladies without delay. Esther was anxious to wait and help Peggy with her toilet, but that young lady was still on her dignity, and by no means anxious to descend to a scene of gaiety for which she had little heart. She refused the offer, therefore, in Mariquita fashion, and the sisters walked dejectedly along the brightly-lit corridors, Mellicent still continuing her melancholy wail, and Esther reflecting sadly that all was vanity, and devoutly wishing herself back in the peaceful atmosphere of the vicarage.

Chapter Twenty Two.

Fire!

It was fully half an hour later when Peggy crept along the passage, and took advantage of a quiet moment to slip into the room and seat herself in a sheltered corner. Quick as she was, however, somebody's eyes were even quicker, for a tall figure stepped before her, and an aggrieved voice cried loudly —

"Well, I hope you are smart enough to satisfy yourself, now that you *are* ready! You have taken long enough, I must say. What about that first waltz that you promised to have with me?"

Peggy drew in her breath with a gasp of dismay.

"Oh, Rob, I am sorry! I forgot all about it. I've been so perturbed. Something awful has occurred. You heard about it, of course—"

"No, I didn't? What on earth," began the boy anxiously; but so soon as he heard the two words "Rosalind's dress!" he shrugged his shoulders in contemptuous indifference. "Oh, that! I heard something about it, but I didn't take much notice. Spilt some ink, didn't you? What's the odds if you did? Accidents will happen, and she has a dozen others to choose from. I don't see anything wrong with the dress. It looks decent enough."

Peggy followed the direction of his eyes, and caught a glimpse of Rosalind floating past on the arm of a tall soldierly youth. She was sparkling with smiles, and looking as fresh and spotless as on the moment when she had stepped across the threshold of her own room. Neither face nor dress bore any trace of the misfortune of an hour before, and Peggy heaved a sigh of relief as she watched her to and fro.

"Jolly enough, isn't she? There's nothing for you to fret about, you see," said Rob consolingly. "She has forgotten all about it, and the best thing you can do is to follow her example. What would you think of some light refreshment? Let's go to the dining-room and drown our sorrows in strawberry ice. Then we can have a waltz, and try a vanilla—and a polka, and some lemonade! That's my idea of enjoying myself. Come along, while you get the chance!—"

"Oh, Rob, you *are* greedy!" protested Peggy; nevertheless she rose blithely enough, and her eyes began to sparkle with some of their wonted vivacity. There was something strong and reassuring about Robert's presence; he looked upon things in such an eminently sensible, matter-of-fact way, that one was ashamed to give way to moods and tenses in his company.

Peggy began to feel that there was still some possibility of happiness in life, and on her way to the door she came face to face with Lady Darcy, who reassured her still further by smiling as amiably as if nothing had happened.

"Well, dear, enjoying yourself? Got plenty of partners?" Then in a whispered aside, "The dress looks all right! Such a clever suggestion of yours. Dear, dear, what a fright we had!" and she swept away, leaving an impression of beauty, grace, and affability which the girl was powerless to resist. When Lady Darcy chose to show herself at her best, there was a charm about her which subjugated all hearts, and, from the moment that the sweet tired eyes smiled into hers, Peggy Saville forgot her troubles and tripped away to eat strawberry ices, and dance over the polished floor with a heart as light as her heels.

One party is very much like another. The room may be larger or smaller, the supper more or less substantial, but the programme is the same in both cases, and there is little to be told about even the grandest of its kind. Somebody wore pink; somebody wore blue; somebody fell down on the floor in the middle of the lancers, which are no longer the stately and dignified dance of yore, but an ungainly romp more befitting a kitchen than a ballroom; somebody went in to supper twice over, and somebody never went at all, but blushed unseen in a corner, thinking longingly of turkey, trifle, and crackers; and then the carriages began to roll up to the door, brothers and sisters paired demurely together, stammered out a bashful "Enjoyed myself so much! Thanks for a pleasant evening," and raced upstairs for coats and shawls.

By half-past twelve all the guests had departed except the

vicarage party, and the sons and daughters of the old squire who lived close by, who had been pressed to stay behind for that last half-hour which is often the most enjoyable of the whole evening.

Lord and Lady Darcy and the grown-up visitors retired into the drawing-room to regale themselves with sandwiches and ices, and the young people stormed the supper-room, interrupted the servants in their work of clearing away the good things, seated themselves indiscriminately on floor, chair, or table, and despatched a second supper with undiminished appetite. Then Esther mounted the platform where the band had been seated, and played a last waltz, and a very last waltz, and "really the last waltz of all." The squire's son played a polka with two fingers, and a great deal of loud pedal, and the fun grew faster and more uproarious with every moment. Even Rosalind threw aside young ladylike affectations and pranced about without thinking of appearances, and when at last the others left the room to prepare for the drive home she seized Peggy's arm in eager excitement.

"Peggy! Peggy! Such a joke! I told them to come back to say good-bye, and I am going to play a twick! I'm going to be a ghost, and glide out from behind the shwubs, and fwighten them. I can do it beautifully. See!" She turned down the gas as she spoke, threw her light gauze skirt over her head, and came creeping across the room with stealthy tread, and arms outstretched, while Peggy clapped her hands in delight.

"Lovely! Lovely! It looks exactly like wings. It makes me quite creepy. Don't come out if Mellicent is alone, whatever you do. She would be scared out of her seven senses. Just float gently along toward them, and keep your hands forward so as to hide your face. They will recognise you if you don't."

"Oh, if you can see my face, we must have less light. There are too many candles, I'll put out the ones on the mantelpiece. Stay where you are, and tell me when it is wight," Rosalind cried gaily, and ran across the room on her tiny pink silk slippers.

So long as she lived Peggy Saville remembered the next

minutes; to the last day of her life she had only to shut her eyes and the scene rose up before her, clear and vivid as in a picture. The stretch of empty room, with its fragrant banks of flowers; the graceful figure flitting across the floor, its outline swathed in folds of misty white; the glimpse of a lovely, laughing face as Rosalind stretched out her arm to reach the silver candelabra, the sudden flare of light which caught the robe of gauze, and swept it into flame. It all happened within the space of a minute, but it was one of those minutes the memory of which no years can destroy. She had hardly time to realise the terror of the situation before Rosalind was rushing towards her with outstretched hands, calling aloud in accents of frenzied appeal—

"Peggy! Peggy! Oh, save me, Peggy! I'm burning! Save me! Save me!"

Chapter Twenty Three.

A Night of Terror.

While the young folks had been enjoying themselves in the ballroom, their elders had found the time hang somewhat heavily on their hands. The evening had not been so interesting to them as to their juniors. Lady Darcy was tired with the preparations of the day, and the countess with her journey from town. Both were fain to yawn behind their fans from time to time, and were longing for the moment to come when they could retire to bed. If only those indefatigable children would say good-night and take themselves off! But the echo of the piano still sounded from the room, and seemed to go on and on, in endless repetition.

Everything comes to those who wait, however—even the conclusion of a ball to the weary chaperon. At long past midnight the strains died away, and in the hope of an early release the ladies roused themselves to fresh conversational effort. What they said was unimportant, and could never be remembered; but at one moment, as it seemed, they were smiling and exchanging their little commonplace amenities, two languid, fine ladies whose aim in life might have been to disguise their own feelings and hide the hearts that God had given them; the next the artificial smiles were wiped away, and they were clinging together, two terrified, cowering women, with a mother's soul in their faces—a mother's love and fear and dread! A piercing cry had sounded through the stillness, and another, and another, and, while they sat paralysed with fear, footsteps came tearing along the passage, the door was burst open, and a wild, dishevelled- looking figure rushed into the room. A curtain was wound round face and figure, but beneath its folds a long white arm gripped convulsively at the air, and two little feet staggered about in pink silk slippers.

Lady Darcy gave a cry of anguish; but her terror seemed to hold her rooted to the spot, and it was her husband who darted forward and caught the swaying figure in his arms. The heavy wrappings came loose in his grasp, and as they did so an unmistakable smell pervaded the room—the smell of singed and burning clothing. A cloud of blackened rags fluttered to the ground as the last fold of the curtain was unloosed, and among them—most pitiful sight of all—were stray gleams of gold where a severed lock of hair lay on the carpet, its end still turned in glistening curl.

"Rosalind! Rosalind!" gasped the poor mother, clutching the arms of her chair, and looking as if she were about to faint herself, as she gazed upon the pitiful figure of her child. The lower portion of Rosalind's dress was practically uninjured, but the gauze skirt and all the frills and puffing round the neck hung in tatters, her hair was singed and roughened, and as the air touched her skin she screamed with pain, and held her hands up to her neck and face.

"Oh! Oh! Oh! I am burning! Cover me up! Cover me up! I shall die! Oh, mother, mother! The pain—the pain!"

She reeled as if about to faint, yet if anyone attempted to approach she beat them off with frantic hands, as if in terror of being touched.

One of the ladies ran forward with a shawl, and wrapped it forcibly round the poor scarred shoulders, while the gentlemen hurried out of the room to send for a doctor and make necessary arrangements. One of the number came back almost immediately, with the news that he had failed to discover the cause of the accident. There was no sign of fire upstairs, the ballroom was dark and deserted, the servants engaged in setting the entertaining rooms in order. For the present, at least, the cause of the accident remained a mystery, and the distracted father and mother occupied themselves in trying to pacify their child.

"I'll carry you upstairs, my darling. We will put something on your skin which will take away the pain. Try to be quiet, and tell us how it happened. What were you doing to set yourself on fire?"

"Peggy! Peggy!" gasped Rosalind faintly. Her strength was failing by this time, and she could hardly speak; but Lady Darcy's face stiffened into an awful anger at the sound ofthat name. She turned like a tigress to her husband, her face quivering with anger.

"That girl again! That wicked girl! It is the second time to-night! She has killed the child; but she shall be punished! I'll have her punished! She shall not kill my child, and go free! I'll—I'll—"

"Hush, hush, Beatrice! Take care! You frighten Rosalind. We must get her to bed. There is not a moment to lose."

Lord Darcy beckoned to one of the servants, who by this time were crowding in at the door, and between them they lifted poor, groaning Rosalind in their arms, and carried her up the staircase, down which she had tripped so gaily a few hours before. Tenderly as they held her, she moaned with every movement, and, when she was laid on her bed, it seemed for a moment as if consciousness were about to forsake her. Then suddenly a light sprung into her eyes. She lifted her hand and gasped out one word—just one word—repeated over and over again in a tone of agonised entreaty.

"Peggy! Peggy! Peggy!"

"Yes, darling, yes! I'll go to her. Be quiet—only be quiet!" Lady Darcy turned away with a shudder as the maid and an old family servant began the task of removing the clothes from Rosalind's writhing limbs, and, seizing her husband by the arm, drew him out on the landing. Her face was white, but her eyes gleamed, and the words hissed as they fell from her lips.

"Find that girl, and turn her out of this house! I will not have her here another hour! Do you hear—not a minute! Send her away at once before I see her! Don't let me see her! I can't be responsible for what I would do!"

"Yes, yes, dear, I'll send her away! Try to calm yourself. Remember you have work to do Rosalind will need you."

The poor old lord went stooping away, his tired face looking aged and haggard with anxiety. His beautiful young daughter was scarcely less dear to him than to her mother, and the sound of her cries cut to his heart; yet in the midst of his anguish he had a pang of compassion for the poor child who, as he believed, was the thoughtless cause of the accident. What agony of remorse must be hers! What torture she would now be suffering!

The guests and servants were standing huddled together on the landing upstairs, or running to and fro to procure what was needed. Every thought was concentrated on Rosalind, and Rosalind alone, and the part of the house where the dance had been held was absolutely deserted.

He took his way along the gaily decorated hall, noted with absent eye the disordered condition of the "harem," which had been pointed out so proudly at the beginning of the evening, and entered the empty room. The lights were out, except for a few candles scattered here and there among the flowers. He walked slowly forward, saw the silver candlestick on the floor before the fireplace, and stood gazing at it with a quick appreciation of what had happened. For some reason or other Rosalind had tried to reach the candle, and the light had caught her gauzy skirt, which had burst into flames. It was easy—terribly easy to imagine; but in what way had Peggy Saville been responsible for the accident, so that her name should sound so persistently on Rosalind's lips,—and who had been the Good Samaritan who had come to the rescue with that thick curtain which had killed the flames before they had time to finish the work of destruction?

Lord Darcy peered curiously round. The oak floor stretched before him dark and still, save where its polished surface reflected the light overhead; but surely in the corner opposite to where he stood there was a darker mass—a shadow deeper than the rest?

He walked towards it, bending forward with straining eyes. Another curtain of the same pattern as that which had enveloped Rosalind—a curtain of rich Oriental hues with an unaccountable patch of white in the centre. What was it? It must be part of the fabric itself. Lord Darcy told himself that he had no doubt on the subject, yet the way across the room seemed unaccountably long, and his heart beat fast with apprehension. In another moment he stood in the corner, and knew too well the meaning of that patch of white, for Peggy Saville lay stretched upon the curtain, motionless, unconscious—to all appearance, dead!

Chapter Twenty Four.

The Valley of the Shadow.

It was one o'clock in the morning when a carriage drove up to the door of the Larches, and Mrs Asplin alighted, all pale, tear-stained, and tremulous. She had been nodding over the fire in her bedroom when the young people had returned with the news of the tragic ending to the night's festivity, and no persuasion or argument could induce her to wait until the next day before flying to Peggy's side.

"No, no!" she cried. "You must not hinder me. If I can't drive, I will walk! I would go to the child to-night, if I had to crawl on my hands and knees! I promised her mother to look after her. How could I stay at home and think of her lying there? Oh, children, children, pray for Peggy! Pray that she may be spared, and that her poor parents may be spared this awful—awful news!"

Then she kissed her own girls, clasped them to her in a passionate embrace, and drove off to the Larches in the carriage which had brought the young people home.

Lady Darcy came out to meet her, and gripped her hand in welcome.

"You have come! I knew you would. I am so thankful to see you. The doctor has come, and will stay all night. He has sent for a nurse—"

"And—my Peggy?"

Lady Darcy's lips quivered.

"Very, very ill—much worse than Rosalind! Her poor little arms! I was so wicked, I thought it was her fault, and I had no pity, and now it seems that she has saved my darling's life. They can't tell us about it yet, but it was she who wrapped the curtain round Rosalind, and burned herself in pressing out the flames. Rosalind kept crying, 'Peggy! Peggy!' and we thought she meant that it was Peggy's fault. We had heard so much of her mischievous tricks. My husband found her lying on the floor. She was unconscious; but she came round when they were dressing her arms. I think she will know you—"

"Take me to her, please!" Mrs Asplin said quickly. She had to wait several moments before she could control her voice sufficiently to add, "And Rosalind, how is she?"

"There is no danger. Her neck is scarred, and her hair singed and burned. She is suffering from the shock, but the doctor says it is not serious. Peggy—"

She paused, and the other walked on resolutely, not daring to ask for the termination of that sentence. She crept into the little room, bent over the bed, and looked down on Peggy's face through a mist of tears. It was drawn and haggard with pain, and the eyes met hers without a ray of light in their hollow depths. That she recognised was evident, but the pain which she was suffering was too intense to leave room for any other feeling. She lay motionless, with her bandaged arms stretched before her, and her face looked so small and white against the pillow that Mrs Asplin trembled to think how little strength was there to fight against the terrible shock and strain. Only once in all that long night did Peggy show any consciousness of her surroundings, but then her eyes lit up with a gleam of remembrance, her lips moved, and Mrs Asplin bent down to catch the faintly whispered words—

"The twenty-sixth—next Monday! Don't tell Arthur!"

"'The twenty-sixth!' What is that, darling? Ah, I remember—Arthur's examination! You mean if he knew you were ill, it would upset him for his work?"

An infinitesimal movement of the head answered "Yes," and she gave the promise in trembling tones—

"No, my precious, we won't tell him. He could not help, and it would only distress you to feel that he was upset. Don't trouble about it, darling. It will be all right."

Then Peggy shut her eyes and wandered away into a strange world, in which accustomed things disappeared, and time was not, and nothing remained but pain and weariness and mystery. Those of us who have come near to death have visited this world too, and know the blackness of it, and the weary waking.

Peggy lay in her little white bed, and heard voices speaking in her ear, and saw strange shapes flit to and fro. Quite suddenly, as it appeared, a face would be bending over her own, and as she watched it with languid curiosity, wondering what manner of thing it could be, it would melt away and vanish in the distance. At other times again it would grow larger and larger, until it assumed gigantic proportions, and she cried out in fear of the huge, saucer-like eyes. There was a weary puzzle in her brain, an effort to understand, but everything seemed mixed up and incomprehensible. She would look round the room and see the sunshine peeping in through the chinks of the blinds, and when she closed her eyes for a moment—just a single fleeting moment—lo! the gas was lit, and someone was nodding in a chair by her side. And it was by no means always the same room. She was tired, and wanted badly to rest, yet she was always rushing about here, there, and everywhere, striving vainly to dress herself in clothes which fell off as soon as they were fastened, hurrying to catch a train to reach a certain destination; but in each instance the end was the same—she was falling, falling, falling—always falling—from the crag of an Alpine precipice, from the pinnacle of a tower, from the top of a flight of stairs. The slip and the terror pursued her wherever she went; she would shriek aloud, and feel soft hands pressed on her cheeks, soft voices murmuring in her ear.

One vision stood out plainly from those nightmare dreams—the vision of a face which suddenly appeared in the midst of the big grey cloud which enveloped her on every side—a beautiful face which was strangely like, and yet unlike, something she had seen long, long ago in a world which she had well-nigh forgotten. It was pale and thin, and the golden hair fell in a short curly crop on the blue garment which was swathed over the shoulders. It was like one of the heads of celestial choir-boys which she had seen on Christmas cards and in books of engravings, yet something about the eyes and mouth seemed familiar. She stared at it curiously, and then suddenly a strange, weak little voice faltered out a well- known name.

"Rosalind!" it cried, and a quick exclamation of joy sounded from the side of the bed. Who had spoken? The first voice had been strangely like her own, but at an immeasurable distance. She shut her eyes to think about it, and the fair- haired vision disappeared, and was seen no more.

There was a big, bearded man also who came in from time to time, and Peggy grew to dread his appearance, for with it came terrible stabbing pain, as if her whole body were on the rack. He was one of the Spanish Inquisitors, of whom she had read, and she was an English prisoner whom he was torturing! Well, he might do his worst! She would die before she would turn traitor and betray her flag and country. The Savilles were a fighting race, and would a thousand times rather face death than dishonour.

One day, when she felt rather stronger than usual, she told him so to his face, and he laughed—she was quite sure he laughed, the hard-hearted wretch! And someone else said,

"Poor little love!" which was surely an extraordinary expression for a Spanish Inquisitor. That was one of the annoying things in this new life—people were so exceedingly stupid in their conversation! Now and again she herself had something which she was especially anxious to say, and when she set it forth with infinite difficulty and pains the only answer which she received was a soothing, "Yes, dear, yes!"

"No, dear, no!" or a still more maddening, "Yes, darling, I quite understand!"—which she knew perfectly well to be an untruth. Really, these good people seemed to think that she was demented, and did not know what she was saying. As a matter of fact, it was exactly the other way about; but she was too tired to argue. And then one day came a sleep when she neither dreamt nor slipped nor fell, but opened her eyes refreshed and cheerful, and beheld Mrs Asplin sitting by a table drinking tea and eating what appeared to be a particularly tempting slice of cake.

"I want some cake!" she said clearly; and Mrs Asplin jumped as if a cannon had been fired off at her ear, and rushed breathlessly to the bedside, stuttering and stammering in amazement—

"Wh-wh-wh-what?"

"Cake!" repeated Peggy shrilly. "I want some! And tea! I want my tea!"

Surely it was a very natural request! What else could you expect from a girl who had been asleep and wakened up feeling hungry? What on earth was there in those commonplace words to make a grown-up woman cry like a baby, and why need everyone in the house rush in and stare at her as if she were a figure in a waxwork? Lord Darcy, Lady Darcy, Rosalind, the old French maid—they were all there—and, as sure as her name was Peggy Saville, they were all four, handkerchief in hand, mopping their eyes like so many marionettes!

Nobody gave her the cake for which she had asked. Peggy considered it exceedingly rude and ill-bred; but while she was thinking of it she grew tired again, and, rolling round into a soft little bundle among the blankets, fell afresh into sweet refreshing slumbers.

Chapter Twenty Five.

Convalescence.

"Convalescence," remarked Peggy elegantly, a week later on, "convalescence is a period not devoid of attraction!" She was lying on a sofa in her bedroom at the Larches, wrapped in her white dressing-gown, and leaning against a nest of pink silk cushions, and, what with a table drawn up by her side laden with grapes and jelly, a pile of Christmas numbers lying close at hand, and the presence of an audience consisting of Rosalind, Lady Darcy, and Mrs Asplin, ready to listen admiringly to her conversation, and to agree enthusiastically with every word she uttered, it did indeed seem as if the position was one which might be endured with fortitude! Many were the questions which had been showered upon her since her return to consciousness, and the listeners never grew tired of listening to her account of the accident. How Rosalind had clutched too carelessly at the slender candlestick, so that it had fallen forward, setting the gauze dress in flames, how she herself had flown out of the room, torn down the curtains which draped the "harem," and had flung them round the frantic, struggling figure. With every day that passed, however, Peggy gained more strength, and was petted to her heart's content by everyone in the house. The old lord kissed her fondly on the cheek, and murmured, "God reward you, my brave girl, for I never can." Lady Darcy shed tears every morning when the burns were dressed, and said, "Oh, Peggy dear, forgive me for being cross, and do, do be sure to use the lotion for your arms regularly every day when you get better!" And the big doctor chucked her under the chin, and cried—

"Well, 'Fighting Saville,' and how are we to-day? You are the pluckiest little patient I've had for a long time. I'll say that for you! Let's have another taste of the rack!" It was all most agreeable and soothing to one's feelings!

One of the first questions Peggy asked after her return to consciousness was as to how much her father and mother had been told of her accident, and whether the news had been sent by letter or cable.

"By letter, dear," Mrs Asplin replied. "We talked it over carefully, and concluded that that would be best. You know, dearie, we were very, very anxious about you for a few days, but the doctor said that it would be useless cabling to your mother, because if all went well you would be up again before she could arrive, and if—if it had gone the other way, Peggy, she could not have been in time. I sent her a long letter, and I have written every mail since, and now we are going to calculate the time when the first letter will arrive, and send a cable to say that you are quite out of danger, and sitting up, and getting hungrier and more mischievous with every dayas it passes!"

"Thank you," said Peggy warmly. "That's very kind. I am glad you thought of that; but will you please promise not to be economical about the cable? They won't care about the money. Spend pounds over it if it is necessary, but do, do manage to make them believe that I am quite perky. Put at the end, 'Peggy says she is perky!' They will know that is genuine, and it will convince them more than anything else." And so those five expressive words went flashing across the world at the end of a long message, and brought comfort to two hearts that had been near to breaking.

So soon as Peggy was pronounced to be out of danger, Mrs Asplin went back to the vicarage, leaving her in the charge of the kind hospital nurse, though for that matter every member of the household took it in turns to wait upon her. A dozen times a day the master and mistress of the house would come into the sick-room to inquire how things were going, or to bring some little gift for the invalid; and as she grew stronger it became the custom for father, mother, and daughter to join her at her early tea. Peggy watched them from her sofa, too weak to speak much, but keenly alive to all that was going on, among other things, to the change which had come over these three persons since she had known them first. Lord Darcy had always been kind and considerate, but his manner seemed gentler and more courteous than ever, while Rosalind's amiability was an hourly surprise, and Lady Darcy's manner had lost much of its snappish discontent. On one occasion, when her husband made some little request, she replied in a tone so sweet and loving that the listener started with surprise. What could it be that had worked this transformation? She did not realise that when the Angel of Death has hovered over a household, and has at last flown away with empty arms, leaving the home untouched, they would be hard hearts that were not touched, ungrateful natures that did not take thought of themselves, and face life with a higher outlook! Lady Darcy's social disappointments seemed light compared with the awful "might have been"; while Rosalind's lamentations over her disfigurement had died away at the sight of Peggy's unconscious form. Perhaps, when Lord Darcy thanked Peggy for all she had done for him and his, he had other thoughts in his mind than the mere physical deliverance of which she had been the instrument!

Arthur had been kept well informed of his sister's recovery, and proved himself the kindest of brothers, sending letters by the dozen, full of such nonsensical jokes, anecdotes, and illustrations, as would have cheered the gloomiest invalid in the world. But the happiest day of all was when the great news arrived that his name was placed first of all in the list of successful candidates. This was indeed tidings of comfort and joy! Peggy clapped her bandaged hands together, and laughed aloud with tears of pain streaming down her face. "Arthur Saville, V.C., Arthur Saville, V.C.!" she cried, and then fell to groaning because some days must still elapse before the medical examination was over, and her hero was set free to hasten to her side.

"And I shall be back at the vicarage then, and we shall all be together! Oh, let us be joyful! How happy I am! What a nice old world it is, after all!" she continued hilariously, while Rosalind gazed at her with reproachful eyes.

"Are you so glad to go away? I shall be vewy, vewy sowwy—I'll miss you awfully. I shall feel that there is nothing to do when you have gone away, Peggy!"—Rosalind hesitated, and looked at her companion in uncertain bashful fashion. "I—I think you like me a little bit now, and I'm vewy fond of you, but you couldn't bear me before we were ill. You might tell me why?"

"I was jealous of you," said Peggy promptly; whereat Rosalind's eyes filled with tears.

"You won't be jealous now!" she said dismally, and raised her head to stare at her own reflection in the mirror. The hair which had once streamed below her waist was now cut short round her head, her face had lost its delicate bloom, and an ugly scar disfigured her throat and the lower portion of one cheek. Beautiful she must always be, with her faultless features and wonderful eyes, but the bloom and radiance of colour which had been her chief charm had disappeared for the time being as completely as though they had never existed.

"I'll love you more," said Peggy reassuringly. "You are ever so much nicer, and you will be as pretty as ever when your hair grows and the marks fade away. I like you better when you are not *quite* so pretty, for you really were disgustingly conceited; weren't you now? You can't deny it."

"Oh, Peggy Saville, and so were you! I saw that the first moment you came into the woom. You flared up like a Turkey cock if anyone dared to offend your dignity, and you were always widing about on your high horse, tossing your head, and using gweat long words."

"That's pride, it's not conceit. It's quite a different thing."

"It's about the same to other people," said Rosalind shrewdly. "We both gave ourselves airs, and the wesult was the same, whatever caused it. I was pwoud of my face, and you were pwoud of your—your—er—family—and your cleverness, and—the twicks you played; so if I confess, you ought to confess too. I'm sorry I aggwavated you, Mawiquita, and took all the pwaise for the decowations. It was howwibly mean, and I don't wonder you were angwy. I'm sorry that I was selfish!"

"I exceedingly regret that I formed a false estimate of your character! Let's be chums!" said Peggy sweetly; and the two girls eyed one another uncertainly for a moment, then bent forward and exchanged a kiss of conciliation, after which unusual display of emotion they were seized with instant embarrassment.

"Hem!" said Peggy. "It's very cold! Fire rather low, I think. Looks as if it were going to snow."

"No," said Rosalind; "I mean—yes. I'll put on some more—I mean coals. In half an hour Esther and Mellicent will be here —"

"Oh, so they will! How lovely!" Peggy seized gladly on the new opening, and proceeded to enlarge on the joy which she felt at the prospect of seeing her friends again, for on that afternoon Robert and the vicarage party were to be allowed to see her for the first time, and to have tea in her room. She had been looking forward to their visit for days, and, new that the longed-for hour was at hand, she was eager to have the lamps lit, and all preparations made for their arrival.

Robert appeared first, having ridden over in advance of the rest. And Rosalind, after going out to greet him, came rushing back, all shaken with laughter, with the information that he had begun to walk on tiptoe the moment that he had left the drawing-room, and was creeping along the passage as if terrified at making a sound.

Peggy craned her head, heard the squeak, squeak of boots coming nearer and nearer, the cautious opening of the door, the heavy breaths of anxiety, and then, crash!—bang!—crash! down flopped the heavy screen round the doorway, and Rob was discovered standing among the ruins in agonies of embarrassment. From his expression of despair, he might have supposed that the shock would kill Peggy outright; but she gulped down her nervousness, and tried her best to reassure him.

"Oh, never mind—never mind! It doesn't matter. Come over here and talk to me. Oh, Rob, Rob, I am so glad to see you!"

Robert stood looking down in silence, while his lips twitched and his eyebrows worked in curious fashion. If it had not been altogether too ridiculous, Peggy would have thought that he felt inclined to cry. But he only grunted, and cried—

"What a face! You had better tuck into as much food as you can, and get some flesh on your bones. It's about as big as the palm of my hand! Never saw such a thing in my life."

"Never mind my face," piped Peggy in her weak little treble. "Sit right down and talk to me. What is the news in the giddy world? Have you heard anything about the prize? When does the result come out? Remember you promised faithfully not to open the paper until we were together. I was so afraid it would come while I was too ill to look at it!"

"I should have waited," said Robert sturdily. "There would have been no interest in the thing without you; but the result won't be given for ten days yet, and by that time you will be with us again. The world hasn't been at all giddy, I can tell you. I never put in a flatter time. Everybody was in the blues, and the house was like a tomb, and a jolly uncomfortable tomb at that. Esther was housekeeper while Mrs Asplin was away, and she starved us! She was in such a mortal fright of being extravagant that she could scarcely give us enough to keep body and soul together, and the things we had were not fit to eat. Nothing but milk puddings and stewed fruit for a week on end. Then we rebelled. I nipped her up in my arms one evening in the schoolroom, and stuck her on the top of the little bookcase. Then we mounted guard around, and set forth our views. It would have killed you to see her perched up there, trying to look prim and to keep up her dignity.

"'Let me down this moment, Robert. Bring a chair and let me get down.'

"'Will you promise to give us a pie to-morrow, then, and a decent sort of a pudding?'

"'It's no business of yours what I give you. You ought to be thankful for good wholesome food!'

"'Milk puddings are not wholesome. They don't agree with us—they are too rich! We should like something a little lighter for a change. Will you swear off milk puddings for the next fortnight if I let you down?'

"'You are a cruel, heartless fellow, Robert Darcy—thinking of puddings when Peggy is ill, and we are all so anxious about her!'

"'Peggy would die at once if she heard how badly you were treating us. Now then, you have kept me waiting for ten minutes, so the price has gone up. Now you'll have to promise a pair of ducks and mince-pies into the bargain! I shall be ashamed of meeting a sheep soon, if we go on eating mutton every day of the week.'

"'Call yourself a gentleman!' says she, tossing her head and withering me with a glance of scorn.

"'I call myself a hungry man, and that's all we are concerned about for the moment,' said I. 'A couple of ducks and two nailing good puddings to-morrow night, or there you sit for the rest of the evening!'

"We went at it hammer and tongs until she was fairly spluttering with rage; but she had to promise before she came down, and we had no more starvation diet after that. Oswald went up to town for a day, and bought a pair of blue silk socks and a tie to match—that's the greatest excitement we have had. The rest has been all worry and grind, and Mellicent on the rampage about Christmas presents. Oh, by the bye, I printed those photographs you wanted to send to your mother, and packed them off by the mail a fortnight ago, so that she would get them in good time for Christmas."

"Rob, you didn't! How noble of you! You really are an admirable person!" Peggy lay back against her pillows and gazed at her "partner" in great contentment of spirit. After living an invalid's life for these past weeks, it was delightfully refreshing to look at the big strong face. The sight of it was like a fresh breeze coming into the close, heated room, and she felt as if some of his superabundant energy had come into her own weak frame.

A little later the vicarage party arrived, and greeted the two convalescents with warmest affection. If they were shocked at the sight of Rosalind's disfigurement and Peggy's emaciation, three out of the four were polite enough to disguise their feelings; but it was too much to expect of Mellicent that she should disguise what she happened to be feeling. She stared and gaped, and stared again, stuttering with consternation—

"Why—why—Rosalind—your hair! It's shorter than mine! It doesn't come down to your shoulders! Did they cut it all off? What did you do with the rest? And your poor cheek! Will you have that mark all your life?"

"I don't know. Mother is going to twy electwicity for it. It will fade a good deal, I suppose, but I shall always be a fwight. I'm twying to wesign myself to be a hideous monster!" sighed Rosalind, turning her head towards the window the while in such a position that the scar was hidden from view, and she looked more like the celestial choir-boy of Peggy's delirium than ever, with the golden locks curling round her neck, and the big eyes raised to the ceiling in a glance of pathetic resignation.

Rob guffawed aloud with the callousness of a brother; but the other two lads gazed at her with an adoring admiration which was balm to her vain little heart. Vain still, for a nature does not change in a day; and, though Rosalind was an infinitely more lovable person now than she had been a few weeks before, the habits of a lifetime were still strong upon her, and she could never by any possibility be indifferent to admiration, or pass a mirror without stopping to examine the progress of that disfiguring scar.

"It wouldn't have mattered half so much if it had been Peggy's face that was spoiled," continued Mellicent, with cruel outspokenness, "and it is only her hands that are hurt. Things always go the wrong way in this world! I never saw anything like it. You know that night-dress bag I was working for mother, Peggy? Well, I only got two skeins of the blue silk, and then if I didn't run short, and they hadn't any more in the shop. The other shades don't match at all, and it looks simply vile. I am going to give it to—ahem! I mean that's the sort of thing that always happens to me—it makes me mad! You can't sew at all, I suppose? What do you do with yourself all day long, now that you are able to get up?"

Peggy's eyes twinkled.

"I sleep," she said slowly, "and eat, and sleep a little more, and eat again, and talk a little bit, roll into bed, and fall fast asleep. *Voilà tout, ma chère! C'est ça que je fais tous les jours*."

Rosalind gave a shriek of laughter at Peggy's French, and Mellicent rolled her eyes to the ceiling.

"How s–imply lovely!" she sighed. "I wish I were you! I'd like to go to bed in November and stay there till May. In a room like this, of course, with everything beautiful and dainty, and a maid to wait upon me. I'd have a fire and an india-rubber hot-water bottle, and I'd lie and sleep, and wake up every now and then, and make the maid read aloud, and bring me my meals on a tray. Nice meals! Real, nice invalidy things, you know, to tempt my appetite." Mellicent's eyes rolled instinctively to the table, where the jelly and the grapes stood together in tempting proximity. She sighed, and brought herself back with an effort to the painful present. "Goodness, Peggy, how funny your hands look! Just like a mummy! What do they look like when the bandages are off? Very horrible?"

"Hideous!" Peggy shrugged her shoulders and wrinkled her nose in disgust. "I am going to try to grow old as fast as I can, so that I can wear mittens and cover them up. I'm really rather distressed about it, because I am so—so addicted to rings, don't you know. They have been a weakness of mine all my life, and I've looked forward to having my fingers simply loaded with them when I grew up. There is one of mother's that I especially admire—a big square emerald surrounded with diamonds. She promised to give it to me on my twenty-first birthday, but, unless my hands look very different by that time, I shall not want to call attention to them. Alack-a-day! I fear I shall never be able to wear a ring —"

"Gracious goodness! Then you can never be married!" ejaculated Mellicent, in a tone of such horrified dismay as evoked a shriek of merriment from the listeners—Peggy's merry trill sounding clear above the rest. It was just delicious to be well again, to sit among her companions and have one of the old hearty laughs over Mellicent's quaint speeches. At that moment she was one of the happiest girls in all the world.

Chapter Twenty Six.

Alas, for Arthur!

A few days later Peggy was driven home to the vicarage, and stood the drive so well that she was able to walk downstairs at tea-time, and sit at the table with only a cushion at her back, to mark her out as an invalid just recovering from a serious illness. There was a special reason why she wished to look well this afternoon, for Arthur was expected by the six o'clock train; and the candidate who had come out first in his examination lists must not have his reception chilled by anxiety or disappointment.

Peggy was attired in her pink dress, and sat roasting before the fire, so as to get some colour into her cheeks. If her face were only the size of the palm of a hand, she was determined that it should at least be rosy; and if she looked very bright, and smiled all the time, perhaps Arthur would not notice how thin she had become.

When half-past six struck, everyone crowded into the schoolroom, and presently a cab drove up to the door, and a modest rap sounded on the knocker.

"That's not Arthur!" cried Mrs Asplin confidently. "He knocks straight on without stopping, peals the bell at the same time, and shouts Christmas carols through the letter-box! He has sent on his luggage, I expect, and is going to pounce in upon us later on."

"Ah, no, that's not Arthur!" assented Peggy; but Mr Asplin turned his head quickly towards the door, as if his ear had caught a familiar note, hesitated for a moment, and then walked quickly into the hall.

"My dear boy!" the listeners heard him cry; and then another voice spoke in reply—Arthur's voice—saying, "How do you do, sir?" in such flat, subdued tones as filled them with amazement.

Mrs Asplin and Peggy turned towards each other with

distended eyes. If Arthur had suddenly slid down the chimney and crawled out on the hearth before them, turned a somersault in at the window, or crawled from beneath the table, it would have caused no astonishment whatever; but that he should ring at the bell, walk quietly into the hall, and wait to hang up his hat like any other ordinary mortal,—this was indeed an unprecedented and extraordinary proceeding! The same explanation darted into both minds. His sister's illness! He was afraid of startling an invalid, and was curbing his overflowing spirits in consideration for her weakness.

Peggy rose from her chair, and stood waiting, with sparkling eyes and burning cheeks. He should see in one glance that she was better—almost well—that there was no need of anxiety on her behalf. And then the tall, handsome figure appeared in the doorway, and Arthur's voice cried—

"Peggikens! Up and dressed! This is better than I hoped. How are you, dear little Peg?"

There was something wrong with the voice, something lacking in the smile; but his sister was too excited to notice it. She stretched out her arms towards him, and raised her weak, quavering little voice in a song of triumph—

"See-ee the conquering he-he-he-he-hero com-ums! Sow-ow-ow-ow-ownd the trumpet, play—a—a—a—"

"Don't, Peg!" cried Arthur sharply. "Don't, dear!" He was standing by her side by this time, and suddenly he wrapped his arms round her and laid his curly head on hers. "I'm plucked, Peg!" he cried, and his voice was full of tears. "Oh, Peg, I'm plucked! It's all over; I can never be a soldier. I'm plucked—plucked—plucked!"

"Arthur dear! Arthur darling!" cried Peggy loudly. She clasped her arms round his neck, and glared over his shoulder, like a tigress whose young has been threatened with danger. "You plucked! My brother plucked! Ho! ho! ho!" She gave a shrill peal of laughter. "It's impossible! You were first of all, the very first. You always are first. Who was wicked enough, and cruel enough, and false enough, to say that Arthur Saville was plucked in an examination?"

"Arthur, my boy, what is it? What does it mean? You told us you were first. How can you possibly be plucked?"

"My—my eyes!" said Arthur faintly. He raised his head from Peggy's shoulder and looked round with a haggard smile. "The medical exam. They would not pass me. I was rather blind when I was here before, but I thought it was with reading too much. I never suspected there was anything really wrong—never for a moment!"

"Your eyes!" The vicar pressed his hand to his forehead, as if unable to grasp this sudden shattering of his hopes. "But— but I don't understand! Your eyes never gave you any trouble when you were here. You were not short-sighted. One knew, of course, that good sight was necessary; but there seemed no weakness in that direction. I can't imagine any cause that can have brought it on."

"I can!" said Arthur drearily. "I got a bad knock at lacrosse two years ago. I didn't tell you about it, for it wasn't worth while; but my eyes were bad for some time after that. I thought they were all right again; but I had to read a lot of things across a room, and made a poor show of it. Then the doctor took me to a window and pointed to an omnibus that was passing.

"'What's the name on that 'bus?' he said. 'What is the colour of that woman's hat? How many horses are there?'

"I guessed. I couldn't see. I made a shot at it, and it was a wrong shot. He was a kind old chap. I think he was sorry for me. I—I came out into the street, and walked about. It was very cold. I tried to write to you, but I couldn't do it—I couldn't put it down in black and white. No V.C. now, little Peg! That's all over. You will have a civilian for your brother, after all!"

He bent down to kiss the girl's cheeks as he spoke, and she threw her arms round his neck and kissed him passionately upon his closed eyelids.

"Dear eyes!" she cried impetuously. "Oh, dear eyes! They are the dearest eyes in all the world, whatever anyone says about them. It doesn't matter what you are—you are myArthur, the best and cleverest brother in all the world. Nobody is like you!"

"You have a fine career before you still, my boy! You will always fight, I hope, and conquer enemies even more powerful than armed men!" cried Mrs Asplin, trembling. "There are more ways than one of being a soldier, Arthur!"

"I know it, mater," said the young man softly. He straightened his back and stood in silence, his head thrown back, his eyes shining with emotion, as fine a specimen of a young English gentleman as one could wish to meet. "I know it," he repeated, and Mrs Asplin turned aside to hide her tears. "Oh, my pretty boy!" she was saying to herself. "Oh, my pretty boy! And I'll never see him in his red coat, riding his horse like a prince among them all! I'll never see the medals on his breast! Oh, my poor lad that has the fighting blood in his veins! It's like tearing the heart out of him to turn Arthur Saville into anything but a soldier. And the poor father—what will he say at all, when he hears this terrible news?" She dared not trust herself to speak again; the others were too much stunned and distressed to make any attempt at consolation, and it was a relief to all when Mellicent's calm, matter-of-fact treble broke the silence.

"Well, for my part, I'm very glad!" she announced slowly. "I'm sorry, of course, if he has to wear spectacles, because they are not becoming, but I'm glad he is not going to be a soldier. I think it's silly having nothing to do but drill in barracks, and pretending to fight when there is no one to fight with. I should hate to be a soldier in times of peace, and it would be fifty thousand times worse in war. Oh, my goodness, shouldn't I be in a fright! I should run away—I know I should; but Arthur would be in the front of every battle, and it's absurd to think that he would not get killed. You know what Arthur is! Did you ever know him have a chance of hurting himself and not taking it? He would be killed in the very first battle—that's my belief—and *then* you would be sorry that you wanted him to be a soldier! Or, if he wasn't killed, he would have his legs shot off. Last time I was in London I saw a man with no legs. He was sitting on a little board with wheels on it, and selling matches in the street. Well, I must say I'd rather have my brother a civilian, as you call it, than have no legs, or be cut in pieces by a lot of nasty naked old savages."

A general smile went round the company. There was no resisting it. Even Arthur's face brightened, and he turned his head and looked at Mellicent with his old twinkling smile.

"Bravo, Chubby!" he cried. "Bravo, Chubby! Commend me to Mellicent for good, sound commonsense. The prospect of squatting on a board, selling matches, is not exhilarating, I must confess. I'm glad there is one person at least who thinks my prospects are improved." He gave a little sigh, which was stifled with praiseworthy quickness. "Well, the worst is over, now that I have told you and written the letter to India. Those were the two things that I dreaded most. Now I shall just have to face life afresh, and see what can be made of it. I must have a talk with you, sir, later on, and get your advice. Cheer up, Peggikens! Cheer up, mater! It's no use grieving over spilt milk, and Christmas is coming. It would never do to be in the dolefuls over Christmas! I've got a boxful of presents upstairs—amused myself with buying them yesterday to pass the time. You come up with me to- night, Peg, and I'll give you a peep. You look better than I expected, dear, but fearsome scraggy! We shall have to pad her out a bit, shan't we, mater? She must have an extra helping of plum-pudding this year."

He rattled on in his own bright style, or in as near an imitation of it as he could manage, and the others tried their best to follow his example and make the evening as cheery as possible. Once or twice the joy of being all together again in health and strength conquered the underlying sorrow, and the laughter rang out as gaily as ever; but the next moment Arthur would draw in his breath with another of those short, stabbing sighs, and Peggy would shiver, and lie back trembling among her pillows. She had no heart to look at Christmas presents that night, but Arthur carried her upstairs in his strong arms, laid her on her bed, and sat beside her for ten minutes' precious private talk.

"It's a facer, Peg," he said. "I can't deny it's a facer. When I walked out of that doctor's room I felt as weak as a child. The shock knocked the strength out of me. I had never thought of anything else but being a soldier, you see, and it's a strange experience to have to face life afresh, with everything that you had expected taken out of it, and nothing ahead but blankness and disappointment. I've been so strong too—as strong as a horse. If it hadn't been for that blow—well, it's over! It's a comfort to me to feel that it was not my own fault. If I'd been lazy or careless, and had failed in the exam., it would have driven me crazy; but this was altogether beyond my control. It is frightfully rough luck, but I don't mean to howl—I must make the best of what's left!"

"Yes, yes, I'm sure you will. You have begun well, for I think you have been wonderfully brave and courageous about it, Arthur dear!"

"Well, of course!" said Arthur softly. "I always meant to be that, Peg; and, as the mater says, it is only another kind of battle. The other would have been easier, but I mean to fight still. I am not going to give up all my dreams. You shall be proud of me yet, though not in the way you expected."

"I never was so proud of you in my life!" Peggy cried. "Never in all my life."

Long after Arthur had kissed her and gone to his own room she lay awake, thinking of his words and of the expression on his handsome face as the firelight played on moistened eye and trembling lip. "I mean to fight."

"You shall be proud of me yet." The words rang in her ears, and would not be silenced. When she fell asleep Arthur was still by her side; the marks of tears were on his face. He was telling her once more the story of disappointment and failure; but she could not listen to him, for her eyes were fixed on something that was pinned on the breast of his coat—a little cross with two words printed across its surface.

In her dream Peggy bent forward, and read those two words with a great rush of joy and exultation.

"For Valour!"

"For Valour!" Yes, yes, it was quite true! Never was soldier flushed with victory more deserving of that decoration than Arthur Saville in his hour of disappointment and failure.

Chapter Twenty Seven.

The Parting of the Ways!

Arthur kept his word, and tried manfully not to let his own disappointment interfere with the enjoyment of Christmas Day.

The party at the vicarage was smaller than usual, for Rob and Oswald had both gone home for the festive season, and he knew well that the knowledge that "Arthur was coming" had seemed the best guarantee of a merry day to those who were left.

Peggy too—poor little Peg, with her bandaged hands and tiny white face—it would never do to grieve her by being depressed and gloomy!

"Begone, dull care!" cried Arthur to himself then, when he awoke on Christmas morning, and, promptly wrapping himself in his dressing-gown, he sallied out on to the landing, where he burst into the strains of "Christians, awake!" with such vigorous brush-and-comb accompaniment on the panels of the doors as startled the household out of their dreams.

"Miserable boy! I was having such a lovely nap! I'll never forgive you!" cried Mrs Asplin's voice, in sleepy wrath.

"Merry Christmas! Merry Christmas!" shouted the girls; and Peggy's clear pipe joined in last of all. "And many of them! Come in! Come in! I was lying awake and longing to see you!"

Arthur put his ruffled head round the door and beamed at the little figure in the bed, as if he had never known a trouble in his life.

"What a wicked story! I heard you snore. Merry Christmas, Peg, and a Happy New Year! And don't you go for to do it again never no more! It's a jolly morning. I'll take you out for a toddle in the garden when we come home from church, if you are a good girl. Will you have your present now, or wait till you get it? It begins with a B. I love my love with a B, because she's a—"

"Oh, Arthur!" interrupted Peggy regretfully. "I haven't half such a nice present for you as I expected. You see I couldn't work anything, and I couldn't get out to the shops, and I hadn't nearly as much money as I expected either. If Rob and I had won that prize, I should have had ten pounds; but the stupid editors have put off announcing the result week after week. They say there were so many competitors; but that's no consolation, for it makes our chance less. I do hope it may be out next week. But, at any rate, I didn't get my ten pounds in time, and there I was, you see, with little money and practically no hands—a—er—a most painful contingency, which I hope it may never be your lot to experience. You must take the will for the deed."

"Oh, I will!" agreed Arthur promptly. "I'll take the will now, and you can follow up with the deed as soon as you get the cash. But no more journeys up to London, my dear, if you love me, and don't use such big words before seven o'clock in the morning, or you'll choke. It's bad for little girls to exert themselves so much. Now I'm going to skate about in the bath for a bit, and tumble into my clothes, and then I'll come back and give you a lift downstairs. You are coming down for breakfast, I suppose?"

"Rather! On Christmas morning! I should just think I was!" cried Peggy emphatically; and Arthur went off to the bathroom, calling in at Max's room *en route*, to squeeze a sponge full of water over that young gentleman's head, and pull the clothes off the bed, by way of giving emphasis to his, "Get up, you lazy beggar! It's the day after to-morrow, and the plum-pudding is waiting!"

Peggy was the only one of the young folks who did not go to church that morning; but she was left in charge of the decorations for the dinner-table, and when this was finished there was so much to think about that the time passed all too quickly.

Last year she and Arthur had spent Christmas with their

mother; now both parents were away in India, and everything was strange and altered. As Peggy sat gazing into the heart of the big gloomy fire, it seemed to her that the year that was passing away would end a complete epoch in her brother's experiences and her own, and that from this hour a new chapter would begin. She herself had come back from the door of death, and had life given, as it were, afresh into her hands. Arthur's longed-for career had been checked at its commencement, and all his plans laid waste. Even the life in the vicarage would henceforth take new conditions, for Rob and Oswald would go up to Oxford at the beginning of the term, and their place be filled by new pupils. There was something solemnising in the consciousness of change which filled the air. One could never tell what might be the next development. Nothing was too unexpected to happen—since Arthur's success had ended in failure, and she herself had received Rosalind's vows of love and friendship.

"Good things have happened as well as bad," acknowledged Peggy honestly; "but how I do hate changes! The new pupils may be the nicest boys in the world, but no one will ever—ever be like Rob, and I'd rather Arthur had been a soldier than anything in the wide world. I wish one could go on being young for ever and ever. It's when you grow old that all these troubles and changes come upon you." And Peggy sighed and wagged her head, oppressed with the weight of fifteen years.

It was a relief to hear the clatter of horses' hoofs, and the sound of voices in the hall, which proved that the church-goers had returned home. Mr and Mrs Asplin had been driven home from church by Lord and Lady Darcy, and the next moment they were in the room, and greeting Peggy with demonstrative affection.

"We couldn't go home without coming to see you, dear," said Lady Darcy fondly. "Rosalind is walking with the rest, and will be here in a few minutes. A merry Christmas to you, darling, and many, many of them. I've brought you a little present which I hope you will like. It's a bangle bracelet—quite a simple one that you can wear every day—and you must think of me sometimes when you put it on."

She touched the spring of a little morocco case as she spoke, and there on the satin lining lay a band of gold, dependent from which hung the sweetest little locket in the world— heart-shaped, studded with pearls, and guarding a ring of hair beneath the glass shield.

Lady Darcy pointed to it in silence—her eyes filling with tears, as they invariably did on any reference to Rosalind's accident, and Peggy's cheeks flushed with pleasure.

"I can't thank you! I really can't," she said. "It is too lovely. You couldn't possibly have given me anything I liked better. I have a predilection for jewellery, and the little locket is too sweet, dangling on that chain! I do love to have something that waggles!" She held up her arm as she spoke, shaking the locket to and fro with a childlike enjoyment, while the two ladies watched her with tender amusement. Lord Darcy had not spoken since his first greeting, but now he came forward, and linking his arm in Peggy's led her to the farther end of the room.

"I have no present for you, my dear—I could not think of one that was good enough—but yesterday I really think I hit on something that would please you. Robert told us how keenly you were feeling your brother's disappointment, and that he was undecided what to try next. Now, I believe I can help him there. I have influence in the Foreign Office, and can ensure him an opening when he is ready for it, if your father agrees that it is desirable. Would that please you, Peggy? If I can help your brother, will it go some little way towards paying the debt I owe you?"

"Oh-h!" cried Peggy rapturously. "Oh!" She clasped Lord Darcy's hands in her own and gazed at him with dilated eyes. "Can you do it? Will you do it? There is nothing in all the world I should like so much. Help Arthur—give him a good chance—and I shall bless you for ever and ever! I could never thank you enough—"

"Well, well, I will write to your father and see what he has to say. I can promise the lad a start at least, and after that his future will be in his own hands, where I think we may safely leave it. Master Arthur is one of the fortunate being's who has an 'open sesame' to all hearts. Mr Asplin assures me that he is as good at work as at play; I have not seen that side of his character, but he has always left a most pleasing impression on my mind, most pleasing." The old lord smiled to himself, and his eyes took a dreamy expression, as if he were recalling to memory the handsome face and strong manly presence of the young fellow of whom he was speaking. "He has been a favourite at our house for some years now, and I shall be glad to do him a service; but remember, Peggy, that when I propose this help, it is, in the first instance at least, for your sake, not his. I tell you this because I think it will give you pleasure to feel that you have been the means of helping your brother. Talk it over with him some time when you are alone together, and then he can come up and see me. To-day we must leave business alone. Here they come! I thought they would not be long after us—"

Even as he spoke voices sounded from the hall, there was a clatter of feet over the tiled flooring, and Mellicent dashed into the room.

"P-P-P-Postman!" she stammered breathlessly. "He is coming! Round the corner! Heaps of letters! Piles of parcels! A hand-cart, and a boy to help him! Here in five minutes! Oh! oh! oh!" She went rushing back to the door, and Rosalind came forward, looking almost her old beautiful self, with her cheeks flushed by the cold air, and the fur collar of her jacket turned up so as to hide the scarred cheek.

"Merry Christmas, Rosalind! How—how nice you look!" cried Peggy, looking up and down the dainty figure with more pleasure in the sight than she could have believed possible a few weeks before. After being accustomed for four long weeks to gaze at those perfectly cut features, Esther's long chin and Mellicent's retroussé nose had been quite a trial to her artistic sensibilities on her return to the vicarage. It was like having a masterpiece taken down from the walls and replaced by an inferior engraving. She gave a sigh of satisfaction as she looked once more at Rosalind's face.

"Mewwy Chwistmas, Peggy! I've missed you fwightfully. I've not been to church, but I dwove down to meet the others, and came to see you. I had to see you on Chwistmas Day. I've had lovely pwesents, and there are more to come. Mother has given you the bwacelet, I see. Is it what you like?"

"My dear, I love it. I'm fearfully addicted to jewellery. I had to put it on at once, and it looks quite elegant on top of the bandages! I'm inexpressibly obliged. I've got heaps of things —books, scent, glove-box, writing-case, a big box coming from India, and—don't tell her—an apron from Mellicent! The most awful thing. I can't think where she found it. Yellow cloth with dog-roses worked in filoselle! Imagine me in a yellow apron with spotty roses around the brim!"

"He! he! I can't! I weally can't. It's too widiculous!" protested Rosalind. "She sent me a twine bag made of netted cotton. It's awfully useful if you use twine, but I never do. Don't say I said so. Who got the night-dwess bag with the two shades of blue that didn't match?"

"Esther! You should have seen her face!" whispered Peggy roguishly, and the girls went into peals of laughter, which brought Robert hurrying across the room to join them.

"Now then, Rosalind; when you have quite done, I should like to speak to Peggy. The compliments of the season to you, Mariquita; I hope I see you well."

Peggy pursed up her lips, and looked him up and down with her dancing hazel eyes.

"Most noble sir, the heavens rain blessings on you—Oh, my goodness, there's the postman!" she said all in one breath; and the partners darted forward side by side towards the front door, where the old postman was already standing, beaming all over his weatherbeaten face, as he began turning out the letters and calling out the names on the envelopes.

"Asplin, Asplin, Saville, Asplin, Saville, Saville, Miss Peggy Saville, Miss Mellercent Asplin, Miss Saville, Miss M. Saville, Miss Peggy Saville."

So the list ran on, with such a constant repetition of the same name that Max exclaimed in disgust, "Who *is* this Miss Peggy Saville that we hear so much about? She's a greedy thing, whoever she may be;" and Mellicent whined out, "I wish I had been at a boarding-school! I wish my relatives lived abroad. There will be none left for me by the time she has finished." Then Arthur thrust forward his mischievous face, and put in a stern inquiry—

"Forbes! Where's that registered letter? That letter with the hundred-pound note. Don't say you haven't got it, for I know better. Hand it over now, without any more bother."

The old postman gave a chuckle of amusement, for this was a standing joke renewed every Christmas that Arthur had spent at the vicarage.

"'Tasn't come ter-day, Muster Saville. Missed the post. 'Twill be coming ter-morrer morning certain!"

"Forbes!" croaked Arthur solemnly. "Reflect! You have a wife and children. This is a serious business. It's ruin, Forbes, that's what it is. R-u-i-n, my friend! Be advised by me, and give it up. The hundred pounds is not worth it, and besides I need it badly. Don't deprive a man of his inheritance!"

"Bless yer rart, I'd bring it yer with pleasure rif I could! Nobody'd bring it quicker ran I would!" cried Forbes, who like everyone else adored the handsome young fellow who was always ready with a joke and a kindly word. "It's comin' for the Noo Year, sir. You mark my words. There's a deal of luck waitin' for yer in the Noo Year!"

Arthur's laugh ended in a sigh, but he thanked the old man for his good wishes, tipped him even more lavishly than usual, and followed his companions to the drawing-room to examine their treasures.

Parcels were put on one side to await more leisurely inspection, but cards and letters were opened at once, and Rob seated himself by Peggy's side as she placed the pile of envelopes on a table in the corner.

"We are partners, you know," he reminded her, "so I think I am entitled to a share in these. What a lot of cards! Who on earth are the senders?"

"My godfathers, and my godmothers, and all my relatives and

friends. The girls at school and some of the teachers. This fat one is from 'Buns'—Miss Baker, the one whose Sunday hat I squashed. She used to say that I was sent to her as wholesome discipline, to prevent her being too happy as a hard-worked teacher in a ladies' school, but she wept bucketfuls when I came away. I liked Buns! This is from Marjorie Riggs, my chum. She had a squint, but a most engaging disposition. This is from Kate Strong: now if there is a girl in the world for whom I cherish an aversion, it is Katie Strong! She is what I call a specious pig, and why she wanted to send me a Christmas card I simply can't imagine. We were on terms of undying hatred. This is from Miss Moss, the pupil teacher. She had chilblains, poor dear, and spoke through her dose. 'You busn't do it, Peggy, you really busn't. It's bost adoying!' Then I did it again, you know, and she sniggered and tried to look cross. This is—I don't know who this is from! It's a man's writing. It looks like a business letter—London postmark—and something printed in white on the seal. What is it? 'The Pic-Pic-Piccadilly'—Robert!" Peggy's voice grew shrill with excitement. "*The Piccadilly Magazine*."

"Wh-at!" Robert grabbed at the envelope, read the words himself, and stared at her with sparkling eyes. "It is! It's the prize, Mariquita! It must be. What else would they write about? Open it and see. Quick! Shall I do it for you?"

"Yes, yes!" cried Peggy breathlessly. She craned her head forward as Rob tore open the envelope, and grasped his arm with both hands. Together they read the typewritten words, together they gasped and panted, and shrieked aloud in joy. "We've done it! We have! We've won the prize! Thirty pounds! Bravo, Rob! Now you can buy your microscope!"—"Good old Mariquita, it's all your doing. Don't speak to us; we are literary people, far above ordinary commonplace creatures like you. Thir-ty pounds! made by our own honest toil. What do you think of that, I'd like to know?"

Each member of the audience thought something different, and said it amid a scene of wild excitement. The elders were pleased and proud, though not above improving the occasion by warnings against secret work, over-anxiety, midnight journeys, etcetera. Mellicent exclaimed, "How jolly! Now you will be able to give presents for the New Year as well as Christmas;" and Arthur said, "Dear Peggums! I always loved you; I took the 'will,' you know, without any grumbling, and now you can follow up with the deed as quickly as you like!" Each one wanted to hold the precious document in his own hands, to read it with his own eyes, and it was handed round and round to be exclaimed over in accents of wonder and admiration, while Rob beamed, and Peggy tossed her pigtail over her shoulder, holding her little head at an angle of complacent satisfaction.

The moment of triumph was very sweet—all the sweeter because of the sorrows of the last few weeks. The partners forgot all the hard work, worry, and exhaustion, and remembered only the joy of success and hope fulfilled. Robert said little in the way of thanks, preferring to wait until he could tell Peggy of his gratitude without an audience to criticise his words; but when his mother began to speak of leaving, it was he who reminded Mrs Asplin of the promise that the invalid should have her first walk on Christmas Day.

"Let us go on ahead, and take her with us until the carriage overtakes us. It will do her no harm. It's bright and dry—"

"Oh, mater, yes! I told Peg I would take her out," chimed in Arthur, starting from his seat by Rosalind's side, and looking quite distressed because he had momentarily forgotten his promise. "Wrap her up well, and we'll take care of her. The air will do her good."

"I think it will, but you must not go far—not an inch beyond the crossroads. Come, Peggy, and I'll dress you myself. I can't trust you to put on enough wraps." Mrs Asplin whisked the girl out of the room, and wrapped her up to such an extent that when she came downstairs again she could only puff and gasp above her muffler, declare that she was choking, and fan herself with her muff. Choking or not, the eyes of the companions brightened as they looked at her, for the scarlet tam-o'-shanter was set at a rakish angle on the dark little head, and Peggy the invalid seemed to have made way for the Peggy of old, with dimpling cheeks and the light of mischief in her eyes.

The moment that Mrs Asplin stopped fumbling with her wraps, she was out at the door, opening her mouth to drink in the fresh chill air, and Robert was at her side before anyone had a chance of superseding him.

"Umph! Isn't it good? I'm stifling for a blow. My lungs are sore for want of exercise. I was longing, longing to get out. Robert, do you realise it? We have won the prize! Can you believe it? It is almost too good to be true. It's the best present of all. Now you can buy your microscope, and get on with your work as you never could before!"

"Yes, and it's all your doing, Mariquita. I could not have pulled it off without your help. If I make anything out of my studies, it will be your doing too. I'll put it down to you, and thank you for it all my life."

"H–m! I don't think I deserve so much praise, but I like it. It's very soothing," said Peggy reflectively. "I'm very happy about it, and I needed something to make me happy, for I felt as blue as indigo this morning. We seem to have come to the end of so many things, and I hate ends. There is this disappointment about Arthur, which spoils all the old plans, and the break-up of our good times here together. I shall miss Oswald. He was a dear old dandy, and his ties were quite an excitement in life; but I simply can't imagine what the house will be like without you, Rob!"

"I shall be here for some weeks every year, and I'll run down for a day or two whenever I can. It won't be good-bye."

"I know—I know! but you will never be one of us again, living in the house, joining in all our jokes. It will be quite a different thing. And you will grow up so quickly at Oxford, and be a man before we know where we are."

"So will you—a woman at least. You are fifteen in January. At seventeen, girls put their hair up and wear long dresses. You will look older than I do, and give yourself as many airs as if you were fifty. I know what girls of seventeen are like. I've met lots of them, and they say, 'That boy!' and toss their heads as if they were a dozen years older than fellows of their own age. I expect you will be as bad as the rest, but you needn't try to snub me. I won't stand it."

"You won't have a chance, for I shan't be here. As soon as my education is finished I am going out to India, to stay until father retires and we come home to settle. So after to-day—"

"After to-day—the deluge! Peggy, I didn't tell you before, but I'm off to-morrow to stay in town until I go up to Oxford on the fourteenth. The pater wants to have me with him, so I shan't see you again for some months. Of course I am glad to be in town for most things, but—"

"Yes, but!" repeated Peggy, and turned a wan little face upon him. "Oh, Rob, it is changing quickly I never thought it would be so soon as this. So it is good-bye. No wonder I felt so blue this morning. It is good-bye for ever to the old life. We shall meet again, oh yes! but it will be different. Some day when I'm old and grown-up I will see in a newspaper the name of a distinguished naturalist and discoverer, and say, 'I used to know him once. He was not at all proud. He used to pull my hair like any ordinary mortal.'

"Some day I shall enter a ballroom, and see a little lady sitting by the door waving her hands in the air, and using words a mile long, and shall say to myself, 'Do my eyes deceive me? Is it indeed the Peggy Pickle of the Past?' and my host will say, 'My good sir, that is the world-famous authoress, Mariquita de Ponsonby Plantagenet Saville!' Stevenson, I assure you, is not in it for flow of language, and she is so proud of herself that she won't speak to anyone under a belted earl."

"That sounds nice!" said Peggy approvingly. "I should like that; but it wouldn't be a ball, you silly boy—it would be a conversazione, where all the clever and celebrated people of London were gathered together, 'To have the honour of meeting Miss Saville.' There would be quite a number of people whom we knew among the Lions. A very grand Lady Somebody or other, the beauty of the season—Rosalind, of course—all sparkling with diamonds, and leaning on the arm of a distinguished-looking gentleman with orders on his breast. That's Arthur. I'm determined that he shall have orders. It's the only thing that could reconcile me to the loss of the Victoria Cross, and a dress-coat is so uninteresting without trimmings! A fat lady would be sitting in a corner prattling about half a dozen subjects all in one moment—that's Mellicent; and a tall, lean lady in spectacles would be imparting useful information to a dandy with an eyeglass stuck in one eye—that's Esther and Oswald! Oh dear, I wonder—I wonder—I wonder! It's like a story-book, Rob, and we are at the end of the first volume. How much shall we have to do with each other in the second and third; and what is going to happen next, and how, and when?"

"We—we have to part, that's the next thing," said Rob sadly. "Here comes the carriage, and Arthur is shouting for us to stop. It's good-bye, for the present, Mariquita; there's no help for it!"

"At the crossroads!" said Peggy slowly, her eye wandering to the sign-board which marked the paths branching north, south, east, and west. She stopped short and stood gazing into his face, her eyes big and solemn, the wind blowing her hair into loose little curls beneath her scarlet cap, her dramatic mind seizing eagerly on the significance of the position. "At the crossroads, Rob, to go our different ways! Good-bye, good-bye! I hate to say it. You—you won't forget me, and like the horrid boys at college better than me, will you, Rob?"

Robert gave a short, strangled little laugh.

"I think—not! Cheer up, partner! We will meet again, and have a better time together than we have had yet. The third volume is always more exciting than the first. I say we shall, and you know when I make up my mind to a thing, it has to be done!"

"Ah, but how?" sighed Peggy faintly. "But how?" Vague prophecies of the future were not much comfort to her in this moment of farewell. She wanted something more definite; but Rob had no time to enter into details, for even as she spoke the carriage drew up beside them, and, while the occupants congratulated Peggy on having walked so far and so well, he could only grip her hand, and take his place in silence beside his sister.

PEGGY STOOD WATCHING, A SOLITARY FIGURE UPON THE ROADSIDE.

Lady Darcy bent forward to smile farewell; Rosalind waved her hand, and then they were off again, driving swiftly homewards, while Peggy stood watching, a solitary figure upon the roadside.

Arthur and his companions hurried forward to join her, afraid lest she should be tired, and overcome with grief by the parting with her friend and partner.

"Poor little Peg! She won't like it a bit," said Arthur. "She's crying! I'm sure she is."

"She is putting her handkerchief to her eyes," said Mellicent.

"We will give her an arm apiece, and take her straight back," said Max anxiously. "It's a shame to have left the poor little soul alone!"

They stared with troubled eyes at the little figure which stood with its back turned towards them, in an attitude of rigid stillness. There was something pathetic about that stillness, with just the flutter of the tell-tale handkerchief, to hint at the quivering face that was hidden from view. The hearts of Peggy's companions were very tender over her at that moment; but even as they planned words of comfort and cheer, she wheeled round suddenly and walked back to meet them.

It was an unusually mild morning for the season of the year, and the sun was shining from a cloudless sky. Its rays fell full upon Peggy's face as she advanced—upon reddened eyes, trembling lips, and two large tears trickling down her cheeks. It was undeniable that she was crying, but she carried her head well back upon her shoulders, rather courting than avoiding observation, and as she drew nearer it became abundantly evident that Peggy had retired in honour of Mariquita, and that consolations had better be deferred to a more promising occasion.

"A most lacerating wind!" she said coolly. "It draws the moisture to my eyes. Quite too piercingly cold, I call it!" and even Mellicent had not the courage to contradict.

And here, dear readers, we leave Peggy Saville at a milestone of her life. In what direction the crossroads led the little company of friends, and what windings of the path brought them once more together, remains still to be told. It was a strange journey, and in their travelling they met many friends with whom all young people are acquainted. The giant barred the way, and had to be overcome before the palace could be reached; the Good Spirit intervened at the right moment to prevent calamity, the prince and princess stepped forward and made life beautiful; for life is the most wonderful fairy tale that was ever written, and full of magic to those who have eyes to see.

Farewell, then, to Peggy Pickle; but if it be the wish of those who have followed her so far, we may meet again with Mariquita Saville, in the glory of sweet and twenty, and learn from her the secret of the years.

The End.

www.ingramcontent.com/pod-product-compliance
Lightning Source LLC
Chambersburg PA
CBHW060803310726
48980CB00002B/217

9783732621606